The Dreamer

THE DREAMLAND SERIES

BOOK I

E.J. Mellow

The Dreamer
Copyright © 2015 E.J. Mellow
All rights reserved.

Published by Four Eyed Owl, Village Station PO Box #204, New York, NY 10014
Editing by Julia McCarthy
Cover Design by E.J. Mellow
Cover Typography by Mercy Lolimen
Cover Photography by Elena Kalis
www.elenakalisphoto.com

ISBN-10: 0996211411
ISBN-13: 978-0-9962114-1-3
ISBN 978-0-9962114-0-6 (ebook)

To all those who dream.
And to my family who taught me how.

Prologue

THE SLEEPING PILLS are small in my hand, nonthreatening and white, but my forearm aches from the weight of them. Bad decisions can be surprisingly heavy.

Glancing into the mirror, I study sunken eyes rimmed with dark shadows and hair that falls disheveled and knotted. I don't know this girl.

Pinching away another wave of frustration that threatens tears, I search back in my mind, disoriented between what is now and what was then. The only certainty I hold on to is that I've begun to hate it here.

Have I gone crazy? Is any of this even real?

As I gaze at the face reflected in front of me, I know there's only one way to answer my questions.

I pop the pills into my mouth and swallow.

Dreams are true while they last,
and do we not live in dreams?
—*Tennyson*

Chapter 1

I MIGHT BE losing my eyesight. That, or I've been staring at my laptop and the slim amount of notes I've written for far too long. It all appears like little blurry ants on my screen. Words, ants, words, ants. I've been attempting to type up the notes from my recent status meeting for the past hour, but since I zoned out and didn't take any in the first place, it's proving rather difficult. This is something that probably shouldn't happen after working for two years at a top New York marketing agency, but what can I say? A lot of things happen in life that shouldn't.

"Mols!" Becca, my best friend since our freshman year of college, leans over the back of my chair. A red lock of her hair falls across my shoulder, and I distractedly push it away, noting that our features couldn't be more contradictory. Becca reminds me of the best parts of summer with her bright sunset mane and eyes the color of freshly cut grass, while I more closely resemble the cold months—dark-brown hair and plain brown eyes. The one visual trait we do share is the spray of freckles on our faces, which we both like to count when the sun harvests them to life in the summer.

"Hey, Bec, how did your meeting go with that director?" I ask as I type usefully vague phrases like "status regroup," "streamline creative," and "circle back to billable and nonbillable" on my screen. Thank you, jargon gods.

Becca slouches into the chair next to me, a familiar posture for her brought on by working as a producer at the agency. "Ugh, not well. You should have seen Tony's face on the call. I had to keep reaching over to squeeze his arm so he wouldn't throw the phone off the table."

I glance at her wryly. "I'm sure you would have gladly kept squeezing even if the call went smoothly."

"Molly!" Becca smacks my shoulder in mock horror as she peers around nervously.

I bite back a laugh, knowing full well I'm not the only one in the office privy to secrets regarding Becca and her work crushes. Tony, a creative director here, is someone Becca has been swooning over for about three years. Did I mention he's married?

Pressing Send on my patchworked e-mail, I lean back, glancing at the clock, and let out a breath I didn't realize I was holding. T-minus seventy-two hours until the weekend.

"So, what do you and Jared have planned for tonight?" Becca rests her cheek in her hand.

"I think he's taking me to Bar Le Duc in the West Village." I close my laptop and swivel to face her.

"Your favorite! Good going, Jared. But I guess it *is* your birthday, so if he didn't bring you somewhere nice, I'd have to make a note on the Discard list."

I barely contain a snort at her need to compartmentalize life into lists. "Yeah, it should be fun. Except I still have to work tonight, so I can't go hog wild and crazy like I know you'd want me to."

"Shit on work. You're pushing a pharmaceutical sleeping pill—those things practically sell themselves! Plus, it's your *birthday*. Jim will understand if you come in a little late and puffy around the eyes…and hopefully lips," she says with a wink.

"Eww, gross." I shove her knee. "If there's anything I've learned, it's that my boss certainly *won't* understand. We have a big meeting with the client tomorrow morning, and I have to get the presentation together." I pop up from my desk and cram my laptop, cell phone, and headphones into my bag.

"Okay, dollface—well, you have fun, and I hope to hear some great birthday fooling around was had." Becca gives me one of her lovely slap-on-the-butt good-byes as I make my way toward the elevators, thinking about the recipient of said fooling around that I'm about to meet.

⊷⊷⊷ ⊶⊶⊶

The evening air is uncharacteristically warm for early spring and adds a lightness to my step as I turn the corner onto Perry Street, catching sight of the man of the hour. Jared leans against a lamppost outside the restaurant, lazily scrolling through his phone, so I take advantage of his averted attention to do my normal ogling. The first time I met Jared, I fantasized that he was born from the pages of a

Jane Austen novel, with the well-bred tilt of his smile and the way his honey-wheat hair had a habit of appearing perfectly windblown. But then I was introduced to his eyes and the power they had to flip from honorable to licentious in a single blink, suggesting he might have come more suitably from a Brontë sister. Just as I'm taking my final visual drag over his dark fitted jeans and snug white oxford shirt, he glances up, hazel eyes growing warm as they find me, and he smiles. A bit flustered, I tuck one side of my hair behind my ear.

"Hey, you." He leans down, giving me a kiss, and I take in his signature guy scent of fresh laundry and cologne. "Happy Birthday."

"Thanks." I smile back. "Shall we?" I motion toward the entrance of the restaurant.

"As they say, 'Age before beauty.'" He gives me a flirty wink.

I roll my eyes. "I'm only twenty-four. Last I looked, you've still got a good three years on me."

His grin grows. "Like I said, '*Age* before beauty.'" He makes his way in front of me.

"Jared!" I jokingly push him from behind, and he turns around, laughing.

"Maybe I should have said, 'Ladies first.'" And with that, he opens the door for me and we walk inside.

·⇥▣◉ ◉▣⇤·

Bar Le Duc is a cute little French restaurant tucked away in the West Village. I found it on one of my random walks through the neighborhood and fell in love. The stone walls with exposed wood beams overhead, light-cream colors, and small three-part French band that croons in the corner evoke an old, dreamy ambiance. The wine is meant to be sipped, and the meals are brought out at a leisurely pace, making the atmosphere a comforting break from the impatience of the city. *This definitely gets you a notch on the Pros list, Jared.*

"You know, we do still have time to order another side for you." I try trapping Jared's fork with mine to keep him from capturing another one of my brussels sprouts. *Then again...*

"But what would be the fun in that?" Jared pops his new conquest into his mouth. "I find that hunting for my food builds up my appetite."

"And it's proving to be quite the appetite." I smile wryly and pull my plate closer.

"Just wait until after dinner—you'll be astounded to see my appetite then." He places his hand on mine and wiggles his eyebrows like a villain.

"Oh, sir, I now see how you ensnare so many ladies." In an exaggerated gesture, I throw my hand over my heart.

"It's true. You should feel lucky that I've spared so much of my time for you tonight. The handful of other maidens I had to cancel on was gut wrenching."

"Well then, dry those tears, for I actually have to finish some work tonight. Those other *maidens* can do with your services after all." I pat his hand playfully.

"Wait...seriously?" Jared slouches in his chair.

Crap.

"Uh...yeah, I'm sorry. I must have forgotten to mention it, but I need to finish a presentation for an early meeting tomorrow." I nervously play with my fork. "Are you mad?" I ask, trying to read any sort of emotion on his face, but he quickly relaxes his forehead.

"No, no, I understand. Work is work. Just thought we could go for drinks or something after this, and then maybe go back to my place. It *is* your birthday, after all."

"I know. Trust me, I wish I didn't have to do this either. I don't know what else to say besides…I'm really sorry." I end my explanation with a *don't be mad, look how cute I am* face.

A small smile creeps across his lips, and he throws up his hands. "You know I can't stay mad when you look at me like that." I hold my expression a bit longer, and Jared begins to laugh. "Man, you're good."

"I *was* the only child. I needed to master the art of getting out of trouble with a single look."

"Well, I'd say you've earned yourself a black belt in that. Poor parents."

"Thanks," I respond smugly.

Jared chuckles and then grows quiet, shifting uncomfortably in his chair. Reaching into his pocket, he pulls out a small navy box. "I was going to do this when we were getting drinks or back at my place, but now that you've forced my hand"—he smiles to show that he's teasing—"I'll give it to you now." With anxious eyes that make him appear younger, vulnerable, and somehow even cuter than usual, he places the box in front of me.

I handle the present with a delicate touch and force a happy look onto my face, hiding the nervous queasiness that always accompanies opening gifts in front of people. To my extreme relief, it's a tasteful silver charm bracelet. "Jared, I love it!" His shoulders relax with my reaction, and he grins.

"I saw it, and it reminded me of you. I know how you like to collect little trinkets wherever you go, so I thought you could collect charms here."

My face flushes at the realization that he knew this about me after only dating for a few months, but I guess the shelf of random objects I have in my apartment gave me away. For every place I visit—city, town, or airport—I like to find a small something to remind me I was there. That, or I have a strange hoarding disorder.

"It's absolutely perfect, really."

Jared helps me clasp it on. "I got you your first charm. I hope you like it—it's of the Empire State Building." He fingers the tiny building that now dangles from my wrist.

Walking around to his side of the table, I give him a kiss.

"Like I said, it's perfect."

⇢▷◎ ◎◁⇠

After dinner, Jared tries to convince me to ditch my work and go for a drink, but I stay firm, promising that I'll make it up to him this weekend. Defeated, he wraps me in his arms and leaves me with a kiss that would raise anyone's blood pressure. *Oh my.*

Heading back to my apartment, which is only a few blocks away on Jones Street, I check my phone to find a missed call and a voicemail from home.

"Happy Birthday to you! Happy Birthday to you! Happy Birthday dear Mols, Happy Birthday to youuuuu!" My parents' voices sing off-key. "Hope you're having a great day, love! Dad and I are eating a cupcake in your honor. Give us a call when you can. Love you!" I smile and am about to hit Redial when the wind picks up and the ominous rumbling of another sporadic April shower sounds in the distance.

I quicken my pace, hoping that I'll make it to my apartment before it starts raining too hard. I'll give them a ring then. I hardly make it another block before the skies open and pour down a monsoon.

Well, Happy Birthday to me.

Cursing six ways til Sunday, I push on, my dress clinging unceremoniously and my feet slipping forward in my heels. Stopping under a doorway to wait it out will only make me more irritable— nobody deserves to stand around in drenched clothes on her birthday—so I keep slopping home as the storm grows increasingly more violent.

My hair's completely soaked, and I'm in the middle of pushing it from my face when a huge crack of lightning flashes nearby. Shocked, I fall forward, dropping my purse, but luckily catch a streetlight to steady myself. I'm about to step away when another loud *CRACK* explodes and the brightest light I've ever seen surrounds me.

Time stops as a million things happen at once: The most excruciating pain I've ever felt extends from the palm of my hand up my arm to envelop me as a scream tries to escape my lips but gets stuck in my throat. My whole body burns like the hottest part of a flame and fights being torn from the inside out. Agonizing splinters of energy course through my body and pierce my brain like a knife jamming into my forehead. Then suddenly, I sense myself lifting off the ground, suspended in midair, and with a rush I slam down onto a hard surface.

Finally, time moves forward and everything goes black.

→▶━◉ ◉━◀←

I'm in nothingness, floating inside a heavy silence. Through the thickness, someone says my name, and I try opening my eyes, but they stay shut. Yet I begin to see things: The color blue pulses in front of me, receding into the deepest crystal-blue eyes I've ever seen. A smile appears. The mouth and eyes are surrounded in blackness, but the form speaks in a calm, deep voice. *You'll be okay, Molly. Trust me.* As soon as the words are uttered, I begin to relax, though I can't pinpoint why the sound of that voice comforts me.

The vision changes, and the silhouette of a city bordered by a never-ending field flashes before me, the dark sky covered with an infinite amount of shooting stars. I take in the smell of night and spice. The vivid blue eyes appear again, this time accompanied by the blurred outline of a man's face, and I desperately try looking through the haze to make him out. His features come into focus for one beat of my heart, and my stomach flutters at the raw, masculine beauty that materializes. He's all darkness and angles and moon-kissed skin hidden under forgotten stubble, sapphire jeweled eyes blazing against the shadows that surround him.

The face begins to blur again as he whispers the words *Terra Somniorum* and cocks his mouth into a mischievous grin. Callused yet soft hands brush across my cheek. *Molly,* he whispers. I can't mistake the urgency in his tone.

Molly.

"Molly." This time it sounds different, muffled and female. Like the shock of jumping into freezing water, I'm swiftly aware of my whole body, and an all-consuming pain radiates throughout me. I moan, forcing my eyes open only to be temporarily blinded by sharp white light. Though it feels like I have earplugs in, I pick up the constant beeping of a heart monitor nearby.

"Oh, Molly! You're awake. Can you hear me?" I carefully turn my head to my mother, sitting next to the bed I'm lying in. I blink.

"Mols, you're in the hospital. You were struck by lightning." Her voice cracks as she grabs my hand and begins to sob.

Chapter 2

I once read somewhere that the odds of getting hit by lightning are one in a million. One in a friggin' million. So, if this situation were to be viewed optimistically, I'm a pretty unique individual. But here's the thing—*I just got hit by lighting on my birthday*, so optimism can go kiss pessimism's butt.

Getting hit by lightning sucks. And I mean, *really* sucks. I could try and give a thousand comparisons for how much it sucks, but I'm not quite sure I'd do it justice, so let's just settle on this one: imagine every horrible, terrible, no-good feeling all rolled into one, multiply it by a thousand, sprinkle on some more suck, drizzle a punch in the face of *kill me now*, and finish it off with a stab (for good measure, of course) of *you've got to be joking*, and then we *might* be close to what it's like.

With that said, one can imagine I'm not currently in the best state of mind.

Nonetheless, my parents, being the saints that they are, try their best to calm me down and explain what happened before the good doctor walks into my room. His thick, dirty-blond hair barely passes the top of the doorframe unscathed, and his blond beard camouflages a natural youthfulness. If not for his white lab coat, I could picture him hanging out on the beach, surfing. He smiles warmly, but given my present mood, he might as well be baring his teeth and hissing.

"Glad to see that you're up, Molly. I'm Dr. Marshall." Grabbing the chart attached to the edge of my bed, he begins scribbling notes while asking me questions.

"How are you feeling?"

I clear my throat, which is raw and dry. "I've felt better," I reply a bit sourly.

Dr. Marshall's smile merely deepens. "Well, your brain seems receptive, which is excellent. And all your vital signs are up to par. I saw to you when you came in, and let me just say, you are one of the luckiest lightning-strike survivors I've ever come across."

My mom absently squeezes my hand, and I gasp in pain. "Oh, sorry!" Flustered, she grabs my arm.

"Ah, Mom!"

"Oh, oh!" She flings her fingers back, realizing her repeated mistake, and flutters them around like individual chickens that just lost their heads. "Are you okay? What should I do? I'm so sorry."

"Mom, just...just sit on your hands or something."

Wide eyed and worried, she does just that.

Dr. Marshall watches with barely contained mirth, and I would scowl at him if it didn't hurt to do so. "Yes"—he nods to my pitiful state—"you're going to feel as if you have a nasty sunburn for a bit. You also have a slightly ruptured left eardrum and second-degree burns where you were wearing a piece of jewelry around your wrist, which I'm sorry to say is ruined. You've suffered a concussion, so you'll probably experience intense headaches, ringing in the ears, dizziness, nausea, and other postconcussion type symptoms."

He rattles these items off like he's talking about the weather, and I suddenly *do* feel all those things, though I'm not sure if it's because the shock is wearing off or my slight tendency toward hypochondria is kicking in. My heart monitor begins to beep faster, and everyone's attention goes to it.

Dr. Marshall chuckles. "Sorry about that. I wasn't trying to frighten you."

"Well, you failed," I mutter.

The doctor's good-natured jovialness is off-putting, given that he's dealing with someone who just got struck by lightning. Can't he see that everyone needs to be as miserable as me?

"Tell me, Molly—do you remember anything that happened last night? Can you tell us *anything* about what you experienced?" He eyes me intently.

"Uh, not really. I just remember that I got scared because some lightning struck close to me, and that's when I nearly fell, so I caught my hand on the lamppost. Then there was a lot of pain, and everything went black." And blue…I remember the color blue but decide to keep that to myself. Who needs a detailed list of all the colors I saw?

My mom lets out a worried moan while my dad stands beside her and squeezes her shoulders. Grouped like that, my parents resemble the picture-perfect suburban couple. My mother in her country-club attire, short brown Mom bob and gold jewelry. My father, with his manicured dark hair and usual court-lawyer attire of starched white oxford shirt and black slacks. The only thing that sets his appearance off is his day-old scruff and sleepless circles rimming his eyes, revealing his true concern that he's trained to conceal for his job.

Dr. Marshall examines me a little longer before restoring his happy expression. "Yes, when you placed your hand on the lamppost, you had direct contact with the strike point. But you still came out with astoundingly minimal casualties. Lightning-strike survivors usually suffer some form of brain damage, permanently or for a couple of weeks. And others have even had their backs broken from a strike."

On command, a tingling sensation dashes up my spine.

"I can't say again how lucky you are to be here with so few casualties. I have no other way to explain it except to blame it on... luck." He clips the chart back to my bed. "We're going to keep you overnight to make sure everything is okay and you don't experience any postseizures."

Postseizures! Umm...what now?

"If you need anything, there's a red button on a cord next to your bed. Just press that and a nurse will be here within seconds. I'll be checking on you tomorrow morning before I sign your release. I've also prescribed you pain medication, and the nurse will be in here shortly to give you something to help you sleep. I want you to come back in a week to tell us how you're faring and to run some tests. Glad you're with us today, Molly. Mr. and Mrs. Spero." He nods toward my parents. Once at the door, he quickly turns back around.

"Oh, and I forgot to mention, sleeping disorders after something like this are also common, so don't be too concerned if your dreams seem...odd. They usually go away with time." He beams another one of his annoyingly chipper smiles and exits the room.

I let out a sigh of relief. That's one problem I won't need to worry about. I don't dream. Replaying the doctor's words in my head, a thousand questions come to mind that conveniently weren't there when I could have asked them. What exactly happened to my body when I got struck? Will I have crazy symptoms in two months that aren't surfacing now, like some sort of late onset? Did this mess up my chance to have kids? Why didn't I ask any of these questions when I had the chance? Doctor, come back!

My mom gently strokes a bandage on my left wrist, bringing my attention to it. Every muscle screams in protest as I gingerly lift it for a closer inspection. "Is this the burn the doctor was talking about?"

"Yes, that's where he said you were wearing a bracelet. I hope it's replaceable. The nurse said it was practically glued to your arm." My mom's brows pinch in with concern.

I frown—Jared's gift, ruined. I'm also a little queasy over her description.

"It was a gift from a friend, for my birthday."

"Well, I'm sure you can get another one." My mom tries desperately to force a happy demeanor.

"Speaking of friends"—my dad takes a seat on my bed—"a young man named Jared came in here earlier while you were still out and brought you flowers." He points to a tasteful bouquet sitting on a small table near the window. My chest fills with warmth at the sight of them.

"You met Jared?" I ask, a little uncomfortable at the thought of them together without me as a buffer...well, at least not a comatose one.

"Yes, oh, and Molly, you should have seen him. He looked absolutely devastated. Kept saying how he blames himself for not convincing you to stay with him yesterday night. He sat with us for a couple of hours while you were asleep. Didn't want to leave your side. He's a very sweet boy."

"He's almost thirty. I don't think that makes him a boy."

She wiggles her hand dismissively. "Nonetheless, he seems very sweet. Are you two dating?"

Oh man, here it comes. "Mom, do we really need to get into this right now? I *did* just get hit by lightning. My relationship status is probably not the most important thing to discuss. What I really want to know is, how did I get here? Who found me?"

My dad tucks in the covers near my feet. "A couple was walking behind you when it all happened. They saw you get hit and called 911. You were out cold from last night to this evening, no movements or anything. Looked like you were just sleeping. They thought you could have been in a coma."

Last night to this evening. So it must be Wednesday afternoon. My head swims again with the realization.

"I'm just happy we're nearby. I would have *died* if we couldn't have gotten here as fast as we did." My mom rubs her delicate fingers against my arm, and I swallow back the threat of tears brought on by my own overwhelming sense of gratitude and shock.

"Getting struck by lightning…what are the odds?" my dad says with a sigh. "You know, I think your grandfather said he got struck when he was a boy."

My mother scoffs. "Who can believe anything that man says?"

My grandfather has always been a bit on the odd side, ever since I was young. He recently had to get a live-in nurse because his mind has finally started to go with old age—practically out of nowhere, he started to rant nonsense about his life that no one in the family had ever heard before, and with my grandmother passed away, there's been no one around to verify.

A knock on the door brings our attention to Becca standing in the entrance with balloons.

⋅⇒◉ ◉⇐⋅

After my parents wander to the hospital cafeteria, Becca saddles up on my bed.

"I was a mess when your mom called. I came as soon as I heard and told work to fuck off. You're obviously more important than that job."

That's when the dam breaks and tears start to fall.

"Oh, Mols, don't cry." She moves to wipe my cheek but pauses. "I can touch you, right? I'm not going to get zapped or anything?" I immediately start to laugh, which makes me wince in pain. Becca smiles sheepishly.

"No, I think you'll be safe."

"Man, babe, I hate to say it, but you have the *worst* luck!"

"Gee, thanks. And here everyone was saying just how lucky I was." I roll my eyes at her. Thankfully, that doesn't hurt.

"I mean, come on. Think about it—getting struck by lightning on your *birthday*! That has to be the single worst birthday present ever." We both start to laugh. I, of course, try my best to keep it at a minimum because my whole body gives me the middle finger when I do.

"Yeah, that does sound pretty bad, not to mention I will *never* go out in a storm again."

"I don't blame you. Neither will I. Your experience, I think, has scared me more than it has you."

I scoff. "I don't know about that."

"Well, you're calmer than I would be. I'd be yelling at the nurses to shoot me up with more painkillers and demanding six or seven brain scans to make sure everything is okay."

"I wasn't so calm earlier...trust me."

Becca nods. "Maybe this will be a good thing. Maybe now you'll realize you have some strange power or discover you're a math wizard. I heard of a guy that suddenly picked up the piano after he got hit. Do you feel like you want to play music?"

I laugh. "No, no music notes coming to me in a vision."

"*Yet*," she adds with a gentle nudge.

My parents and Becca hang out for a little longer before a nurse enters, announcing that I need to get some sleep. Everyone says their good-byes, telling me they'll be back in the morning for my release. One of the nurses—I learn her name is Julie—changes the bandages on my wrist before pressing a button that's attached to an IV in my arm. Cool liquid flows into my veins, and slowly my eyes droop to a close.

⋅→▣ ▣←⋅

I'm gently being carried through the air while the sound of crickets surrounds me. The darkness softly begins to dissipate like a fog being burnt away by the sun, and I find myself standing in a large field at night. The tall grass tickles my bare ankles as I gaze around. Familiarity swarms me, but I can't put my finger on why. I have a desire to reach out and touch the air in front of me, but I'm constricted by an invisible source containing me in a small, cool bubble.

There's a bright light in the distance. The skyline of a city pushes up and out of the empty field that surrounds it, the only structure in sight. With no roads leading to or from it, the metropolis seems to float in its own pulsing glow. A gentle wind stirs the leaves in a tree, and I turn to a solitary elm standing at the top of a small hill a few yards away. As I study it, my eyes are drawn into the night sky that covers the land like a blanket, and I gasp.

Instead of blackness, the sky is painted with thousands of shooting stars. Constant white lights zoom past overhead, and gazing at it too long has the effect of making the world spin very fast. Still, it retains an intensely mesmerizing beauty, like watching the hypnotic flow of the northern lights. And yet...I feel that I have seen this before. But how is that possible?

A movement draws my attention to a shadowy figure leaning against the tree. My stomach tightens in fear, and I search my surroundings, thinking I should run, but I'm completely exposed.

When I glance back, I'm suddenly standing inches from the tree, and I take a staggering step away in shock. I watch, my heart racing, as the figure moves from the shadows and into the soft night's light.

It's a man about my age, maybe a few years older. He's dressed all in black—black boots, black pants, black T-shirt—and has a strange strap around his torso, pressing taut against a lean, muscular body that is evident even through his shirt. An object that resembles a quiver rests on his back, but I see no arrows. His arms are delicately lined with muscles, and his face is cast down, blocking out any details. He wears a buzzed military-type haircut that is raven-black in color.

I hold my breath as he tilts his head up; he will see me in seconds. But when his eyes go to mine, they hold no acknowledgment—as if they can't see me at all—before they continue toward the sky. His eyes—I take a breath in again—seem so familiar, so brilliantly blue. Where have I seen them before? I study his features, which seem carved from a master's hand, from the sharp cut of his cheekbones down to his prominent, straight nose and angular jaw that shows through his scruff. I stay silent, not wanting to interrupt the songs of the crickets that fill the night or the man who stands in front of me. When he lets out a gentle sigh, I have an instant desire to reach out and touch him—in that moment, he seems to shoulder a sadness, a stoic sensibility.

His gaze dances back in my direction, and the blueness of it penetrates through my core, sending shivers along my spine. Not until the moment passes do I realize he's not looking at me, but past me, toward the city in the distance. He shakes his head as if discarding some thought and moves his face into an amused smile, transforming his features into an even more unbearably heart-stopping sight.

Adjusting the strap around his shoulder, he walks forward, and I stand stock still with wide eyes as his tall form crosses my path without a hint of awareness of my presence. The smell of night and spice play off his body as the breeze glides by, and it's intoxicating. His movements are graceful and strong as he makes his way toward the city in the distance, and I grow panicked, not wanting him to leave. I try taking a step in his direction, but my feet are rooted to the ground, the grass holding my ankles in place, an invisible shield keeping me still. I try calling out to him, but no sound escapes me.

My heart flips when he abruptly stops. Turning around, his gaze slides over my form as if he senses someone's there. His eyes narrow, looking hard in my direction, and I have a desperate desire to stay invisible and be seen all at once. Finally he relaxes and turns once again, setting off at a jog toward his destination.

With his departure, the grassy hills begin to morph and move and grow into mountains. I'm lost while floating between them with no sense of direction. My body courses through images that make no sense and colors that I can taste. A familiar sapphire blue expands in front, and I will myself forward, letting it wrap around me, cooling my skin. Just as my body is slowly being swallowed into it, my eyes jerk open to a sunlit room and the rhythmic beeping of a heart monitor nearby.

Chapter 3

"GOOD MORNING, MOLLY." Nurse Julie enters my room carrying a tray of standard hospital breakfast food. My head's heavy, like I had too much to drink the night before, and it takes a few seconds to re-orient myself to my surroundings. "How are we feeling?" She pulls over a wheeled cart and places the tray on my bed. I swallow the taste of sleep in my mouth.

"My head hurts a bit and my body's sore, but it doesn't feel like it's on fire anymore."

She nods. "That's excellent. You're probably going to have a headache for a little while, but don't worry. There was nothing wrong with your scans. It's your concussion giving you that pain. Your muscles will also be sore because the strike basically gave your body one large charley horse."

"How pleasant," I say both to her comment and to my breakfast that suspiciously jiggles when I poke it. *Yum.*

After getting down a few bites of the plastic-tasting food, I grab some toiletries and ask the nurse to help me into the bathroom. I have enough strength to stand on my own and walk, but every muscle screams in protest. Once I'm in front of the mirror, I grip the sink until my knuckles are white to keep from falling over with shock. I look *horrible*! Why didn't anyone tell me? My hair is all over the place, I have dark circles under my eyes, and my lips resemble those on a petrified mummy. I push away the horrible thought that Jared saw me like this.

Yes, even after getting hit by lightning, I remain vain.

Once showered, my rat's nest of hair combed and a two-inch thick glob of lip balm smeared on my cracked lips, I step out of the bathroom to find Becca and my mom standing in my room.

"How do you feel?" Mom takes my arm, helping me to the bed.

"Better," I say, even as I let out a breath like I just ran a marathon.

Becca places a bag next to me. "I stopped off at your apartment and brought you some clothes. The dress you were wearing when you came in obviously isn't going to make it back out."

"That's what happens when you splurge. God smites you down," I retort. Becca and I both giggle, but our smirks are quickly wiped away by my mom's disapproving eyes.

"I don't know how you girls can joke about this."

"You know what they say, Mrs. Spero—laughter *is* the best medicine."

My mom shakes her head while reaching into her purse, and I hold back an appreciative smile when Becca sneaks me a wink.

That evening, I walk through the door to my studio apartment on the second floor of a small building on Jones Street. My mom fusses and flutters over me while Dad watches on, sympathetic but amused. *The big jerk.* Thankfully, after Becca ensures that I'll be left in her capable hands and I promise that I'm fine and I'll call in the morning, my parents leave with a teary-eyed good-bye, making their journey home.

I change into the coziest clothes I own, and Becca whips up scrambled eggs and toast for dinner, declaring that breakfast is the most comforting food in the world, and at this moment, I have to agree.

"Have you checked your phone, Mols? I bet you've got some messages waiting for you."

I haven't even thought about my phone, assuming everything that was on me was ruined when I got hit. But then I remember dropping my purse right before the accident, which must have saved it.

I carefully clamber off my bed, which also functions as a couch and dining table—studio apartments in New York are just the best—and find my phone in a plastic bag with other contents from that night. Plugging it in to bring it back to life, my hand vibrates with an onslaught of missed messages. I haven't felt this popular since Amanda Reynolds told all the girls in our middle school class that I was the first to get my period. Flipping through a couple of texts from coworkers, I stop on one from Jim saying how worried he is and that I can take as much time as I need.

"Looks like Jim actually has a heart." I glance at Becca, who's scarfing down her food while watching a rerun of *Friends*.

"It's because he has the hots for you."

"*Eww* gross! Add nausea to my ailments, why don't you."

"Oh, sorry," she says with false concern. "I meant to say he's absolutely repulsed by your face."

"Thank you—much better."

I flip to the couple of texts from Jared.

Hope you got home okay, started raining pretty hard. Had a great time. Happy Birthday again!

Hey, just wanted to make sure all is okay. Didn't hear from you last night.

You probably won't get this until you're back at apt. Went to hospital to see you. You were still asleep. Really worried about you. Pls let me know how you are.

I quickly text him back.

Hey, sorry I never got these until now. Thought my phone was toast. I'm doing much better. Bec is here w/ me staying the night.

A second after I sent the message I get another from him.

Good to see your phone is still up and running and so are you. Was really worried. Crazy night. I wish I could replace Becca's spot right now.

The last comment has me smiling.

Yeah my birthday has a whole new event to celebrate w/ it now. And you can take up a spot tomorrow night :)

"What's making you so happy over there?" Becca teases. "I think I can guess." Before I can answer, my phone vibrates again.

I'd like to take up a spot permanently, but if it's just tomorrow night, I'll take what I can get. See you then.

My stomach tightens a little when I read the word "permanently." Not really knowing how to respond, I text back the only thing that comes to mind.

Gnight.

"Wellllll?" Becca whines from the bed. "If you don't spill, I'm going to eat the rest of your eggs. I've already started on your toast."

"Jared texted me. He's going to come over tomorrow night."

Becca shoots me a wicked grin. "You guys are going to have the best sex. Nothing like a man thinking he almost lost a woman."

I roll my eyes. "I don't even know if I'm allowed to have sex. It's only been three days."

Becca gapes. "Well, you better call up Dr. What's-His-Nuts and ask! That's an important detail." Ignoring her, I pick up my plate, shoveling the remainder of my eggs into my mouth, and give her a satisfying smirk as I chew.

After washing up and taking some pain meds, I crawl into bed. Becca wiggles under the sheets next to me. "It's just like college days. Except the event prior would have been you holding my hair back over the toilet."

"Ah, the memories," I say, and we both laugh. A long pensive silence follows.

"Mols?"

"Mmm?"

"I'm really happy you're okay." She rolls over and puts her arm around me. "I don't know what I would do if anything happened to you." Becca hardly shows emotion like this, and when she does, I'm usually waiting for the punch line. This time it never comes.

"Love you, Bec."

"Love you too, Mols."

We both close our eyes and let the sound of honking on the streets below rock us to sleep.

I begin to dream of something familiar. I'm floating over a nearly empty field at night. A solitary elm tree rests in the distance. My body's warm with light, as bright as a star, and I move faster and faster, racing toward the tree. A shock of penetrating, ice-cold water bursts across my skin, and I smack down to the earth. My vision goes dark.

Gradually, I hear movement around me. Feet stepping on grass. The sound of crickets chirping. A soft, cool breeze brushes across my skin. I open my eyes to the sky, my view partially blocked by the leaves of a tree. The part of the sky I can see is streaked with white lights zipping past. I've dreamt of this place before. I've seen this tree and felt this grass beneath me. I'm so at ease lying in this familiar place. No pain comes from my head here, and I want to stay like this forever.

I'm brought out of my reverie by a girl's whispers. I chance a look around to see two figures standing at my right, looking down at me. They are both completely dressed in black with some object strapped to each of their backs. One is a girl with almost white-blonde hair and fragile features. From the dark silhouette of her body, I can tell she's as skinny as a stick. The other figure is a man with short-cropped raven hair and two-day stubble, which, coupled with his attire, allows him to seamlessly camouflage into the dark surroundings. His pale skin is what sets him apart from the backdrop, along with the brightest blue eyes I've ever seen.

Those eyes.

I stare into them, trying to stir up the memory that is swimming around in my head suggesting I've seen them before. All I can currently deduce from the rapid beating of my heart and the tense heat in my belly is that I must find him attractive. And if anyone else were seeing what I'm seeing, I don't think they would blame me.

The girl next to the shadowed man whispers fervently in his ear as he stands still, arms crossed over his chest, studying me intently.

"It's a Dreamer," he finally says, his voice deep and rich. The girl flinches at his volume used but follows suit.

"I see that it's a Dreamer, Dev. But what is she doing *here*?" The light, twinkling quality of her voice contradicts the vehemence of her tone. *Do they think I can't hear them?*

The girl paces to his other side while gazing at me warily, her blonde locks pushing forward to cast shadows around her face. Even with her features slightly obscured, her beauty is obvious. I begin to wonder if this dream is going to be all about supermodels, which would definitely make it a nightmare.

"I'm not sure. Something must have gotten crossed on the journey to her landscape," he says while turning his attention to the night sky.

"That's never happened before. It's impossible." The girl puts her hands on her hips in bewilderment and faces him.

Dev—I'm guessing his name—shifts his weight and scratches his stubble-filled chin, regarding me like I'm a car with a flat. "Well, it's happened now."

This whole time I've kept quiet, and I decide it's time to say something.

"Excuse me." I begin to sit up.

Dev stands perfectly still, his face subtly lighting up with curiosity. The girl, on the other hand, takes a step back, steadying herself like she's about to throttle me.

"Whoa." I put up my hands, indicating my nonviolent intent. "I'm not going to do anything but stand. Can I do that?" I fix my gaze from one to the other questioningly.

"She can hear us." The girl tries to whisper sideways through her mouth.

Is she kidding me? "Of course I can hear you! What's going on? Where am I? Who are you guys?" My numbness upon waking here has quickly evaporated and is replaced instead by slight hysteria.

"Inquisitive, isn't she?" Dev arches one of his brows in amusement.

I let out a frustrated sigh. "*Please* stop talking like I'm not right in front of you. Like I said, I can hear you. And I have a name. It's Molly."

The girl is about to say something, when Dev puts his hand up to quiet her. "Hi, Molly." He flashes a lopsided grin. "What's going on is that you're *dreaming*." He elongates the word dreaming while wiggling his fingers as if he's telling a spooky story. "*Where* you are is in your dream. *Who* we are... Well, we're obviously figments of your imagination."

Chapter 4

IN THE BEGINNING of my junior year of high school, life decided to play a practical joke on me by hilariously messing up my schedule and placing me in advanced calculus. Now, I like to think I'm of reasonable intelligence, *but* ordinary differential equations and myself...we don't really hang in the same comprehension circles. So, try as I might to follow my teacher's logic in how he got $3f''(x) + 5xf(x)$ to equal eleven, I never quite understood. His answer in no way, shape, or form resembled mine, and this misalignment—this complete confusion of how point A got to point B—is kind of where I'm at right now.

"*Dreaming?*" I repeat dubiously.

The girl glances sideways at Dev and presses her lips together.

"Yes, dreaming. You know, a series of thoughts, images, sensations occurring in a person's mind during sleep," he says casually.

The three of us stare at one another, the background of chirping crickets providing the perfect sound effect for my skeptical silence.

Eventually, the girl shifts uncomfortably and peeks over her shoulder toward the glowing light in the distance. At least a mile away is a cluster of illuminated skyscrapers and other tall buildings jutting into the night sky. Something about it jars my memory.

As I wait for recognition, a slight breeze tickles grass across my bare thigh, and I realize I'm in my pajamas...*braless* in my pajamas.

Oh God!

I none-too-subtly cover myself with my hands, and Dev chuckles. All sorts of cockiness flows off him, and I'm not sure if I like it or hate it.

"We should go." The girl adjusts the strap around her chest, showing me a glimpse of the object on her back. It's an empty quiver, no arrows in sight.

Dev doesn't move but rather continues to watch me with the same amused smile from when I first spoke. Squirming under his scrutiny, I'm about to tell him to take a picture because it'll last longer, when his friend forcefully whispers his name.

"Aveline, we can't leave her here."

"And why not?"

"It's not safe. We can't have her wandering around. This has never happened before that either you or I can ever recall."

"Okay, so what do *you* suggest we do?"

The tone they take with each other makes me wonder if they are brother and sister. But their drastic difference in hair color and size leads me to believe they aren't. Maybe they're dating?

Dev pensively rubs a hand over his short black hair. "We need to make sure she's okay until she wakes up."

"Ha!" Aveline throws up her hands. "You'd like that, wouldn't you? What even makes you think she *will* wake up? I for one don't want to waste my day sticking around to find out. We have patrols to run."

"Don't you mean night?" It comes out of my mouth before I realize that I'm speaking.

Aveline flashes me a murderous glare. "Excuse me?" She sneers, the twinkling tone all but lost from her voice.

"Well...you said you didn't want to waste your *day*, but it's obviously night out." I gesture at everything around us.

Aveline makes a weird snorting-laughing sound. "Yeah, okay, *night*...whatever you say, Dreamer." She rolls her eyes and flashes a *see, a waste of time* face at Dev.

He's looking at me with that smirk again, and I grow flush, then a little angry that this guy can evoke such an immediate reaction from me. *What are you, thirteen? Pull yourself together.*

Wanting to quickly change the subject, I ask, "Why do you keep calling me *Dreamer*?"

The girl ignores me. "Okay, Dev, I've obviously lost you. I'm going to finish the rounds because *that's* what we are here to do. If you want to stay and play babysitter, be my guest."

"This is what Tim would want us to do, Ave. You know if we leave now, with her still here, and something happens, we would get strung out by our toes in City Hall. Aren't you in the least bit curious?"

Aveline flicks a glance my way. "No."

Dev shakes his head in resignation. "Fine, go. But I'm staying put and making sure she gets back okay."

"All we need to do is leave and then report this to Tim. He'll take care of it."

"We can report it *after* she leaves."

I can't stand it anymore.

"Uh, excuse me again, guys, but *where* am I leaving to? I still don't understand anything that's happening."

"Whatever, Dev. I'm going. You have fun with *that.*" Aveline jerks her chin in my direction before turning and jogging toward the glowing lights of the city.

⊷═◉ ◉═⊶

As Aveline's retreating form gets smaller and smaller, I slowly realize I'm now alone with this guy, practically in my underwear. Perfect.

Returning my attention to Dev, I find him leaning cross-armed against the tree, and something about his amused disposition and the way he regards me with a calculated fervor threatens any composure I might intend to have in front of him. He instantly annoys me.

With that realized, I decide the best course of action is to disregard his presence. Maybe if I ignore him, he'll somehow vanish. A girl can dream, right?

Pushing myself up, I'm midway to standing when cool, strong hands clasp around my arms and help me the rest of the way. I jerk my head up—now inches away from Dev. He smells uniquely of night and spice, and I work hard not to lean in and breathe in his skin. His attention's focused on my bandaged wrist, and I subconsciously hide it from view. His eyes lock to mine, the rich blue that fills them causing me to shiver.

"Are you cold?" he asks in a husky voice while still holding me.

I pull away, clearing my throat. "No," I say and begin brushing the grass off my bare legs and butt.

"Need help?"

I glance back, a bit shocked at his candor. "*No.*"

He holds up his hands while taking a step back. "Just trying to be polite." With the wry grin that grows, I highly doubt that's all he was trying to be.

Turning away, I take a better look around, straining to find what's beyond the rolling field. The only thing visible is the city straight ahead, its glow like a warm welcoming beacon. Besides that, there's nothing but the endless field stretching to the horizon. I wonder which way the sun will rise and search for the moon—there is none. The only illumination comes solely from the bright moving stars above and the distant metropolis.

"So, where are we?"

His answering silence has me glancing over my shoulder to him. He once again leans against the tree. All he needs is a cigarette hanging loosely from his mouth to finish the bad-boy vibe he's exuding. I raise an eyebrow in an *I'm waiting* gesture.

"We're in your dream," he says casually.

"Really?" My tone still dubious. "Then who are you? I've never seen you before. So how am I recalling you here?" When I say I've never seen him, it feels like a lie.

"Isn't it obvious?" He gestures with his hands, showcasing his body. "I'm the man of your dreams."

My eyes snap wide as Dev works hard to suppress a laugh. "I highly doubt that," I say dryly and turn away, annoyed. I need to go over my options. This guy, Dev, certainly isn't giving me any answers. He says I'm dreaming, but I honestly can't remember the last dream I ever had. I always just wake up blank.

Without returning my attention to Dev, I move forward, deciding I might as well walk around while I'm here.

"Where are you going?" He jogs up next to me.

"Oh, so you're allowed to ask questions, but I'm not?" I study the grass for any rocks or weird night creatures I might unwillingly introduce to my exposed feet.

"If I recall correctly, you've asked questions."

"Yeah, none of which you've answered truthfully." I take a left, heading parallel to the city.

"Why do you think I haven't answered truthfully?" He turns around to walk backward in front of me, forcing me to look at his smirk, which I'm starting to believe is his face's default expression.

"Because I don't dream."

He stops abruptly, and I almost walk into him.

"What did you say?" All amusement drains from his face, leaving a determined and slightly concerned countenance. So much for default expressions.

"I said, I don't dream. Well, not really, not like this." I gesture around us.

"You don't *dream*?" His tone suggests I've just admitted something horribly wrong about myself.

"Uh...not really. I mean, we all dream, I guess, right? At least that's what they say. I can never remember them when I wake up though. I don't know. I've just never felt so awake in a dream before. Like right now, I find it impossible that I could be sleeping when... when I can feel and smell and see so much." Impulsively, I take a deep breath in through my nose, closing my eyes and tasting the rich night air in the back of my throat. I slowly open my eyes again to Dev regarding me with a new look of interest. I swallow and take a step back. "Yeah, well, you get what I mean."

He doesn't say anything, just keeps staring at me, and I tuck one side of my hair behind my ear, looking anywhere but at him.

"You do realize people consider staring to be rude," I manage to finally say.

"Am I making you uncomfortable?"

I steal a glance his way, determined not to let the playful smile he wears bother me, and I'm about to retort with some sarcastic insult, when his eyes hold me in a trance. I know I should look away, but I can't find the strength. It's as if a lasso has wrapped itself around my head, forcing it forward. His eyes are so blue. Staring into them, I think of a rich cloudless sky above a tropical ocean, waves crashing around me and warm sand under my feet. A strange coldness wraps around my mind, making me slightly dizzy.

Suddenly, just as I imagined it, the heat from the sun beats down on my skin and small grains of sand push through my toes. The gentle roar of waves tumbling on a beach fills my ears.

Dev gasps and shifts his gaze from mine. With that break in contact, my lungs fill with air, softening the ache that comes from holding your breath. I blink a few times, getting my mind back in order to find we are no longer in a field at night but standing instead on a tiny island. I take a couple of steps back in astonishment. Aqua-blue waves sift up and down on the shoreline, and an azure, sunny sky hangs over our heads. I turn in a circle, staring off into the distance. Surrounding us farther away is the night and grassy field, and in another direction the single elm tree where I first woke to this place. It's almost as if a spotlight illusion is shining down right where we are standing, making it into a tropical island.

"Whoa!"

Walking to the shoreline, I dip my foot into the tide. It's cool and slippery. It feels so real. I breathe in deeply, smelling the salty ocean, and bury the tops of my feet in the sand, reveling in the fact that I was just tickling them with grass seconds before.

"This is crazy! I…" Turning back to my companion, I find him lying on the sand, eyes closed, letting the sun's rays bake into him, a ridiculously childish grin plastered on his face. His skin seems too pale to be in a place as bright as this, and his all-black combat uniform clashes rather comically with the tropical setting.

Stifling a laugh, I walk over and sit beside him. "What are you doing?"

He rolls to his side, propping his head up with one hand, and his shirt shifts upward, exposing a portion of his muscular stomach. He stares at me with excitement, like he just found buried treasure.

"What are you thinking about?" he asks.

The question catches me off guard given that I was just checking out his abs. "What do you mean?"

"What were you thinking about a couple moments ago? When we were in the field?"

"Uh…nothing. I can't remember." I answer too quickly, and Dev merely smiles.

I flip back to that moment, to being transfixed by his eyes and how they reminded me of the sea. But I will absolutely not tell him that. I'm pretty certain his neck isn't strong enough to hold up any more of an inflated head.

Dev plucks something from the sand and begins to roll it over in his hand. It's a perfectly formed seashell, one that a hermit crab would make its home. He turns it around, tracing the spiral design with his long, graceful fingers as if it's the first time he's ever laid eyes upon such a thing.

"That's a good find. You usually don't get one completely intact like that."

He looks up. "Yes," he says, studying me again. "It is a good find." His gaze is searing, and I turn from him, uncomfortable and a bit flustered with the emotions suddenly bouncing around inside me.

Time passes with us both staring out across the small sea toward the edge of the illusion where the night grass touches its liquid horizon. I absentmindedly play with my bandaged wrist, soaking in the peace.

"What happened?" Dev asks, breaking the silence. He gently pulls my left arm toward him. His touch cools my skin even though the sun above bathes us with warmth. I pull my arm back and cradle it protectively against my stomach.

"I have a burn."

His brows pinch in with concern. "A burn? Did you do it to yourself?"

"Oh no! Nothing like that."

"Like what, then?"

"You'd never believe me if I told you."

"Try me."

I laugh lightly. "Okay, I got struck by lightning."

His eyes go wide and then small as he obviously tries wrapping his head around the idea, and then he says something that surprises me.

"Right now? Before you came here?"

"No, and I guess yes…" I say, a bit confused by the question. "A couple of days ago. Why?"

He stays silent, gaze locked to the sky, and I'm not sure if I imagine it, but his face relaxes as if finally understanding something.

"But that doesn't explain your wrist being bandaged."

"I was wearing jewelry, and it burned me when I got hit." I have a strange, disembodied feeling when I talk about the accident, as if all of that happened to a different Molly than the one sitting here.

Deciding to change the subject, I ask, "So does this kind of thing happen often?" I nod to our surroundings.

"No…" He looks around. "I wouldn't say that it does."

I take in the rhythmic crashing of waves mixed with the light chirping of insects in the distant field. It's the most soothing mixture. "Well, I really hope I don't forget this dream."

Dev turns to me, seemingly conflicted. He opens his mouth to say something but then closes it, a desire ever present in his eyes. Still remaining silent, he simply looks away, sighing, and pushes his lips into a tiny smile. I have a weird sense that I've seen this expression on him before, but I can't recall from where.

He reveals the shell again and pensively flips it over in his hands. I'm about to push him on his thoughts, when something touches my legs. The sensation starts at my feet and creeps up my back. I search around in a slight panic, seeing nothing but sand. The feeling continues, and my legs become caught by an invisible force.

"What's happening?" I ask Dev as my heartbeat quickens.

Sadness momentarily flashes on his face. "You're waking up."

"Waking up?"

Just as I utter the words, I feel my bed around me, the sheets tangled in between my legs. Dev begins to blur and fade into the light that surrounds us, and my heart lurches with a sense of loss. I gasp, reaching out to grab his hand to keep me in this place, but in that moment, I blink.

And when my eyes open, Manhattan morning light fills my studio, and the buzzing of my alarm clock counts away the seconds I'm no longer asleep.

Chapter 5

"UGH, MOLS, THAT is the *worst* sound to be woken up to," a girl whines at my side.

Small pieces of memory float back to me—one being that Becca slept over last night. She reaches across me and slaps the alarm quiet, flopping back to her side of the bed. "Ahh, so much better. Man, you wake up early for work."

I read the numbers 7:30 on the clock and turn away in disgust—I didn't remember to shut off my alarm the night before. My head's extremely heavy, like I was forced awake in the middle of a deep sleep. Visions of a field at night and a man in black move across my eyelids as I hold them closed. Blue eyes and a seashell.

None of it makes any sense, and the longer I stay awake, the farther away these memories slip.

Becca moves from the bed, and immediately the temperature under the sheets shifts, leaving a cold pocket of air in her place. She peeks out the window to check the weather. From where I'm lying, I can tell it's going to be a sunny day.

"Thank God it's Friday!" Becca exclaims, her red bedhead like a lion's mane around her face.

"How are you feeling, chicken?"

"I'm okay," I rasp in a sleep-ridden voice. "My head still hurts, and I'm already tired of saying that, which means you're probably tired of hearing it."

She huffs dramatically and creeps back onto the bed, gently poking me over and over. "I will never be tired of hearing anything you say," she consoles in a mothering voice.

"Ah, stop!" I squirm in discomfort and laugh simultaneously. My body is still sore, but not as much as yesterday.

"We can't have you feeling sorry for yourself!" Becca jumps up and heads toward the bathroom.

"I never knew you to be a morning person, Bec." I slowly sit up, testing for any dizzy spells—none come.

"Yeah, that's because I'm not—can't you tell? This is grumpy me." As she sees me sit up, she furrows her brow. "Mols, you don't have to work today. Go back to sleep. It's way too early to start your day unless you have a boring job to go to." She closes the door behind her and the shower begins to run.

Becca's right. I should try to go back to sleep, but I have a feeling I won't be able to. Plus, something about the thought of sleeping makes me nervous. I look around my studio, strangely noticing all the blue things I own. The picture frame on the wall, the knobs on my dresser, a pair of shoes on my floor, a shirt peeking out of my drawer…blue, blue, blue. When did I become obsessed with the color blue? I blink away the feeling that my brain is trying to remind me of something, and get out of bed. Yeah, definitely can't go back to sleep.

⟶▷ ◁⟵

After Becca leaves for work—reminding me that I need to fill her in on what happens tonight with Jared and to call her if I need anything—I make some breakfast. Putting two pieces of bread into the toaster, I lean against the counter that separates my bedroom from my kitchen. I stare out my windows that sit in the far end of my studio, watching the light slowly rise. My head's groggy, and I'm not sure if it's from the lightning, the pain meds, or the strange feeling of a dream I had during the night. But I never remember my dreams.

My toast pops up like a demonic jack-in-the-box, jolting me back to the present. Pinning the bread with my best death glare, I smear jelly on it more forcefully than necessary.

Sitting by the windows, I eat my breakfast and watch the Manhattanites make their commutes. Some are in nicely suited business outfits, others in casual clothes, parents walking with their kids to school, hipsters on bikes with one side of their pants rolled up. The hustle and bustle of the city makes me feel less alone up here, gazing out.

As I wonder about their lives, if they like their jobs, their spouses, boyfriends, girlfriends, or kids, a pit in my stomach grows, and I shake my head, knowing the cause. I've always felt silly for feeling sorry for myself or catching myself in a depressed mood. My life is nothing to be sad about. I live in one of the greatest cities in the world, have a well-paying job, a family that loves me, an amazing best friend, and a guy that seems to think I'm pretty great. But even with all that, at times I still find myself lonely, removed from things. I can't shake the feeling that something is missing from my life, and I drive myself crazy trying to figure out what it is. I have a habit of watching people—resting my eyes on the ones that look happy, trying to see how they do it.

This isn't to say that I'm crippled with depression, which would be melodramatic. The only way I know how to describe it is that I feel like there's an invisible hole inside my being. This can't be all I'm meant for: a nine-to-five job, five days a week. It's like a piece of me was displaced at birth, and I need to find it so I can be whole again.

So, I keep my eyes open, watching for that thing that can unlock what I'm searching for and lead me to where I'm meant to be.

I don't know how long I've been staring out the window. When my phone buzzes, I glance at the clock and see it's close to noon. I've been sitting here for almost three hours!

Holy moly.

I jump up and immediately regret it. My knees give way from being in the same position for so long, and I'm still achy from the accident. I fall flat onto my bed and lie there pathetically for a second, slightly out of breath, before regaining my bearings and crawling to my phone. It's a text from Jared, asking if we are still on for tonight. After confirming and settling on a time for him to come over, I glance down to my wrinkled pajamas, complete with jelly stain. Sexy. I can only imagine what my hair looks like.

Throwing my dish in the sink, I strip off my clothes and prepare myself for a five-hour shower.

⇥✦ ✦⇤

My door buzzes precisely at six o'clock, and I let Jared up. Leaving my front door ajar, I quickly check myself in the bathroom mirror.

My dark-brown hair falls past my shoulders in waves, my long-sleeved V-neck gray shirt hints at my cleavage, and my black skinny jeans hug me in all the right places. Not too bad. Except for the bandage around my wrist, there's no hint of what happened a few days ago. Five-hour showers are so worth it. Sorry, environment, but it's true.

My front door swings open and Jared strides in, holding a bag of Chinese takeout and two DVDs. He wears a sky-blue collared shirt under a chestnut leather jacket and the same dark fitted jeans from the other night. I love those jeans. At the sight of his height and build, I immediately want to push him on the bed and forget about dinner.

"Hi there, beautiful," he says, placing the food and DVDs on my kitchen counter and walking over to me. He wraps me in his arms, sending shivers along my body from the outside cold he still wears. I look up into his warm hazel eyes.

"Hey, back at ya, handsome."

"I was so worried about you." He gently pulls me in for a kiss.

"I'm sorry," I mumble against his lips, "but now I'm right as rain." I flash a smile.

Jared steps back to hold me at arm's length, his concerned expression slowly relaxing into a devilish grin.

"What?"

"Only you could get struck by lightning a week ago and still look this hot."

He swiftly lifts me off of my feet and carries me to my bed as I giggle like a pathetic schoolgirl.

Pathetic being the key word.

Placing me down, he strips out of his jacket, fully exposing his blue shirt underneath. Something about the color jars my nerves, and my stomach tightens. I hardly have time to react when he leans over and swoops one arm under my back, raising my body to his. He gently kisses me, and my mouth opens invitingly. He tastes like spearmint gum. My legs wrap around his calves, pulling him closer, and a deep groan escapes him.

"Let me know if I'm hurting you," he says softly.

"You're not," I reply breathless. My head swims with yearning as heat pulses between us. I'm about to roll on top of him, when my phone rings. We both freeze at the invasive sound.

"It's probably my mother," I whisper against his mouth. He exhales and suddenly releases his full body weight, pinning me to the bed. I laugh uselessly, trying to shove him off, my muscles still sore. "Jared, I need to take this. I forgot to call her today."

He rolls to the side, allowing my escape.

"Hi, Mom."

"Molly? Why haven't you called me today!?" She bellows out from the phone, and I wince, moving the speaker from my ear.

"I'm so sorry. I've been doing things all day and lost track of time"—*a.k.a. eating and staring out my window.*

"Well, I've been waiting for you to call me since this morning. It's six thirty! And what do you mean, doing things all day? You should be *resting.*"

"Mom, I'm *so* sorry," I say again. "I didn't mean that I was running around or anything. I've just got a lot on my mind."

Jared glances at me, and I shrug, attempting to mime that I'm making things up as I go along. My mom sighs on the other end of the line.

"I'm sorry too, Mols. I'm just your mother, and you're my baby. I worry about you, and you promised you'd call me every day. Can't a mother worry?"

I laugh at her question. "Of course a mother can worry. But I'm *fine*. My day was relaxing and pretty uneventful. Jared's over now, and we're about to eat dinner."

"Oh, Jared! Tell him I said hi."

"My mom says 'Hi,' Jared."

"Hi, Kathy." I'm slightly shocked that he knows my mom's first name, but then I guess my parents would have introduced themselves at the hospital. Jared kisses me on the forehead before pushing off the bed and begins to unload the takeout.

"What are you guys going to do tonight?" Her tone is much more chipper than when I first picked up the phone.

"Laying low, eating some Chinese, and watching some movies. What are you and Dad doing?"

"We have a dinner to go to that some of his law school friends are hosting. In fact, we're about to run out the door now. But I wanted to make sure you were okay before we went."

"Well, I'm doing great, so don't worry. My head hardly hurts anymore, and my body isn't nearly as sore. Tell Dad I said hi and I love him."

Jared starts humming some tune as he grabs dishes from the cupboards, and I smile.

"I will," my mom says. "Oh! And before I forget, you need to call your grandfather too and let him know you're okay. When we told him what happened, he started to have one of his nervous fits."

I can sense Mom rolling her eyes. I also know from whom I inherited that trait. "Yes, okay, I'll try to remember to give him a call."

"Good, good. All right, you and Jared have fun tonight, and I love you."

"Love you too, Mom."

Hanging up, I continue to watch Jared making himself at home in my kitchen. His ease and relaxation in my small apartment is kind of cute. When he catches me eyeing him, he shoots me a shy, curious smile. Cute just got upgraded to adorable.

After we're done filling our faces with Chinese, we settle in to watch the movies.

"So what have you brought?"

He flashes an excited grin. "What do you think?"

I stare at him blankly, really having no clue. He chuckles and tosses the two movies onto the bed, where I'm sitting cross-legged. "You really think I'd miss the chance to finish this series with you? As soon as you suggested watching the first one, I knew you were a keeper."

I smirk, reading the titles: *Die Hard 2* and *Die Hard: With a Vengeance*. I've been into good cop/bad cop dramas since I was little. I think it's my dad's influence, being that that's his alter ego's fantasy profession.

"You don't find a lady that likes cop movies every day. Gotta take advantage when you do." He wraps his arms around my waist and gently pulls me toward him, softly running kisses along my earlobe. I squirm, and before I can become completely distracted, escape his hold.

"I know for a fact we won't be watching much of anything if you keep that up."

"I'm willing to risk it if you are." His gaze is sinful.

"I have no doubt that you would, but here's the thing"—I pop the first movie into my player—"you might have underestimated my fandom for this genre. Especially where Brucey is concerned."

"Brucey?"

"Yup, Bruce Willis. If there's a chance to see him in action *and* to hear him lay down some Grade A puns, well that's it, game over. You'll know where to find me."

Jared raises his eyebrows. "Should I be worried?"

I sigh as the man himself fills the screen. "Always."

After getting my vitamin B fix—much to Jared's amusement—we get ready for bed. Despite not doing much today, I'm absolutely drained.

"Tired?" he asks as we push ourselves into my cool sheets.

"Extremely." I wiggle my way into his strong arms.

"Too bad, because you look absolutely edible in your little pajama set."

Normally I wear mannish baggy clothes when I sleep alone, but on the occasions when a guy comes around, I try to be a little enticing. My Road Runner boxer shorts I'll save for month six.

Even though Jared's mouth is gentle and coaxing, he seems to catch on to the seriousness of my exhaustion, because he laughs warmly and kisses my cheek instead. "I had a great time tonight," he whispers. "And I'm really glad you're okay." His features are content and relaxed in the dim light.

"Me too." I run my fingers across his jaw. "To both of those things."

He smiles before kissing me once more. "G'night, Molly."

"G'night," I say and pull his arms tighter around me. It only takes a moment before we both drift off to sleep.

-→•▭◉ ◎▭•←-

The darkness envelops my body like a warm blanket as I propel forward. I'm completely weightless as I soar above a grassy field, and I wonder if this is what it's like to be a ghost. The crisp fragrance of night hits my face, welcoming me in a refreshing caress. I pass over a familiar tree and continue onward. A city rises in the distance as I draw nearer. A fortified wall surrounds its perimeter. I fly past the wall and above the city, swimming in and out of the tall buildings.

As I look around in wonder, I note that this metropolis seems to have the same characteristics as any other: glass-and-metal skyscrapers desperately reach toward the zooming stars above—a lover trying to return to its mate. Brick-and-marble apartment buildings along with sidewalks and parks fill the guts of the city, coiling around tall structures in a grid formation.

The one thing that does seem out of place is the complete absence of cars. It's the cleanest city I've ever seen. No graffiti covers any surface or wall, no garbage wraps along the streets, and no steam rises from drains. The people beneath me ride sleek bikes, skateboard, or walk. Their dark clothes camouflage them into the night-filled city, bringing to mind a symbiotic existence with their surroundings and making it difficult to distinguish how many people are truly below.

I continue to travel deeper into the metropolis that's covered in a cool blanket of white-blue light, reminiscent of the hottest part of a flame. Victorian lampposts line the modern sidewalks, housing this swirling bright mixture of colors. Transfixed by the movement inside these lamps, a feeling of embarrassment washes over me. It's as if I'm glancing at something so pure and vulnerable that I need to look away. *What a funny dream this is.*

As I pass over certain city squares, I notice strange, glowing circular pods tucked away into corners. White light blazes from their centers as people pop in and out like they are walking through an invisible door.

A whooshing sound passes by, and I glance up, startled at what I hadn't noticed until now. There are zipline cables everywhere, with dozens of people zooming from building to building. They grasp sticks that look like archery bows slung over the lines, and familiar-looking tubes sit on their backs.

My body changes direction, descending toward the fire escape of a brick apartment building. I reach out, grabbing hold of the metal balcony, and place my feet down, my body registering gravity once again.

I stand on the fire escape—about six flights up—and watch clusters of people hustle on the streets below. I tip my head up to the night sky, studying the familiar captivating shooting stars, and that's when it all comes crashing back to me.

I've been here before. Not to this city, but to this place with the sky that zooms overhead. I remember the large field I flew over earlier and the solitary tree. A memory of a man's face begins to take shape, but it's dashed away by the sound of voices behind me.

Turning around to one of the apartment's windows, I peek inside. There's a small kitchen that's separated from a dining room and living room by a bar countertop. The room and kitchen are modern in design, like an apartment one would find in New York: chrome countertops, glass-and-metal kitchen cabinets, and rich wooden floors. The only thing out of sorts is the lighting, which looks like same material and colors I saw in the lanterns on the street below. The interior bright blue-white substance swirls and coils around itself, and again the familiar feelings creep over me.

A girl walks into the room beyond the kitchen, placing a bowl on the dining room table. Her long blonde hair is pulled up into a ponytail, revealing pale skin that's high in contrast against her dark-black clothes. The name Aveline pops into my head.

"I don't know why you're so calm about this," the girl says in a slightly frustrated tone as an older man strides into view. He looks late forties and has short brown hair that's salted with bits of gray. His wide shoulders pull the limits of his black uniform, and with his tall frame and thick beard, he reminds me of an old sea captain. Pulling out a chair at the head of the table, he sits.

"I'm calm because there's nothing to get excited about yet." He moves the newly placed bowl closer to him.

"Exactly...yet! What happens if she comes back? You should have seen him. It was like the sky opened up and poured down the heavens." The man is unmoved and pops whatever he just plucked from the bowl into his mouth. "Seriously, Tim, he keeps droning on about how this could be the key to winning against the Metus. But he can't even explain how!" When she realizes he's not going to say anything, she throws up her hands. "Gah! You're almost as bad as he is."

Tim leans back, rolling another item from the bowl between his thumb and pointer finger. It looks like a grape. Placing it into his mouth, he doesn't speak until he's finished chewing. "Like I said before, at the moment there's nothing to get worked up about. We don't know if she's coming back, and even if she does, it could mean nothing. All in due time, Aveline, all in due time."

Her name *is* Aveline! Why did I know that?

"What you both should be doing is concentrating on your rounds." He goes on. "We can't have either one of you busy thinking about 'could bes' and 'what ifs' when you're out on patrol. That's how someone gets hurt. Especially with the higher number of sightings we've encountered lately."

I stare into the apartment like a deer in headlights. I can't shake the feeling that they are talking about me. But nothing else makes any sense. Something called the Metus? What is this place?

"You know, I think I could find others who would agree with me that being a Peeping Tom *might* be more rude than staring." A familiar, deep voice comes from my right.

I jump back, my stomach clenching in fright as I take in the appearance of a man casually sitting on the metal stairs that lead up to the next landing. Even in the shadows I can make out his half-upturned lips that form an amused smile. My cheeks redden as I connect with his blazing blue eyes—eyes that I feel have captured me before.

He chuckles at whatever face I'm making, and in my shock all I manage to whisper is, "Dev."

Chapter 6

I STAND RIGID against the far railing of the fire escape. My heart beats erratically against my chest, a million thoughts rapidly shuffling through my mind. How did he get there? I didn't hear a thing. Was he sitting there this whole time? Taking in his familiar face, I'm not sure if my heart palpitations are from being scared so bad I nearly peed myself or because of whom I'm looking at.

"You remember my name." Dev leans forward, bathing the side of his face with the light that escapes from the apartment window. My mind swirls, trying to recollect where I've seen him before and why I know his name.

"I...I've met you before?" I stammer, more of a question than a statement.

He's silent for a moment, assessing me. "I don't know, Molly. You tell me."

The sound of my name on his lips makes my heart do another little leap. He knows me too. Letting go of the railing, I stand tall, feigning confidence. "Yes, I think we've met before. A lot of this seems familiar. Not really the interior of this city, but..." I trail off, thinking of the field I flew over earlier and the single elm tree.

"But…" Dev coaxes.

"But I know you, and I know that girl in there." I point toward the window. "You obviously know me too, since you said my name."

"Interesting" is his only reply, which has me frowning.

Not sure where to go from here, I'm caught off guard when he suddenly stands, taking up most of the small space. I stumble back in shock and hit the railing hard. In my flustered state, I lose my balance and lean over the metal edge, about to fall. Before I can get a scream out, strong hands catch around my waist and pull me up. I'm breathing heavy as my mind slowly processes that I'm standing safe and not painting the cement red below.

That's when I realize my arms are tightly wrapped around Dev's neck and my face is buried into his hard chest. Unable to stop myself, I take in his fresh scent of night and spice, and my brain stirs with a confused longing. My body that was chilled with fright is now flush as we press tight against one another. I glance into his sapphire eyes, unable to move my hands, and my stomach tightens at our facial proximity.

"You're a jumpy one, aren't you?" Dev says with a smile.

Instantly, I push away, and he chuckles.

"I was only going to open the window," he says, crouching down to the glass. "Oh, and by the way…" He looks back in my direction, slowly gliding his gaze up my body. "I like your outfit tonight *much* more than last night." He finishes with a crude eyebrow raise before jumping inside. I'm left standing with mouth slightly ajar, glancing at my clothes. Or should I say underwear.

"Shit."

I'm wearing exactly what I wore when I crawled into bed with Jared. A tight, small gray camisole and snug gray-and-white polka-dot shorts. Not leaving much to the imagination. I don't know if this is worse than dreaming you're naked in front of your whole high school class.

Yeah, it's worse.

Coaching myself into believing this situation is not at all embarrassing, I cover my exposed chest and bend down, peering inside the open window. Dev is already standing where Aveline and the man are, and after saying a few words, they both turn in my direction.

"Great," I mutter.

Now that my cover is blown and I feel like an idiot out here, I make my way through the window. I'm about to set my feet on the kitchen floor when someone helps me the rest of the way. I glance down to Dev's hands on my hips, his fingers grazing my bare skin where my camisole hitched up.

Umm...

I step away and scoot my shirt down. Could I feel any more naked? "I can climb into a window, thank you very much," I state in composed agitation, hoping anger works as the cover-up for my flushed expression.

"We can never be too sure, now can we?" Dev leans in and winks. My mouth gapes open again at his blatant vulgarity, and his attention is brought to my lips.

Oh dear Lord. He's all kinds of wrong.

I pull myself together by making a disgusted noise and glance to the other people in the apartment. This guy is making me feel crazy.

"Tim, this is the wonder I was telling you about." Dev turns to his companions, who both now stand, and I can't mistake Aveline's eyes growing beady as she scrutinizes my presence and attire.

Awesome. If she didn't like me before, she probably hates me now. And who can blame her? I would hate me in my current state too.

"Ah, Molly is it? Welcome to our home. My name is Timon, but please call me Tim."

He extends his hand for me to take, and his grip is firm but comforting and just as warm as his smile. Stepping back, he looks me over. I would probably blush again if my cheeks weren't already permanently stained red with mortification from this entire evening. "Aveline, why don't you go and see if you can find something for our guest to wear that might make her a little more comfortable." He glances at the girl, who still has her vengeful glare boring a hole into my face.

"*Aveline.*"

She eyes him with disdain before turning toward one of the hallways. Dev chuckles under his breath as she passes, and she loses none of her momentum as she shoves him from the side, causing him to laugh harder. I realize that his hubris doesn't get under just my skin, and I suddenly want to befriend this girl, even though it seems like that's the last thing in the world she wants to happen.

Now that I'm inside, I take a moment to study the apartment. The white walls shape a perfect square, housing a late '60's-style sunken living room in the middle. Rich cream leather couches sit in the center along with a glass coffee table, all of which face a modern-looking fireplace inset in the farthest wall from us. The off-white coloring of the walls mixes into a strange cool-warm hue from the glowing fire and the blue-white of the lighting fixtures around the apartment. Two hallways go off on either end of the room, but they are cast in shadow so that it's hard to discern how long they are and what is beyond. The dining table sits in front of the open-style kitchen and seats six, making me wonder how many people live here.

Dev pulls out one of the chairs and sits. Leaning back, he puts his hands in his pockets and extends his long legs in front of him, crossing them at the ankle. Our eyes lock briefly before I look away.

"Dev, don't be rude by sitting first." Tim's brows pinch in with disapproval. "Have I taught you nothing of manners?"

"Would you like to take a seat, Molly?" Dev says in a musically polite tone as he gracefully waves his arm out, displaying the other chairs. Before I can respond, Aveline stomps back into the room and throws clothes onto the table.

"I don't really have anything in *your* size," she slightly sneers. "So I thought these stretchy pants could accommodate the difference." I pick up what looks like spandex yoga pants, but the material is much tougher and thicker. "This is one of my *bigger* shirts." She hands me a soft black T-shirt like the ones they all wear. I don't know why she keeps referencing the size of the clothes—I'm not fat, but I guess compared to her rail-thin frame I would seem slightly Amazonian. *Excuse me if I have curves.*

"And you'll just have to make do with these boots—which I want back, by the way." She hands me black combat boots.

"Uh, thanks." I hold the clothes awkwardly in my arms.

"Dev, can you please show Molly where the bathroom is?" Tim requests pleasantly. Dev stands without a word and moves toward the hallway on the other side of the room. I hesitate for a moment before following.

We walk a short distance in the dark hall before Dev stops in front of an open door, flicks on the light, and gestures for me to enter. I carefully step around him so as not to touch any part of his body. Turning, I catch him watching me strangely, and I clear my throat. "Thanks."

"My pleasure," he says in an exaggerated velvety smooth voice before disappearing back down the dark hall. I gently shut the door and lean against it, clutching the clothes to my chest.

This is all so insane. How can this be a dream?

I survey the small bathroom. It's modern, white, and sparse, reminding me of what a serial killer's bathroom could look like: easy to bleach.

Dropping the clothes to the ground, I begin to dress. I throw the black T-shirt over my camisole, and even though Aveline said it was her *biggest* one, it still hugs parts of my body, specifically the bosom area. I take slight solace when I see that it's a crew collar.

I slip out of my shorts and slide into the black pants. The material clings tightly to every curve of my legs and butt. Though it's an extremely flexible fabric, I can tell that it's protective of every inch of my skin beneath, like some sort of body armor. Lastly, I tug on the black boots that reach a little bit higher than my ankles. I sigh... at least something fits me. I lace them up over my pants and, standing on my tippy-toes, glance into the mirror to see my full figure.

I bark out a laugh. I would never wear something like this. I look like some sort of dominatrix searching for a pet. Even with the pants covering me completely, I feel more exposed than I did in my tiny shorts. They are just so tight. Aveline really is a stick.

Pulling my hair into a ponytail with a tie I find around my wrist, I take a deep breath and exit the bathroom. Approaching the end of the hallway, I catch the three of them sitting around the dining table talking in fast whispers, and I grow uneasy.

Dev sits at the head of the table and sees me reenter first. His eyes go wide and then slowly grow dark and a bit frightening as he takes in my appearance. My stomach turns at the thought that I must look more ridiculous than I presumed. Deciding I won't let this bother me any more than it already has, I raise my chin and pull out a chair next to Tim, who, like everyone else, has stopped talking.

Tim recovers faster than the others. "If I didn't know better, I would have thought you belonged here, Molly. Those clothes suit you very nicely."

"Really? I feel kind of ridiculous in them, to be honest. I don't normally wear anything like this."

"Obviously," Aveline mutters under her breath, and I give her a cold look. Yeah, I don't know about the befriending thing anymore.

Dev suppresses a chuckle, and I refuse to acknowledge him.

"So, Timon, that's an interesting name. I've never heard it before," I say, letting his charming face set me at ease.

"Yes, it's not that common. It's a biblical name and means wisdom." Given the meaning, it's very fitting. He seems to exude his namesake in those sparkling brown eyes.

"Everyone's name has a meaning. *Aveline*, for example"—he motions toward her—"means life." He flashes her a radiant, fatherly smile, and she holds his look with apparent love. I wonder who this guy is to them.

"Dev"—he places his hand on Dev's muscular shoulder—"is short for *Devlin*, of Irish origin, and means fierce courage." Dev seems slightly embarrassed at the sound of his full name, and Aveline chuckles.

"What?" I ask, not seeing the humor.

"*Devlin* thinks his name sounds feminine." Aveline laughs again, and the sound is light and twinkles like bells. It's an infectious sound, and I find myself growing happy listening to it. I much prefer her this way.

Dev scours and pushes her shoulder. "Shut up." This makes her giggle more, and Tim smiles, watching their sibling-like exchange. Seeing how they must interact on a daily basis, laughing and joking and teasing each other, I feel slightly removed from this close-knit group.

"So, Molly, where you come from, you have a last name as well. What is it?" Tim asks.

A bit confused by the phrasing of his question, I say, "Spero, uh, my last name is Spero." Everyone goes quiet. Dev, Aveline, and Tim share a stunned look. "What? What is it? Does it mean something bad?" I ask, glancing from face to face.

Tim clears his throat. "Molly, which originates from Mary, can mean star of the sea. And Spero…" He pauses, making eye contact with Dev. "Spero means hope. So your full name can translate to mean—"

"Star of Hope," Dev finishes in a whisper.

⊷═◉ ◉═⊶

"Star of Hope," I repeat. "Okay…so?"

All three of them stare at me. Aveline's familiar frown is back. Tim studies me intently, and Dev…well, Dev looks like he's trying to see inside my soul. His blue eyes grow slightly unfocused as if he's remembering something.

"Why are you guys looking at me like that? It's just a name." I laugh lightly, trying to bring the mood back to the levity of earlier.

"You must excuse us," Tim says. "Here, names have great meaning and importance. It's sort of prophetic for what one will be capable of accomplishing."

My eyes narrow. "Where is *here*?"

Without missing a beat, Tim gently pats me on the back. "We'll just have to see, won't we?"

Another nonanswer. "What does that even mean?" I can't hide the exasperation in my tone.

Tim doesn't expand; instead, he displays a sad, understanding smile. I'm so sick of getting this look. Why is no one answering me? First, Dev out on the fire escape, and now Tim. And what's so secretive that they can't tell me? If I'm only dreaming, then what's the big deal? God, I want to pull my hair out from agitation.

Throwing my elbows on the table, I place my face in my hands, letting out a giant sigh. Not the most mature way to act, but at this particular moment I don't really care. These people have already seen me in my underwear.

The snap of the logs crackling in the fireplace grows louder as the silence stretches through the apartment. I know everyone's attention is on me, but I refuse to acknowledge them. My mind is in overdrive trying to come up with answers to where I am and what's going on. Could this really be a dream? I remember being with Jared and getting into bed and falling asleep. And then it's like I just woke up here...

I whip my head up. "Dev, you said out on the fire escape that you liked what I was wearing tonight better than what I was wearing last night..."

Dev's smile is impish. "You liked that, huh."

I wave my hand like I'm swatting away a fly. "No, I mean, you said you saw me *last night.*"

He suddenly grows serious and something about the fact that I was able to remove his self-satisfied grin pleases me. "Did I say that?" he asks innocently.

"You just admitted you did." I scowl. "You *also* said to Tim that I'm the *wonder* you were telling him about. If we've never met, how could you talk about me?" Seconds tick by as we hold each other's gaze, mine growing more confident now that I know I've caught him, and his looking more aggravated that he was obviously caught.

The sound of metal scraping against the wooden floor draws my attention to Aveline standing. "I know you two would love to stare into each other's eyes all day, but we have rounds to make, Dev." She hits him on the shoulder. He holds me captive a second longer before a small, mischievous expression creeps across his mouth, and he stands.

"That's it? You're not going to explain yourself?"

"I have nothing to explain." Dev calmly turns around.

Have I mentioned that I find this guy annoying?

I watch in aggravated silence as they open a closet hidden against the wall adjacent to the front door. It's so seamlessly placed that I didn't notice it earlier when I came in. The two doors let out a huff of air as they smoothly open and track into the walls. A bright blue-white light shines out. Inside are all sorts of strange, innocuous-looking black objects encased in a glowing plush material, as if they are being charged by it. There are long black sticks, black baseball-sized spheres, and cubes. In the center are three familiar-looking quivers, and above each are smooth black batons. Dev and

Aveline each pick up a quiver, leaving the third in the center, and collect the batons.

Dev gracefully handles the objects like they are old friends and straps the quiver to his back, allowing the black baton to be sucked inside. An image of him standing over me in the field with a quiver strapped in the same place flashes through my mind. When was that?

"All right, Tim, we'll catch you later." Aveline walks toward the front door but stops short when she realizes Dev isn't following. Instead, he's staring at me.

"Well, aren't you coming?" he asks me.

"Uh, what?" Aveline's voice rings out. "She is so *not* coming with us!"

"Of course she is."

"AAARGH" Aveline yells and points toward Dev. "See this, Tim? *See*! This is exactly what I was talking about! He's lost his mind."

"I resent that statement." Dev casually leans against the wall, pretending to clean his nails. Aveline takes in a calming breath and closes her eyes, seeming to count in her head.

Girl, I know how you feel.

"Dev," she says in a forced, pleasant tone, "please explain to me why Molly needs to come with us?"

"Because it would be fun."

"Fun," she repeats.

"Yes, fun."

"So it would be *fun*, not dangerous and probably illegal, and the stupidest idea anyone has ever had in the entire existence of mankind?"

"Nope. Just fun." Dev pushes off the wall and strides toward me.

After Aveline listed all those points, maybe it is best if I stay here. Plus, it's probably safer for both Dev and I if we remain a safe distance from one another. "It's okay. I don't mind staying with Tim."

"Nope. You're coming with us." He grips my arm, pulling me awkwardly to my feet. My anger dissipates slightly with his touch and the thought that I might gain some answers by seeing wherever it is they're going.

Could I be any more desperate for answers? No, no, I couldn't.

"Are you sure this is a good idea?" Concern is etched on Tim's face.

"I think it's one of the best ideas I've ever had." Dev guides me toward the exit before I can find another reason for staying behind. Aveline shoots him a death stare as he marches past and completely ignores me. "Ladies first." He opens the front door to a dimly lit hallway.

His comment brings me back to my birthday dinner with Jared, and I grin at the memory. Dev blinks a few times at my pleased expression and then gives me one of his knee-weakening smiles.

Immediately, my face falls. "I wasn't smiling at you."

"I see." He glances around. "So it was for the other man who opened the door for you."

"As a matter of fact, it was," I say and breeze past him.

Their apartment is at the end of a long, dark hallway, and I head in the only direction possible—straight. Dev is close behind, and I'm suddenly aware, once again, of my tight pants.

I chance a glance over my shoulder and catch Dev's eyes as they come up from exactly where I thought they would be. He gives me a wicked smile. "Pig," I bite out and turn away, not mistaking Dev's low laughter from hearing my comment. I bristle.

Stopping at the elevator at the end of the hall, Dev presses the Up button.

"Where are we going?"

"To the roof," he answers as the doors ding open, and we step inside. It's just as dark in this elevator as it is in the hall. Aveline presses buttons that are filled with Roman numerals on a keypad, and we start to ascend. I'm standing in the corner with Dev a little way in front of me, and I feel so small behind his towering body.

Being this close, I can't help but check out his muscular arm that's practically grazing my face with its proximity. Dev casually holds the strap around his chest, flexing his bicep, which I have no doubt he's doing on purpose. Furtively glancing up, I study his profile. He truly is gorgeous, even if it pains me to admit it. Maybe I don't hate him so much.

Just then he bumps his arm into my face, snapping me out of my ogling. He chuckles lightly. "Oh, sorry about that," he says while still facing forward.

Yeah, never mind. I definitely hate him.

Chapter 7

THE ELEVATOR DOORS open, and I'm immediately hit with the slight chill of night. We exit onto the roof, which seems like any other roof except for the large platform that sits at the end farthest from us. The platform is constructed of black metal, and a large pole protrudes from the back with a thick wire attached to the top that disappears into the city. On closer inspection, I realize it's one end of a zipline, like the other thousands I saw crossing the metropolis.

Aveline and Dev walk quickly onto the structure as I stay at the base of the stairs, unsure of what to do.

Dev turns around. "What's the matter?"

"Uh…" I glance around, uncertain.

He smiles as he descends the stairs and extends his hand. I look at it like he's offering me a gun—shocked, slightly afraid, and clueless as to what I'm supposed to do with it. He sighs and grabs my hand, leading me up. His skin is cool and slightly rough with calluses.

Once I'm on the platform, I notice a lit bull's-eye for a landing zone along the base. Aveline is over near a keypad, typing in numbers, which again are displayed as Roman numerals. She hits a blue button and the thick zipline cord retracts into the pole and then shoots out again like venom from a snake's mouth. It now faces an entirely different direction.

Dropping my hand, Dev reaches over his shoulder as if to grab an invisible arrow. A black baton jumps from his quiver with a suctioning sound, and he snatches it from the air. He shakes it quickly in front of him and two ends snap out from either side, now looking like an archery bow without its string. I blink in astonishment.

Dev holds the object out for me to examine. "This is called an Arcus, but you would probably call it a bow."

I nod because that's exactly what I called it. "Where's the string?"

"The string retracts for when we need it, but the Arcus is also used for getting around." He points to the zipline as if that explains everything.

It doesn't.

He smiles sweetly at my confusion. "Can I show you?"

"Uh, I don't know..." I say, uncomfortable with his sudden genuine display of warmth.

Aveline lets out an exasperated huff. "You guys are ridiculous. Dev, I'll see you on the other side."

In one fluid movement, she snaps her baton into the long bow, runs, and leaps to the zipline, raising the bow to straddle the cable. With a firm grip on either handle, she flies away into the city at a sickening speed.

My body sways with nausea... Is that what I have to do?

"It looks worse than it is. You'll be perfectly safe."

Why don't I believe him?

"Really, I think you'll actually love it," he coaxes. "It's a strangely liberating feeling. Flying." There's a slight ache in his tone on the last word. His face is completely relaxed, devoid of its usual self-assuredness. He looks so beautiful like this, innocent even.

"You'll be okay, Molly. Trust me."

He holds out his hand without moving his eyes from mine.

Trust me...

Hearing those words gives me a ghostly sense of déjà vu.

Do I trust him? Of course not, I just met him... Yet, everything seems so familiar to me. But how could I ever forget meeting someone like him? Forget being in a place like this?

"Okay..." I tentatively take his hand.

His answering smile lifts my heart, and I quickly look away before the small wall I built with this man comes crumbling down. I just have to remind myself that he's usually an annoying twit. A gorgeous, annoying twit...

"I have a safety cord that harnesses you to me," he explains as he leads me to the center of the illuminated circle. "So you don't have to worry about losing your grip."

He pulls a thin but obviously strong cord from one side of his quiver.

"Come here."

He turns me so I'm facing forward on the platform and standing directly in front of him. The glittering city expands around us. "I'm going to strap you into me and then show you how you're supposed to hold the Arcus on the zipline."

Before I can get an "okay" out, I'm quickly pressed against his warm, hard chest. My mind goes soft as my breathing deepens, feeling my backside fitting to him perfectly. I swallow.

"I don't think this is a good idea, actually." I move to step out of this intimate position, but his grip on me tightens.

"Molly, relax." His breath tickles my exposed neck, and goose bumps explode on my skin.

"I can control the speed by gripping the ends of the Arcus here." He cages me in by placing his arms in front of me, displaying the bow. "To slow down, I just squeeze the handles, and the Arcus will grip the cable line harder. See?" Dev tightens and relaxes his grip on the ends, which resemble brake levers on a bike. The space in the middle of the bow, where the zipline wire goes, pinches in.

I nod.

"Okay, now hold this while I strap you in."

I was expecting the bow to be heavy, but it's surprisingly light, as if it was made from some sort of durable aluminum. It fits in my hands perfectly, and I grip it like I'm used to holding such an instrument.

The material of the handles feels like leather but looks more like rubber. I wonder how they can get rubber to feel like this. I'm about to ask, when Dev's fingers move into the side of my waistband.

"What are you doing?!" I smack his hands and step away.

"Ow!" He shakes out his fingers and stares at me in shock before rolling his head back in a belly-exploding laugh, the sound deep and warm,

"I'm glad you find taking advantage of me so funny."

Dev wipes a tear from his eye. "You, Molly, might just be the end of me."

"Promise?" I mumble.

He shakes his head, still smiling. "I need to get at the loops in your pants—they run around the front of your waistband and are what acts as the harness."

"Oh."

"Yeah, *oh*. Trust me, if I wanted to go *there*, we would have already been *there*."

I've never rolled my eyes so fast in my life. "Please, you are *not* my type."

He moves closer. "But don't you remember? I'm the man of your dreams."

Before I can blink, he whips me back against his body, and I suck in air while growing paralyzed as his fingers skillfully find all the loops in my pants. He guides the cord through the harness, grazing the length of my midriff the whole way. Once through the last hoop, he straps the tip into the other side of his quiver. It's like a seat belt is tied tightly around my waist, pulling me to him. With my eyes wide and, I'm sure, my face beet red, I fit snugly to Dev's body. His chest rises and falls with each breath, and I can't tell if it's his heart or mine that's beating so fast.

"You can let go of the Arcus now," he says softly in my ear, pulling the bow from my aching grip. With a hand on my hip, he guides our now attached bodies back to the center of the circle.

Breathe. Breathe.

He steps onto a small glowing button, and the landing zone rises. I grab his wrist to steady myself, and his soft laughter reverberates through my body, making me want to lean in closer.

"So jumpy," he says, and I allow myself to smile, certain that he can't see it. The platform stops much closer to the zipline, and Dev's hand falls away, relieving my body of his touch. "I'm going to attach the Arcus to the line, and then I'm going to need you to lift your arms up and wrap your hands inside the extension loops."

He holds the bow out in front again, indicating the two loops that now extend on either end of the bow like tassels on a kid's bicycle handle.

"Ready?" he asks gently.

"What do I do once we get going?" I want to ask a million questions not just because I have them but also to stall. I'm not really an adrenaline junkie kind of gal.

"You don't need to do anything but hold on and try to be loose with your body. The line will guide us to where we need to go. Just enjoy yourself."

Sure, enjoy myself while I'm falling down a multiple-story building to my likely death. Easy enough.

"Any more questions?"

"None that will get me out of doing this," I say dryly, making Dev laugh once more.

He fits the Arcus to the line, smoothly moving it back and forth. His toned stomach contracts with the motion, the proximity of our bodies acting like a medieval torture of wills.

"Can you reach up and grab the extension handles?"

I have to stand on my tiptoes to do so, acutely aware that this pushes my backside into his groin. I hear him suck in air, and I hold my eyes shut in mortification.

Clearing his throat, he walks us to the end of the platform. I peek over the ledge and practically seize at the distance below. The ground looks miles away, and I can't help building a detailed vision of my body splayed across the cement. Standing up straight, I internally do the sign of the cross and try backing away.

"Ya know, now that I'm thinking about it, maybe I should stay with Tim. He did seem to think this was a bad idea, and looking at it from this angle, I have to agree with him."

"Don't worry—this will be great. Got a good grip?"

Before I can say no, he pushes off the platform, and we go barreling down into the open air. My stomach drops out and is left somewhere on the platform as my body is violently pushed back against Dev's. The wind whips against my eyes, and I can hear someone screaming.

Just as I understand that it's my own desperate expression of fear and excitement tearing out of my vocal cords, a weird out-of-body experience surrounds me.

I shut my eyes tight, and when I open them again, I'm sitting upright in my bed, sweating and panting in the dark.

Chapter 8

"BABE, ARE YOU okay?" I jump at the gruff voice that mumbles from the other side of my bed. Jared lies there rubbing his eyes. "What time is it?"

I glance at the clock, still clutching the sheets tightly in my hands, trying to regulate my breathing. "It's still the middle of the night. Go back to sleep," I say softly. Jared murmurs his consent before slipping back into slumber.

I sit immobile, staring into the darkness. What was that? Was I really dreaming? I move my tongue around my dry mouth and swallow. My throat's sore. Did I scream out loud or just in my sleep?

My mind feels strange. As if I spun around in circles and suddenly stopped, my brain trying to catch up with the twirling movement.

A cool breeze comes in through the open window, sending a chill across my skin. I settle my eyes over my gray camisole and polka-dot shorts, my limbs feeling oddly exposed.

Exiting the bed, I pad over to my kitchen, needing a second before I even attempt to try to sleep. I remember flying down a zipline with a man, his face all but a blur, and my stomach tightens at the thought that I don't remember who he was.

Pouring myself a glass of OJ, I press the cool cup into my hand and lean against the counter. My hazy, sleep-ridden mind starts to clear, pushing away any detailed memory of my dream.

I freeze, realizing that something inside me doesn't want the dream to slip away. My heart picks up again, and I can't explain why, but a sadness tugs at my chest. What is happening to me? I've never experienced this after sleeping before…not until the accident.

Panic explodes around me. Did it mess up my brain? Why do I feel like I've had a similar dream before? I stare at a blue hand towel that's draped over my kitchen sink. My drink stops halfway to my lips as I lock on to the object. Blue, his eyes are blue…

"Mols, what are you doing?" Jared sleepily calls out from my bed again, interrupting my spiraling thoughts.

I clear my throat. "I just needed something to drink. I'll be back in a second." Finishing my OJ, I place the glass in the sink.

I'm fine. This is all fine. It's just the Chinese I ate before we went to bed. I'm never eating Chinese again.

As I crawl back under my sheets, Jared shifts over, holding me to his warm body. This is real—this man behind me is real. All that other stuff was just a dream. Taking in a large breath of air, I snuggle into his chest.

I lie there staring out my dark window, trying to keep my eyes open as long as I can, listening to Jared's rhythmic breathing against my neck and the casual honking of cars below.

Eventually my eyes begin to sting with exhaustion, and I slowly allow them to close.

⊷⟞⟝⊶

My mind floats through nothingness again, stretching itself into the expansion of endless space. Slowly, a hard, damp substance materializes against my back. I move my body cautiously, relieved at its response. I breathe in deep, tasting and smelling a familiar fragrance. My ears pick up bugs chirping, and my heart pumps excitedly in my chest, remembering where I must be.

Finally, I open my eyes.

I'm lying in tall grass, the night sky above twirling with shooting stars, and a grin spreads across my face. I'm back.

Why does this make me happy?

I turn to a large tree, and like quick synapses, the memories of this place flood my mind. The dark field, the illuminated city in the distance, the beautiful star-filled sky. Three familiar faces dressed in black. This place has become the sole focus of my dreams. Like my brain is a record stuck on the same note.

All the panic I had before I closed my eyes vanishes now that I'm here, and I marvel that all this could merely be in my imagination.

I play with the grass in front of my crossed legs, noticing I'm once again in my provocative pajamas. The tight black clothes must have vanished when I woke with a start. Why do I remember more about this place when I'm here but can't seem to when I'm back in my apartment?

Gazing toward the city that I know I've traveled to before, I watch the surrounding glow expand and contract like a beating heart.

"Beautiful, isn't it?"

I whip my head around, my stomach filling with nervous flutters as I take in my new companion. "How do you do that?" I ask, wrapping my arms around my knees—an attempt to cover myself.

"Do what?" Dev gracefully plops himself beside me.

"Know where I'll be and then sneak up on me like that?"

He shrugs. "I have my ways."

I let out a resigned sigh, slowly growing accustom to never getting an answer in this place.

Dev stretches his legs and leans back on his arms, looking like a lazy farm boy on break. With his attention on the city, I'm tempted to trace his profile with the tip of my finger. I turn away and place my chin on my knees.

"I have to be careful next time and try not to scare you as much," he says, extending a shy smile at my bemused expression. "You woke up."

I nod, visions of the two of us tied together pummeling toward the city flashing in my mind. These dreams are almost like reentering a part in a book that was dog-eared, continuing right where I left off the last time I awoke.

"Is this really a dream?"

Dev studies me intently before looking away. "I'll either have to be more careful, or you'll have to build up some courage to not be frightened so easily," he continues.

I sigh at him ignoring yet another question, before asking another. "Do you still need to do your rounds?"

"You're remembering more," he says, sitting up. "You were gone longer than it probably felt."

"You know, none of you guys ever give any answers that make sense. I just want to know why I keep dreaming of this place, if I *am* dreaming, like you say." I give Dev one of my imploringly desperate looks. "*Please.*"

With a small smile, he shakes his head. "I don't know why you keep coming here."

Though not helpful, his answer sounds genuine. I also notice that he says "coming here" and not "dreaming." "But you have some theories?"

He smirks. "I always have my theories."

When he doesn't enlighten me to what these are—big surprise there—we sit side by side in comfortable silence. The touch of the cool night passes over us, mixing with the peaceful symphony of insects in the grass.

"What's that?" I ask, noticing Dev spinning something between his hands.

He quickly palms the object, bringing it around to his other side. I'm not positive, but I think I saw a familiar-looking shell.

"Come on—what are you hiding?"

Reaching out, I coax him to hand over whatever he's concealing. He wears a playful smile that slips away when he sees my arm. Noticing that I've extended my bandaged wrist, I move it away, but Dev gingerly grabs my hand and brings it closer.

"No! I don't think you should do that," I say as he begins to unwrap the bandage, remembering what the doctor told me about exposing the burn too much. He holds me steady.

"Do you want this to heal?"

"What?"

"It's a simple question. Do you want this to heal?" He nods to my bandage.

"Of course I do." I furrow my brows. "I want nothing more than for it to heal so I don't have to wear this stupid thing."

As soon as I finish speaking, the coolness of his hands seep through the bandage and reaches my skin. The sensation startles me, and I try tugging my arm back, but Dev laces his long fingers with mine, holding me in place. After a beat he continues to unwrap the dressing, my newly exposed skin feeling sensitive in the fresh air.

My breath catches at what I'm pretty sure shouldn't be there. The puffy, raw skin I was used to seeing circle my wrist is now nothing more than an ugly scab. How did it heal so fast? I slowly turn my hand over, lightly touching it to make sure it's real.

"The mind is a powerful thing, Molly. Always remember that."

He looks so much older in this moment...his eyes seem to hold centuries of secrets. I wonder what his age actually is. I thought he was just a few years older than myself, but now that I see his face smoothly lit by the night sky, empty of anything but a gentle expression, he possesses something ancient.

"What type of jewelry were you wearing?" He brings me back to the present by lightly stroking the sensitive part of my wrist.

I hold in a shiver. "Um, a charm bracelet. It was a gift for my birthday."

He removes his hand. "Who gave it to you?"

I hesitate. Jared obviously gave it to me, but do I just say that? Then Dev will ask who Jared is, and for some reason I'm reluctant to admit what he might be to me.

I tuck my hair behind my ear. "A guy."

Dev searches my eyes as I try to read how my answer might have affected him—deep down, I know I desperately want it to.

Dear Lord! What is wrong with me? This guy isn't even real! And isn't this the same man who made me furious earlier tonight?

"What do you do when you're awake?"

"What?"

"What do you do when you're not here? Do you have a job?"

"Uh, yes I have a job…" I hesitate, confused by the change of subject. "It's all very boring though."

He pushes me to explain, asking question after question about my mundane existence.

Slowly, his voice begins to fade and sound distant. I dig my fingers into the grass in an attempt to hold myself here, and Dev flashes me a sad smile.

"I'm waking up, aren't I?"

"Yes."

"But I wanted to ask *you* questions now."

He reaches out, grazing my cheek with his hand. The sensation of his touch is barely there as my body has begun to recognize another surrounding. "There will be plenty of time for that." His voice is buried under layers, and my heart trembles that there might not be. Will I dream of this again?

With that last thought, light fills my vision, and my eyes flutter open to early morning rays stretching into my window, laying their gentle warmth on my skin like a touch I long to remember.

Chapter 9

THE DELICIOUS SMELL of waffles tickles my nose, and the sound of plates being taken out reminds me that someone else is in my apartment. Slowly rolling onto my side, I spot Jared standing in my kitchen in only his boxers. His bare torso ripples gracefully with the small movement of him forking a waffle from the maker and plopping it on a plate. I feel far away watching him, my eyes registering his presence but my mind still in another place with another man.

Jared smiles and asks me something, which I don't catch. I'm still remembering the guy that I was sitting with in a field only moments ago, his sapphire eyes and the small, intimate gesture of his hand on my cheek. I can't shake the feeling of bereavement that is starting to make a home in my chest.

"Molly?"

I snap into focus and see Jared sitting on my bed. His hand rests on my hip, stroking it rhythmically.

"Are you okay?" he asks gently, his handsome face softly lit from the morning light and his light-brown hair disheveled with bedhead.

"Yes, I've just been having strange dreams."

"Yeah, I forgot that you woke up last night. What are they about?"

I try to recall what I remembered only moments ago, but whatever it was has gone. A hazy, dark wall has gone up in its place, and I frown. "I don't remember." The words act as the last deadlock to my recollections.

"Well, you're no longer dreaming, so you don't have to worry." He continues to rub my hip. *No longer dreaming*—those words knock me back hard with dysphoria.

What's going on?

I quickly shake my head and mold my features into a picture of happiness. Mom always said you can't feel sad while you smile. I test her theory. "Did you make me waffles?" I reach out to him, focusing on the reality of Jared being here, reminding myself that everything is fine.

"That I did! Now get up and let's eat before I decide that breakfast should get cold while we play here." He kisses me chastely while slapping me on the butt.

I duck into the bathroom to freshen up, and after I'm done brushing my teeth and taming my disheveled hair, I unwrap my burn to put on a fresh bandage.

Looking down at my wrist, my stomach instantly twists and a cry jolts from my mouth. The skin that I swear was raw and red the last time I checked is now practically healed. The only remnant is a gross-looking scab.

Holy Moses! How is this possible?

"What's wrong?" Jared has opened the bathroom door and is watching me with concern. I glance from his face back to my wrist, then to his face again, at a loss for words. "Molly, what are you doing? You're acting strange," he says impatiently.

"I...I...look!" My brain suddenly lacks the ability to form a sentence, so I shove my wrist toward him.

His brows knit together, clearly not understanding.

"It's scabbed."

"Yes...I see that," he says like I've lost my mind. I'm starting to feel like maybe I have. "Isn't this a good thing? Doesn't that mean it's healing?" Jared takes my wrist that's still shoved in his face and steps into the bathroom.

"Yes, that means it's healing...but how can it heal so fast? I don't think it should be scabbed yet. I swear it wasn't like this yesterday."

Jared chuckles. "Babe, you're acting so crazy. You got struck on Tuesday. It's now Saturday. A couple of days can do wonders, and who knows what kind of advanced medicine they have now for this kind of stuff. It's probably some top-of-the-line ointment."

He holds my arm up, inspecting it again.

"Judging by the looks of this, it definitely is." Jared continues to talk, but I tune him out, remembering someone else holding my wrist, callused yet gentle hands unwrapping my bandages. The images of another man come in flashes, and it's hard to discern what they all mean or if they are even real.

A voice brings me back, and Jared's arms encircle my shoulders. "Hello, earth to Molly," he whispers in my ear. "Where'd you go just then?"

"Nowhere," I return too quickly. "I was trying to remember what Dr. Marshall told me about the ointment." I step out of the bathroom before he has a chance to realize I'm lying.

"Now let's eat some waffles!" I say, pushing away the trepidation I feel looming in my mind about what could possibly be happening to me.

⟶▒◉ ◉▒⟵

After eating an obscene amount of syrupy goodness, my phone rings, and Becca's signature goofy face pops up on the screen.

"Hello there," I say into the phone.

"Who is this?" she says back.

I roll my eyes, knowing the conversation we're about to have. "It's me, Molly."

"Hmm, Molly? Oh yes, I know a couple of Mollys. Now tell me, is this the Molly that wants to meet her best friend for some much-needed window shopping, *or* is this the old-maid Molly that likes to sit in her cramped apartment in day-old pajamas, saying 'woe is me' while looking out of her window?"

She knows both of those Mollys very well.

"I think you've reached the window-shopping Molly today." I smile.

Jared shakes his head while putting the dishes in the sink—he's begun to understand this routine.

"Perfect! Let's say *that* Molly meets me downstairs at her building in thirty minutes?"

"Sounds like a plan. I'll see you then." I hang up and push Jared away from the sink. "You cooked, I clean," I say, my mood in a much better place than when I first woke up.

Jared wraps his strong arms around my waist and pushes my hair off my shoulders, kissing my skin. It's hard to concentrate on washing the dishes when he does that. "I would try to seduce you, but what I have in store takes more than thirty minutes," he says suggestively in my ear. My skin prickles with goose bumps from his warm breath against my neck.

"Oh yeah?"

"Mmhmm," he murmurs as he turns me around to face him, pulling my soapy hands above my head and pushing them against the cabinet while pinning me to the counter with his hips.

I breathe in deeply as he leans in and gently parts my lips with his. Day-old scruff scratches my skin as he slowly increases his apparent appetite for my mouth. I moan, feeling the desire he creates pool in my body.

Without warning, he pushes away with a devil of a smile.

"That's for you to catalogue for next time." He kisses me chastely on the head before walking toward his discarded clothes.

What the...

I follow his movements, still stunned from that sudden, delicious accosting. Narrowing my eyes, I splash water in his direction from the faucet. "You're the worst!" I yell.

He picks up his leather jacket, shielding himself from my onslaught, and chuckles.

"Watch it—this is designer!" he yells back between laughs.

I splash him harder.

⊷⧉ ⧉⊶

It's a bright, crisp day as Jared and I sit outside on my stoop waiting for Becca. I told him he didn't have to wait, but he said that nothing could outweigh the importance of spending more time with me. He really knows how to charm a girl.

"Hey there, love bugs." Becca walks up, looking cute and fresh in her early spring getup. Designer straight-leg jeans fit snugly against her long, lean legs, stopping at her tan ankle boots. She wears a slightly-too-big knit green sweater, which sets off her vibrant apricot hair, and big round tortoiseshell sunglasses sit on her delicate nose. I know the only reason she's single is because she wants to be.

"Hey." Jared greets her with a hug.

"I hope you two had an interesting enough night that I'll be entertained with the details later."

Jared laughs. "I guess you and I will just have to wait and see." He places his arm around me as I purse my lips at the two.

"All right, as much as I like looking at you, Jared, it's time for you to mosey on outta here. Girl time, and stores need us," Becca mumbles while applying some lip gloss.

Jared shakes his head before turning toward me. "You go back for your checkup on Tuesday, right?" he asks, and I nod. Tuesday is the day Dr. Marshall scheduled me to come in to readminister tests. "So you won't be returning to work until after you hear what he says?"

"Yeah. He needs to run some tests to see how I'm doing before he gives me the green light."

"Great, then can we plan to see each other early in the week?"

"Yeah, I think we can manage that."

"Good." Jared gives me a quick kiss. "Then I'll text you later. Have fun depleting your bank accounts, ladies," he says in jest before heading to his apartment.

"If both of you weren't so good looking, I'd never put up with being around all that PDA," Becca says while we make our way toward Bleecker Street.

"Then be thankful that we are."

"Har har. Soooo, spill! How was the sex?" She leans in, lowering her glasses.

"We didn't actually have sex." I wait less than a second to get the immediate response I know is coming.

"WHAAAAAT!?" Two passing women stare at us for a second before returning to their routines, unfazed by random New York pedestrian outbursts. "How could you guys *not* have sex? Have I taught you nothing?" She's absolutely appalled.

"It's not that we didn't *try*, but things kept coming up, like *you* calling me to hang out and not giving us any time in between." I mockingly glare at her.

"Oh, *sweetie*, all you had to say was, 'Becca, I need more time to bone,' and I would have *completely* understood."

I roll my eyes. I don't know why my sex life is so intriguing to her. Probably because it's rare and thus makes it more of a scandal for Becca—God knows how she loves a scandal.

"So what did *you* do last night?" I change gears as we stop in front of a shoe store. Becca leans down, studying a pair of strappy pink pumps.

"I went out for drinks with some of the peeps from work. Wasn't really that great."

"Why wasn't it that great?" We walk to the next store window.

"Todd's wife was there."

Oh boy.

With that, the conversation is closed. I don't know why Becca pursues this guy—she's so smart and gorgeous. Why muddle yourself up with a married man when you can have any number of attainable men—men that I know have thrown themselves at her? But this conversation was already had, and resulted in a week of the silent treatment from both of us.

Skipping to the next topic.

"Bec, look at this." I push the cuff to my jean jacket up over my wrist and gently unwrap the thin bandage.

She wrinkles her nose. "Gross."

"Yeah, I know, but it's actually supposed to look like this... Well, in time it was supposed to."

"Okay." She wears a *so what* expression.

"It didn't look like this yesterday. It was still all red and blistery."

"That's great then! Means it's healing fast."

"Yes, but don't you find it weird that it kind of just...healed like this overnight?" I'm trying to bring the abnormality of this situation to light without sounding like a nut.

"I guess..." Becca's slightly distracted by a cute guy passing by in a soccer uniform who gives her a winning smile. She turns back to me. "But I mean, they have all sorts of crazy new medicine these days. I'm sure Dr. What's-His-Nuts gave you some of the good stuff."

"His name is Dr. Marshall, and yeah, that's what Jared said." I look at my wrist again. Is it really as easy as that? Maybe I'm making too big of a deal out of it.

"See? Jared knows his shit, so don't worry about it." She smiles, wrapping her arm around my shoulders and giving a little squeeze. "I mean, if you're still weirded out about it, call up the doc."

"No, you're right. It's the medicine—I just thought it was crazy." I shrug, wrapping my wrist up again. I have no desire to call Dr. Marshall. For some reason he makes me feel weird. He's always so smiley, too smiley.

"You hungry?" Becca asks, her mind already moving on. "Let's get something light in this café up ahead." Holding on to my jacket sleeve, she pulls me forward.

New York has a magical pulse on the first warm days after winter. People come out of their miniature apartments after hibernation, stretching and prancing about, showcasing their still-pale limbs that were wrapped like pigs in a blanket from the cold. People even smile at strangers courteously—a gesture that will evaporate in a few days' time with the accustomed warmth.

My mother calls while Becca and I sip our coffees and judge some of the new fashion that passes by. I quickly let Mom know I'm fine and getting some fresh air with Becca, apologizing again that she had to call me first.

"The world is really sick." Becca shoves away the newspaper she's reading in disgust.

"Why? What's going on?" I place my phone back in my bag.

"Some teenagers in Europe burned down a bunch of buildings while people were sleeping inside. It's the third case like this in the past month."

"That's horrible!"

"Yeah," Becca agrees, glancing down at the paper again. We both sit in silence for a second.

"So what do you think? Up for going out tonight?" Becca picks up the last of her muffin and pops it in her mouth. I smile at her vitality.

"Yeah, actually—I don't think I can spend another night in that studio prison." I sip my coffee.

"I don't know why you're not into moving to Brooklyn like I did. You'd have double the space."

"Yeah, I know, but I can't part with Manhattan yet. I just love this neighborhood. It only feels cramped because I've practically been in my room night and day."

"Whatever you need to tell yourself," she says wryly.

Becca's been pushing for me to move to Brooklyn ever since she did a year ago. I know it's mainly because she can't stand not living in the same neighborhood as me, since we used to be room-mates when we first moved to the City.

"All right, so where should we get silly tonight?" she asks with excitement.

"I don't really care, but I know I shouldn't get *too* silly." I'm not sure if I'm even supposed to be drinking. I should have paid more attention when the nurse was giving me the rundown, but I *was* just struck by lightning. I think I get a pass for being out of it.

"Yeah, *oookay*. Will you have some sort of radioactive reaction to alcohol or something?"

I chuckle. "No, I don't think that was a listed side effect."

"Good, then it's a date! Let's meet at The Wicker Horse, since it's close to you. I've been wanting to check it out, and I hear it has some yummy men on Saturdays." She rubs her hands together sinfully.

I smile at my crazy friend. This is exactly what I need to relax—forget the last couple of days and definitely forget how lost and confused I've been every time I wake up.

I just need to remember not to mix the alcohol with my painkillers.

Chapter 10

THERE'S NO LINE when I walk into the bar—a good sign for how the rest of the night will go. I glance around the typical West Village watering hole: distressed wood fills every inch, mixing with modern brushed-metal accents, and the patrons are cast in a flattering light by a soft yellow glow.

I find Becca at a corner cocktail table. "Hey." I reach over and hug her before sitting down at one of the tall stools.

"Isn't this place great?" She beams while taking in all the men who are meandering in front of us.

"Yeah, as soon as I saw no line, I was sold. Do you need a refill?" I gesture to her half-empty beer bottle.

"Yeah, but just get me whatever you're having."

I walk to the bar and try to make space between two men. They both look like tools to me, so I have no problem trying to flag down the male bartender first, even though they were here before me. I mean, they don't call us New Yorkers for our manners.

"Hey there, whatcha drinking?" One of the tools with a—yes, I think that is what I'm seeing—popped collar asks me. He has a boyish face and is probably younger than me.

"Alcohol," I answer pointedly.

"Oooo, Jerry, I think that means she's not interested." Tool number two laughs from his side. Jerry mocks a wounded heart by placing his hand over it, grimacing.

"Ya got me good, midnight. Ya got me good."

"Midnight?" I ask, curious about his strange pet name.

He smiles, his confidence building now that he has obtained my interest. "Just when I saw you with your black silky hair and dark eyes, you reminded me of looking into midnight. A very *sexy* midnight." He leans in so I can smell his beer breath. *Oh God.* I lean back.

"These guys bothering you?" A deep voice resonates from behind me. All three of us turn to take in a very tall, disarmingly built blond man, hands resting casually inside the front pockets of his black jeans. Even in this unthreatening pose, he projects ass-kicking abilities, and my two companions can feel it. I look from one to the other as each takes a step away from me, and I smile up at my savior.

"Not anymore."

Blondie moves between broken-hearted Jerry and me and leans down on the bar so I don't have to strain my neck to see him. His skin has a brownish hue, like he is of exotic island descent, and it's deepened by his golden surfer hair and black attire. His beautiful hazel eyes spark gold in the candlelight, and as he moves closer, I notice his scent of sunshine and night all mixed together—it's surprisingly pleasant and partly familiar.

"Didn't mean to intervene where I might not have been needed, but those two didn't seem like your type." He flashes me perfect white teeth.

"No, I'm happy that you did, thank you." I grin. "I stopped being interested in popped collars as soon as I saw them happening." Blondie laughs warmly, bringing the attention of the second female bartender toward us.

"Can I get something for you?" she asks flirtatiously. He returns her smile with one of his own, and I catch the red glow spread over her cheeks. This guy knows what he's carrying around.

"Yeah, I'd like a scotch, neat, please, and my friend here will have..." He turns to me.

"Oh, uh, two vodka tonics, please."

"And two vodka tonics." The bartender blinks a few times before leaving to make our drinks. "My name is Rae." He extends his hand, and I can't help but think how uncannily appropriate his name is.

"Molly."

His grip is firm and warm. "So, Molly, who's the second drink for?" he asks, leaning on the bar with one elbow. He looks goofy bent over this much to be eye level with me.

"A friend. She's sitting over there." I point in the general direction of our table, where large crowds of people now block it.

He nods in understanding. A protective gleam in his eyes disappears, making me realize it was there in the first place. Is he interested in me?

The bartender comes back and hands all three of the drinks to Rae, telling him they're on the house. He gives her a wink and thanks her. She blushes deeper and hesitantly turns to the next patron. Rae drops a fifty on the bar anyway. High roller.

"Here you go." He hands me my drinks.

"Thanks, I really appreciate it."

"No problem. It was nice to meet you, Molly. If you ever need saving from popped collars again, just look for the tallest guy in the room." He flashes his pearly whites before turning around and walking to the other side of the bar.

I guess the answer to my question is: definitely *not* interested. I've never had a man buy me a drink before, let alone two drinks, without ulterior motives.

I return to Becca, who is trying to give a guy the hint that she's not into him. I push my way between him and her, turning my back to the guy. Becca smiles, relieved, and takes her drink.

"Thanks, that guy didn't get it." She sips on the tiny useless straw that always accompanies these kinds of drinks and scans the bar. "So, anyone that you think I'd be into?"

"What? I'm being left out of tonight's vulturing?"

Becca scoffs. "Molly, you're with Jared!"

"We haven't talked about being exclusive. I don't even know if I want that." Becca blinks at me like I've just sprouted six noses.

"Listen, let me ask you something." She puts down her drink. "If you found out tomorrow that Jared went out and hooked up with a girl tonight, would you be mad?"

That sentence alone makes me see red.

"Exactly," Becca says, seeing my expression. "So you guys are exclusive. I don't know why you're so hesitant about him. It's obvious he's madly in love with you. But hey, if you're not into it, I will gladly take him off your hands." She finishes by tipping her drink my way and scans the bar.

"Oh *my*, who is that tall glass of sunshine?!" Becca asks. I follow her gaze to Rae standing a couple of tables down, staring in our direction while two girls try desperately to get his attention. When we catch eyes, he smiles and waves. I wave back.

Becca grabs my hand. "Uh, excuse me, miss? You *know* him?!"

"Hey, careful." I gently take my arm from her grasp. "This is the one with the burn."

"Oh, sorry! But wait, you have to explain how you know that beautiful species of a man!"

"Well, maybe we can have him explain." I nod toward Rae, who is steadily approaching. Becca sits up straighter, flattening her extremely flattering eggplant-colored top, and brings her long hair in front of her shoulders. Is she actually nervous? She's never nervous around men.

"Hey, Molly. So, this is the recipient of the other drink I bought?" Rae stands at our table, swirling the scotch in his glass while appraising Becca.

"You bought me my drink?" she asks with slight shock.

"Yup, how's it tasting?" He smiles and moves closer to her, obviously liking what he sees.

"It tastes exactly like a free drink should taste—*delicious*. I might be in the mood for another." She flashes him one of her enticing grins. Boy, I hope this guy is ready for her.

"Rae, this is one of my favorite people in the world, Becca." I start the introduction before I completely lose her to our new acquaintance.

"Pleased to meet you." Rae takes her outstretched hand and brings it to his lips.

My jaw drops, and Becca glances at me, wide eyed. That's a lot different than the handshake he gave me. I know in that moment that Becca is a goner for this exotic Prince Charming. She quickly asks him to join us.

Rae is laid back and charismatic, acutely aware of Becca at his side, and I catch him brush his hand over her thigh more than once under the table. His presence doesn't go unnoticed by the other females in the bar, who are leering at us with green eyes of jealousy.

"Let's do shots!" Becca proclaims with delight.

"I'm game," I say, feeling the effects of my previous two drinks and accepting the carefree whims of my friend. She winks at me before jumping up and going to the bar. I smile at Rae, happy at how our night is turning out for Becca. He surprises me by wearing a contemplative expression.

"Do you think you should be drinking so much?" he asks, leaning in and speaking softly.

"What do you mean?"

"I don't think alcohol is the best choice since you just got hit by lightning," he says authoritatively.

Whoa.

When did I tell him that?

I stare at him, wide eyed, unable to respond for a moment. I try to sift through the past hour of conversation, but the alcohol in my blood is making it all a little fuzzy. Deciding that we must have talked about it, I respond, "I don't think a shot will kill me."

I maintain a playful tone, but I'm a little resentful of this guy—we just met!—trying to school me on what is and isn't good for me.

Becca saunters back just as Rae is about to say something else. He quickly paints his face into the blithe countenance he was wearing earlier. I eye him suspiciously.

"Did I miss anything good?" Becca asks as she places the three shot glasses on the table.

"Nope, we were just talking about how lucky I was to bump into Molly tonight." Rae smiles at Becca.

"Oh?" She looks back and forth between the two of us.

"Because then I wouldn't have had the pleasure of meeting you." He finishes by bringing her into his side. She all but swoons in his arms. I pick up one of the shots and shoot it back. *Ugh, tequila.* It burns the whole way down.

"Hey! We were supposed to do them together!" Becca scowls. I just shrug. Rae frowns.

I suddenly want to get ass-ripping drunk.

Two drinks and another shot later, I need to go home. I'm starting to sweat from the increase of body heat coming off the influx of people walking into the bar and the abundance of alcohol burning its way through my veins.

"Hey, guys, I think I'm going to get out of here." I work hard not to slur any of my words.

Rae and Becca have been leaning toward each other, talking about something that kept making Rae laugh. Ever heard of a room? Preferably one I'm not in, kids.

"Aww, no, Mols! We were just saying how we should find another bar, one a little more quiet." Becca wraps her arm around my shoulder and gives me a look that fully explains what she really means by "quiet."

Yeeeah, definitely not sticking around for that.

"You guys keep hanging out. I'm feeling really tired. I probably should've been in bed hours ago." I nudge her side, signaling that I really don't mind and she should stay out. She grins before switching to her serious face.

"You okay to go home by yourself?"

"Yeah, of course. I'll grab a cab. Don't worry about me." I stand and Rae stands with me. I smile at the gentlemanlike gesture. He'll treat Becca well.

"Rae, it was a pleasure to meet you. Thanks for saving me from the bro-squad earlier." I strain to hug him around the neck, even in my heels.

"Anything for a friend."

For some reason, it doesn't sound like he's referring to me, but I'm too drunk to contemplate anything more than putting one foot in front of the other without falling. Really shouldn't have done that last shot.

"I'm sure I'll be seeing you again," he says while tugging Becca to him. I hear her sigh. Yup, she's got it bad.

"I hope so too," I say genuinely.

Even though Rae confused me at points tonight, I'm strangely comfortable around him. It could be because of his naturally gregarious disposition or the fact that I'm pretty drunk. I'd like to go with the former.

It takes a couple of tries with my keys to finally get my door open. I imagine tiny shot glasses with wings are flapping around my head, and I swat at them as I stumble over my threshold. My temples throb, and I curse that I can't take any of my pain medication.

Managing to chug a glass of water, I slide my body over my bed. My phone beeps from my purse. With great effort I collect it to see a text from Jared, but since my vision is too blurry to read anything, I throw it to the side and rest my face back on my cool sheets. Letting out a contented sigh, I'm slightly aware that I'm still fully clothed, but way too relaxed in my current state to care. I close my eyes and push away the spinning that reminds me that I'll hate myself in the morning.

As I drift into the darkness, I can already begin to smell the refreshing scent of night, and my memories thrust through the intoxication of my brain to tell me I'm on my way back to a place that is only unlocked when I sleep.

With no great effort, I welcome it forward.

Chapter 11

ROLLING TO MY side, I moan as a million tiny monsters hack away at my brain. I hate tiny, brain-hacking monsters. A piece of grass tickles the inside of my nose, and I brush it away, groaning at the effect that such a meager movement has on my distressed head.

I manage to slowly rest on my back and open my eyes, gazing up at the small burning orbs in the distance, shooting across the dark abyss of the sky. I'm in the same place I dreamt of last night (and I'm pretty sure the nights prior as well). My recollection of this place only resurfaces when I'm here.

I take in a few deep breaths, trying to settle the queasy feeling in my stomach, and gingerly sit up. To my right is the familiar tree that I'm beginning to believe is my dream's favorite starting point. The branches loom over me, casting a shadow on the grass below. I crawl to the tree and sit against its trunk, leaning my head on the cool wood and closing my eyes.

"Had a little too much fun?"

I jump at the familiar husky voice, aggravating my nausea. "Please *stop* doing that," I groan.

The soft laughter that follows causes a dozen memories to tear through me like birds catching flight. I don't need to see his face to know who it is, but I look over anyway. Dev leans against the tree, staring down at me. Even from my low vantage point, I can make out his darkly handsome face and signature amused smile.

I give another groan and roll forward, putting my head in my hands. *Just kill me now.* I hate that he's seeing me like this. I feel Dev take a seat beside me, and even though I'm in pain, my body reacts instantly to his proximity, calming the sharp throb in my head and dissolving me into liquid heat.

"What's the celebration?" he asks.

"Being a Saturday," I grunt out.

"Hmm."

Silence.

"I think I like what you normally sleep in compared to this." He tugs at the blazer I fell asleep in.

Couldn't even take off your jacket, Molly? I bring up the image of my revealing sleepwear, and with my head still in my hands, say, "I think that should offend me, but I feel too horrible to care at the moment."

He chuckles.

The other times I've found myself here, I've never really felt the usual aches and pains of when I was awake. This is decidedly different. Picking my head up, I glance at Dev, catching the small amount of concern etched on his face. When our eyes meet, he shifts back to amusement.

"Dev?"

"Yes, Molly?" he says, lacing my name with a prick of pleasure, which makes my stomach tighten again, though not from alcohol.

"Why do I still feel drunk here if I'm supposed to be dreaming?"

He studies me before scratching his scruff, apparently debating if he should answer. "Well, your mind here is the same mind you've got when you're awake. So, if your brain is still drunk right before you go to sleep, why wouldn't it stay that way when you're asleep?"

I guess that logic makes sense.

"So I guess that means I really am dreaming. None of this is real?" I motion to our surroundings.

He quirks his mouth up and lightly knocks his shoulder into mine. "It would seem so, wouldn't it?"

I sigh and turn away. *It was worth a try.*

Dev stands, extending his hand, and I follow the length of it all the way up to his face, momentarily mesmerized by the inviting blue eyes staring down into mine. "Come on," he says while wiggling his fingers. "I want to show you something."

As he helps me up, I lose my balance and fall forward, grabbing his arm to steady myself. I don't know if it's a subconscious impulse or something I've less-than-subconsciously wanted to do since the first moment I saw him, but my hand inadvertently squeezes Dev's smoothly sculpted bicep.

"Molly..." Dev laughs. "Are you feeling my muscle?"

I think I just died inside.

"What? No!" I take a few staggering steps back.

Oh God! Why can't I wake up when something like this happens?

"I mean, you're welcome to feel them." He teasingly extends his flexed arm.

"Just...shut up." I slap his impressively rock-hard arm and he laughs again. "Actually...you know what?" I say, annoyed. "I don't think I'm in the mood to see whatever it is you want to show me after all." I hardly take a step away when Dev hooks one of his arms around my waist and easily twirls me to face him.

"I'd rather not be manhandled," I say through gritted teeth, trying to regain some composure and ignoring my lurching stomach.

"So you think I'm a man?" His eyes sparkle with humor.

"Gah!" Raising my hands, I push him off and walk away. I can't win with this guy. "Whatever. Let's go see what's so great."

Tight-lipped from suppressing a smile, Dev quickly falls into step beside me.

After a while of trudging in my suede heels and having them stick more than once in the soft ground, I decide it would be better to take them off. Unsuccessfully balancing on one leg to remove my shoes, I gratefully grab the hand Dev offers. When I'm finally barefoot, I try to remove my hand from his, but he doesn't let go.

He looks at our connection with an unreadable expression and interlocks his fingers with mine. My heart begins to skip like rocks over a pond, and I'm confused and slightly flustered by Dev's actions. But what worries me the most is that I have no desire to remove my hand from his.

He begins to walk again, seemingly oblivious or indifferent to our hand-in-hand situation.

I feel anything *but* indifferent.

His skin is cool and strong between my fingers, and my stomach tightens as his thumb begins to circle the sensitive part of my palm, sending scorching desire for him to areas besides my hand.

I swallow.

This isn't good.

We eventually reach a small plateau where the grass stops and a light gravel paves the ground. I follow the new terrain with my eyes and stop when it disappears over a ledge. Dev reluctantly lets go as I slowly step forward, and my jaw goes slack from the expansion of the wonder before me.

A huge gaping canyon that seems miles wide and miles deep stretches out in front of me. With the low glow of the night, it's hard to discern what colors lace through the expanded mass and what sits at the bottom. In this darkness, it goes on endlessly.

My stomach does a little flip, and I step back from the ledge. "This is amazing," I whisper, as though any noise is too loud for this commanding place.

"I come here every so often," Dev says from behind me. "It's strangely humbling to look at something bigger than yourself."

I smile, picturing him here alone, reflective. The image is at odds with how I perceive him. "I've wondered what was beyond the field—if it kept on going," I say as I glance back toward him.

Dev sits on a rock facing the canyon and pats the surface next to him invitingly. Taking a seat, we both gaze into the silent night. When his thigh brushes against mine from our close proximity, I grow flush and decide to take off my blazer, hoping it will cool me down. I quickly realize this makes the heat much worse. Our bare arms touch, and the contact creates a fever inside my skin that travels deep.

I need us to talk about something, *anything*, and fast.

"So, do you think you'll ever explain why you always know when I'm here?"

His lips twitch. "One day, if you're lucky, I'll show you."

"What does that even mean?"

"You'll understand when the time's right."

I shake my head. "Well, can you at least give me a straight answer about something when I'm awake?"

Dev looks at me hesitantly. "I can try."

"Why can't I remember you when I wake up?"

Pain flutters across his features and then is gone. He stands and walks to the lip of the canyon. I stare at his tensed back as a moment of silence passes before he speaks. "Your brain is completely closed off when you sleep, only concentrating on resting. So it's easier for you to remember me here than out there." He gestures vaguely to the space in front of us. "When you wake up, you have a lot more to think about, so the things that happen while you sleep get pushed to the back of your mind."

I make my way to stand beside him. "So will I remember that you just told me this?"

He turns, glancing down at me. "I'm not really sure. I'm still trying to figure out how much you'll remember." His eyes shine, reflecting the shooting stars above and in this moment seem completely open for me to dive into.

"Why? What else is there to tell me?"

He takes a step forward and pushes a strand of hair behind my ear. I try very hard to keep my breathing steady. "There's nothing else. I'm not sure why I said those things. You must be making them up for me to say."

I'm not convinced. I wasn't thinking of anything for him to say. Could I really be conjuring this whole place into existence? Is he really just a dream? Feeling more confused than ever, I turn away.

"Mols…" He says my name like a caress.

I've never heard him call me by my nickname, and it does strange things to my body. I look back and catch the conflict in his features: frustration, sadness, acceptance. That's when another memory bursts through my vision, like a bright flash from a bulb. Dev and I are on a beach, and he's giving me the same torn look. Another flash. The first night, when he couldn't see me. The night he and Aveline found me lying under the tree. Our surroundings changing when Dev's sea-blue eyes remind me of the ocean. The apartment and Tim. Our bodies pressed together on the zipline. All these moments string together, bringing me back to the present.

A tingling sensation runs up my spine and races the length of my arms. I take in a shaky breath. This can't be just a dream.

"Are you cold?" he asks as he skims my now goose-bumped skin, making me shiver even more. I shake my head. "If it makes you feel any better," he says in a soft, deep voice, "I never forget *you* when you leave." Blood rushes to my cheeks, and I'm thankful for the constant coverage of night this land provides.

Dev moves closer, and I close my eyes, unsure of what to do, knowing that what I *truly* want to do makes no sense.

He's not real.

But the smell of him, as I breathe in, seems impossible to fake.

"Molly, I can't explain it, but there's something about you that makes me know this is all happening for a reason," he says so quietly I can barely hear him. I'm inches away from being able to kiss his dangerously sensual mouth. "You're my hope." He places his hand on my cheek, and I understand the reference he's making to my last name. The air between our bodies crackles with an angry desire for one of us to close the gap, and I'm about to be that one, when a strange orange glow rises in the distance.

Dev quickly takes a step back, turning to stare at a light that seems to be coming from a massive fire in the direction we just came. He curses and moves toward the brightness, dowsing the blaze that was almost ignited between us.

"What is it?" I call out in concern.

He spins around, blinking as though he forgot for a moment I was with him. He curses again. "You have to wake up now," he says in a commanding tone. Still reeling from our almost-passionate exchange, I don't completely grasp what he's saying. He takes quick, long strides back to me and grabs my shoulders. "Listen, you have to wake up. I have to go," he repeats, a little softer but with urgency.

"I'll go with you."

He immediately shakes his head. "No. That's not an option."

"Well, I'm not staying here."

"I know. You're going to wake up."

I eye him defiantly. "How? You can't make me."

Dev glances quickly at the ravine. The crooked smile that morphs onto his face scares me a little, and I take a step back. He follows me with a step forward.

"Dev?" I say his name like I'm not quite sure that this is the same man who was, until recently, gently stroking my cheek.

"I'm extremely sorry, but it's for your own good." He continues to move closer. My feet touch the lip of the canyon.

"What is?" I dare to ask.

"This."

And then he shoves me over the ledge.

For one tenth of a second, I lock on to Dev's apologetic eyes before I let out an earsplitting scream and race the gathering blackness to my imminent and unexpected death.

Chapter 12

I JERK TO the side of my bed, choking on my own cries. I thrash violently and grip my sheets, trying to claw my way out of the hurtling sensation of falling off a cliff.

Holy shit!

My heart's plastered between my ribs, forcing itself to keep beating. A cold sweat erupts on my skin as it realizes it's not torn apart on a rocky floor. When my mind disengages from the horrid fate within my dream, the late onset of last night's intoxication wretches in my stomach. I quickly run to the toilet and expel every last substance residing in my abdomen.

The bathroom floor's cold tiles press up against my back as salty tears run down my cheeks. Completely distraught, I can do nothing but lie still and tell myself to breathe. After some time, my heart slows to a normal pace, and the hypersensitivity of my skin subsides to the typical ache that accompanies a hangover. I can tell it's early morning by the mild light filtering through my open bathroom door.

I blink at the ceiling, remembering everything—remembering Dev, meeting him in the field, being in the city, on the roof, walking with him barefoot in the grass, the giant ravine, feeling him push me over the ledge.

He pushed me over the ledge!

My throat tightens at the memory that violently forced me awake. I scream in outrage, banging my heels and fists on the floor like an irate child, ignoring the wave of nausea caused by the sudden movement. I'm filled with anger, which quickly shifts to betrayal and resigned sadness.

What the fuck is going on?!

It all felt so real, but...I'm not dead, which means it couldn't have been. Yesterday, I blamed my weird dreams on the Chinese —today, could I blame nearly dying in them on the alcohol?

It's just that I see everything so clearly in my mind. The door that normally locks these memories away is ajar, and I'm able to coalesce some of the puzzle pieces. I remember the giant field and the shooting stars, the brightly lit metropolis with people all in black, and sapphire eyes that rest inside a rough and gorgeous face. I swallow back the confusing feeling of desire that last image produces.

Pushing myself up, I lean on my sink, staring at my reflection in the mirror. Wearing the same clothes from last night, I look exactly how I feel—like I was put through the spin cycle mentally and physically. Grabbing my toothbrush, I quickly attempt to rid myself of the acidic layer that envelops my tumultuous morning.

These are just dreams, Molly, just dreams.

I wonder if the more times I say it, I'll eventually bring myself to believe it.

Drying my hair with a towel, I step out of the shower feeling like a new person. The pounding of my head softly dispersed with each second I stood under the kneading, warm water, washing away any residual anger I still held clenched in my fists.

My phone chirps with a new text from Becca, and I quickly call her.

"Would you call me crazy if I told you I'm in love?" She picks up on the first ring.

I smile at her ridiculousness and sit on the edge of my bed. "I already call you crazy, so I don't see how this would make a difference."

"Well, Rae is the most perfect specimen of man I have ever come across."

"Oh, yeah?" I say, amused.

"We stayed out so late, talking and laughing. I have no idea what time I actually made it back to my apartment."

"Well, I'm glad you made it back and didn't just dive straight into his."

She *tsk*s into the phone. "*He* is not a one-nighter. I knew that as soon as I saw that he could still tower over me in my heels."

I laugh. "Yeah, he's mad tall. I didn't know how to give him a nonawkward hug good-bye."

She giggles. "And he was *such* a gentleman. We didn't do anything more than kiss. But trust me, I ran through every excruciating alternative in my head. The only thing on my con list is that he's only in town for work, so I don't know how long he'll actually be here."

"Oh really? Where's he from?"

"California." She sighs.

This doesn't really surprise me, given that he looked like he was specifically made for the sunny Pacific Coast. "Hmm, and what does he do?"

"He didn't really give too many details about what he's doing here, just that he deals with some sort of life insurance. I don't know. I honestly blacked out at points in our conversation because his yummy face was too distracting!"

I laugh again. "Oh boy, Bec, you're in trouble."

"I know!" She practically squeals. "And want to know the best part?"

"What?"

"We have a date Monday night!"

"That's great!" Becca hasn't been on a proper date in a while. She's more into the bag-and-tag relationships these days.

"Yeah! Self-restraint might have something going for it after all." I'm amused that she just echoed exactly what I was thinking. "So how are you feeling today? You were pretty plastered."

That doesn't even begin to describe how I was last night. "I was an absolute mess this morning—I even got sick."

"Gross. Rookie moves. You should eat something greasy. That always does the trick."

A bacon, egg, and cheese sandwich does sound finger-licking good right about now. My stomach growls in agreement. "Yeah, you're probably right. I'll go get something from the deli." I pause, wondering whether or not to tell Becca about my crazy dreams, and decide it wouldn't hurt—I always end up telling her everything anyway. "So you're probably going to make fun of me for what I'm about to say—"

"Molly, I never make fun of you!"

"Yeah, okay, what about that time when my thong was showing above my pants at work and you didn't tell me until after lunch?" She breaks down in hysteria on the other line. "Yeah, exactly." I frown.

"Okay…okay," she gasps through laughs, "but I was trying to help you out and let people see your sexy side."

"Whatever."

"*Molly*! Tell me what you wanted to say. If I laugh, I will put you on mute so you can't hear."

I roll my eyes. "Okay, well…have you ever had dreams that last more than one night? Like you keep dreaming the same dream?"

"Hmm…like the classic 'I dreamt I was naked at school' dream?"

"No, not exactly—just a dream I guess, but it seems to play out like a TV show, and I'm the main character."

"Sounds awesome," she says. "What's the dream about?"

The question catches me unprepared. I don't really know what it's about, just that I keep having the same one, in the same place, with the same characters… Well, one character in particular. "I don't really know, but there's this guy—"

"OH! A sex dream!"

"No, no! Nothing like that," I respond quickly. "Never mind—it's probably because of the accident, or maybe something I keep eating."

"Mhmm, well, my diagnosis is that you're probably sexually frustrated and should bone Jared already. I mean, how long has it even been? *Two weeks*? Trust me, that will take care of everything, you'll see."

I chuckle at her precision-focused mind. "Thank you, Practitioner Becca. I'll take that under advisement."

"Good. Send the check for this session to my receptionist," Becca quips. "So you're still out tomorrow, right?"

"Yeah, I guess so. Though I'm tempted to come in. I'm just so bored during the day."

Becca sucks in air. "Molly, if I see an *inch* of you at work, I will personally knock you out and drag you back to your apartment. No one expects you back for another week or two. You are surprisingly resilient after getting hit by friggin' lightning."

I know what she's saying is true. I researched other survivors online and realized how extremely messed up I could have been from my accident. I have no idea why I am able to walk away with so few casualties. "I know you're right."

"*Duh* I'm right. Work on how to relax or something. You gotta take the days off when you can."

I'm midway up my stairs, on my way back from Sunday afternoon grocery shopping, when my phone rings in my satchel. I scramble to my door so I can set my bags down and answer.

"Hey," I say breathlessly.

"Hey, you okay?" Jared asks.

"Yeah, I was just getting back from food shopping."

"Oh."

"What's going on?" I ask as I begin to empty the bags.

"I wanted to see how you were. You didn't return my text last night, so I was getting a little worried."

Crap. "Ah, yeah, sorry about that. I went out drinking with Becca and passed out before I saw it. I was kind of a mess this morning and forgot about it." A little white lie never hurts.

"Oh—well, that's okay." I can't mistake the slight hurt in his tone.

"Yeah, I'm really, *really* sorry. It's purely an airhead move on my part."

"No, I understand. Don't worry about it, just glad to know you're okay."

I smile at his concern. "I can always make it up to you..." I say suggestively as I reach into a bag and take out the bushel of bananas. *How appropriate.*

"Hmm, what do you have in mind?"

"Well, I could do some extreme forms of 'making it up to you' on Monday night."

He laughs lightly. "I think I can be into that plan."

"Good, then it's a date." I spread out on my bed, feeling the effects of a bad night's sleep. "So what did *you* do last night?"

"Nothing crazy. Met up with some of the guys and watched the baseball game. Then I had to finish up some paperwork for a company we're meeting with this week."

I yawn. "Man, sounds like you had a better night than me."

"Yeah, it was an *insane* time." He chuckles through the phone. "Okay, Mols, just wanted to say hi and see if you were alive. I have to grab a bite with my boss. He wants to review what I worked on last night." He sighs.

"A guy can't catch a break."

After we hang up, I whip up a quick dinner and watch some news. The anchorman goes on and on about a horrible gang brawl that happened in Kansas. Two groups from opposing towns played out the *West Side Story* last night, sans synchronized finger snapping.

What could possibly be so important to make people hate like that? Picking up the remote, I click off the TV.

With my body aching for some much-needed sleep, I clean up and pull out my pajamas. For some reason the idea of going to bed is starting to make me nervous. I think it's because I'm scared of what I might or might not find when I close my eyes, and whether or not a certain someone will make his star appearance again. Now that I'm beginning to remember my dreams, my mind is tied in a knot of anxiety—partially because remembering my dreams is a new experience, but also because they don't feel like dreams at all but more like another life I'm living.

This thought in particular is what has me worried that I might be losing it. And at twenty-four, no less. If only I was eighty, when becoming senile was the next stage, and I could wear my Depends in comfort knowing this was merely nature's way.

Crawling into bed, I stretch out my still-achy limbs before scrunching into a fetal ball of comfort and hugging my pillow. As soon as I close my eyes, my mind instantly shuts off from this world and drifts into another.

⇥ ⇤

My body is weightless for a few moments before gravity wraps its inevitable arms around me, and I open my eyes to a dark, grassy landscape. Once aware of my surroundings, the details of all I've experienced here pour into my memory. Like a matchstick catching fire, my mind prickles as I remember the very last thing that happened. Dev pushed me off a cliff.

That son of a bitch.

Rapidly I sit up, searching for the one person I'm ready to explode on. Where is he?! I'm going to kill him for what he did. I might have had a day to calm down, but now that I'm back. My vengefulness erupts like a weed escaping cement.

I spin in a quick circle, preparing myself for Dev to pop up out of nowhere, but after scanning my surroundings, I stop dead upon seeing another form leaning against the tree. My heart hiccups in fear.

"Who's there?" I call out to the thin, lanky figure standing completely in shadow.

"Calm down, Molly," a familiar feminine voice chimes.

Instantly I relax as the individual moves into the soft light. Her waist-long blonde hair moves in the breeze, and her skin radiates like porcelain in the darkness. "Aveline?" I can't hide my shock. "What are you doing here?"

She gracefully continues toward me and throws a bundle at my feet. "Change into these." Her tone is clipped, revealing a no-nonsense attitude.

"Why? What is it?" I pick up the black mass and untie the string that's around it. Black combat boots fall to the ground in a heavy thud and I catch the black T-shirt and pants. "Oh," I say after comprehension sets in. "Um, okay."

No one seems to be around for miles, but I still hide under the tree's dark canopy to change. I'd rather show a little civility in front of Aveline whenever possible. She doesn't say anything as I change, merely picks nonexistent lint from her black T-shirt and faces away. These clothes are much more comfortable than the previous ones I borrowed from her. The pants are made from similar material, and while still snug, they don't leave me feeling like I'm wearing a leotard. The T-shirt fits exactly like one I would buy.

"Why are the clothes always black?" I walk to Aveline.

"They just are," she answers with boredom.

I suppress an eye roll in response to her haughty demeanor. "Well, thanks for bringing me a change of clothes." I push for killing with kindness. She starts to walk fast in the direction of the city, and I quicken my pace to catch up to her.

"If Dev wasn't like a brother to me, I wouldn't be bringing you anything."

On the other hand, I might have to kill her with something else. "Where are we going?" I try for another topic.

"You'll see" is her only reply as she sets off at a jog.

Chapter 13

We stop at the base of the giant wall that acts as a fortification to the city. I tip my head up, studying its impressive reflective surface. It stands at least seven stories high and appears to be made out of one solid piece of metal.

Looking up, Aveline walks its length and I follow. When she finds what she's searching for, she reaches behind her to the opening of the quiver that's tightly strapped to her back. A black baton shoots out in a puff of air and she grabs it, fluidly bringing it down to her side. She repeats the motion, and a second baton flies out.

"Here." She hands me the newly acquired baton. "You're going to have to be a quick learner, because I'm no teacher and I hate repeating myself." I can only nod, as the anticipation for what I'm about to experience has dried my mouth shut. "Take the collapsed Arcus in your dominant hand like this." She extends her arm out and holds the baton parallel to the ground. I do the same. "Now, bring your hand out like you're punching someone in the face, and squeeze as you do so." She demonstrates as she gives me these instructions. Two semiarched attachments fly out from either side of the baton, creating the same sleek Arcus that Dev showed me on the roof.

With my arm in the proper position, I take a breath and quickly punch my hand out, not forgetting to squeeze. The effect is like activating a switchblade. I grin wide in triumph.

Aveline nods—her only sign of congratulation. "Okay, there's a lot of things the Arcus can do, but you don't need to know everything. Right now there's only two things I need you to do. First, we are going to grapple onto that zipline platform." She points to a black platform that sits a little over the edge of the wall. A long pole extends skyward, exactly like the pole I saw on their apartment roof, and at the top is a small hook that I can barely make out from this distance.

Aveline beckons for me to come closer, and she turns her Arcus over, indicating two buttons that sit on either side of the groove in the middle that straddles the zipline cord. "See these two buttons?" She points back and forth to them. I nod. "You need to press the right one to aim and the left one to shoot. The end of the grapple is extremely magnetic, so if you're marginally close to your target, your Arcus will find it. You're going to aim by holding and lifting up like this." She wraps her hands around the instrument and spreads her fingers over the length of the Arcus so that her thumbs rest perfectly above each button. She holds the device up toward the platform.

"When I push the button on the right, you'll see a laser target shoot out so that I can accurately pinpoint where my grapple hook will go." She pushes the button and a red beam extends out, resting its concentrated dot on the hook atop the pole. It reminds me of something from a hi-tech spy movie. "You with me so far?" she asks, still aiming her Arcus up.

"Yeah." I nod.

"Good. Okay, so now this left button"—she lifts her left thumb, showing it to me—"it's going to shoot out the grapple and attach to that hook." She pushes it, and a whooshing sound snakes out as the grappling cord flies from inside the Arcus toward its destination. It quickly lands true, and her line becomes taut.

"Now, when I push both the left and right buttons at once, it's going to retract the cord and carry me up to the platform. Make sure you have a good hold, or you'll be left where you're standing, and your Arcus will fly off without you." She gives me a serious face, expecting me to tell her I understand, which I do. "Good, then I'll see you at the top." She presses both buttons and quickly ascends to the platform, easily placing her foot on the lip and walking out of view.

I take in a breath. I can't believe I'm about to do this.

"Your turn," Aveline calls down.

Moving to where she was standing, I mimic how Aveline instructed me to hold and aim the Arcus. I press the first button, and a thrill goes through me as the red laser pointer shoots out. I aim so that it rests on the hook...hopefully. Taking a deep breath, I push the left button. My arms give a little as the grapple shoots out and sticks to where I aimed.

"Yes!" I hiss in excitement. One less reason for Aveline to detest me.

"Good job," she calls down, and my eyes go wide at a non-sarcastic compliment coming from her. And no one's even here to witness it. *Pity*.

Remembering what I have to do next, I fidget for a second. I have to stay calm or I might wake up, repeating what happened the last time I was on the zipline with Dev. I tighten my grip on the Arcus and press the buttons.

My feet leave the ground in a rush, and a little squeal escapes me. Before I can think, I'm near the platform, and Aveline's grabbing my shirt to bring me forward. Once I step on, she tells me to press both buttons again to release the grapple. Looking behind me, I see the outstretched city and beam. "That was awesome!"

Ignoring my elation, Aveline pushes a button on the ground near the circular landing zone. Just like before, the platform rises so we are closer to the zipline cord.

"I'm not as *keen* on snuggling up to you as Dev is, so you'll have to do this next part on your own too," she says, causing me to grow awkward remembering Dev's body intimately hooked to mine. "I already programmed this line for our destination, so just straddle the cord with your Arcus, and you'll eventually get to where we need to be." I glance up, surprised by all the cables jutting from the top of the pole. Aveline is pointing at the line in the center. "Now watch what I do and follow." She extends her instrument over the center line and glides the Arcus back and forth, making sure it's in place. She turns to me. "Remember, hold on." With those last words she pushes off and goes barreling into the city.

Shit.

I can't believe I'm about to do this—by myself. Shouldn't I have some sort of harness? What happens when my hands get tired and I can't hold on any longer? I curse again, wishing I had thought to ask Aveline these things. Though she didn't really seem too enthused to instruct me any more than necessary.

Taking a large breath to clear my head, I walk to the cord and swing my Arcus over. It locks in place, and I smoothly slide it back and forth, pumping the confidence that says I can do this into my veins.

Stay calm, breathe.

I repeat the words once more before I rip the Band-Aid off and push away from the landing. The wind whips through my hair and over my body as I zoom between buildings. The feeling is exhilarating! I'm not sure if I'm less scared because I already experienced this with Dev, but my heart pumps in excitement, and my face is plastered with an ear-to-ear grin.

I catch glimpses of other people passing by on other lines, reminding me of a subway system in the air. I relax my grip, feeling the effects of some sort of natural stickiness holding my hands in place, and let my body take the turns the line delegates. Below, the city streaks by in a blur as I careen forward over lit sidewalks and dozens of people in black, none of whom take notice of my moving form. I'm just another person traveling among many.

Eventually, I begin to zip between more dated, classical buildings, indicating that I'm entering the older part of the city. The modern structures recede as I find myself flying into an open space. Below me lies a beautifully manicured tree-lined square. Grecian-style buildings jut up gracefully, and one in particular seems to be the main attraction. Sitting in the back center of the square, the large building has crowds of people walking in and out of its impressive entrance. Giant marble ionic columns line the expansion of its façade, supporting an impressively carved frieze that sits below another ornately decorated pediment. In the center of the triangle pediment lies a simple, carved *T S*. I wonder what those letters mean. Rising from the top of the building is a massive domed roof.

My zipline ends at a landing platform close to the impressive building, where Aveline waits next to an Asian girl who's also dressed in black. They exchange words while watching me approach.

My stomach tightens as I realize Aveline never told me how to land. I instinctively clench my grip on the Arcus handles, relieved when I feel myself slowing. As I draw near, Aveline and the other girl walk to either side of me, catching my waist and easing me to a stop. Unhooking the Arcus from the cable, my arms only slightly ache and I let out a breath, thankful that my landing was more graceful than anticipated. My heart still pounds from the ride.

The sound of clapping and a familiar laugh turns my attention to Dev stepping onto the platform, wearing a huge knee-weakening smile.

"You're a natural," he says with pride.

A vengeful flame flickers in my gut, and despite my easily manifested anger, I manage to move my mouth up in warmth. Reading my expression, Dev's face radiates with joy. I slowly approach him.

"Hey," he says gently down to me.

"Oh hello," I sweetly purr. Then I pull my hand back and slap him across the face.

Dev holds his cheek in shock, and Aveline guffaws with her friend behind me. I watch as the bemusement slowly leaves his face, replaced by a heated and entertained expression. I work hard to ignore the pulling sensation in my abdomen and stay angry.

"If you EVER do that to me again," I growl through clenched teeth, "you will wish *you* were the one plummeting down that canyon instead."

He attempts to mold his features into a look of severity while saying, "Yes, ma'am." But the task proves too great, and he's once more smiling playfully. My hand itches to slap him again, and I'm unsure when I became a person who *slapped* anyone. Coincidentally, my answer is literally staring at me.

"You know, Molly, that might have been the most redeeming thing I've ever seen you do." Aveline comes to our side along with her companion.

"I think you're the first girl who's actually acted on what quite a few of us have wanted to do for a while," the other girl says with a smile. "I'm Brenna." She extends her delicate hand.

"Molly," I say while shaking it.

Brenna has beautiful clear features and eyes as black as night. Her raven hair is cut in a sharp angle right under her chin. She's young, maybe in her midteens, and I can't help but wonder what her purpose is here. "Yes, I've heard a lot about you." She quickly glances to Aveline.

"Oh?" I raise my eyebrows, knowing none of what she's heard was probably good if it was coming from Aveline.

Dev wraps his arm around my shoulders, turning me in the direction of the stairs. "We've got to get going, Ave, or we'll be late."

Walking away, I steal a glance back to Brenna, who has resumed what I'm assuming is her post at the platform. New travelers have already begun to land.

The three of us make our way down a cobblestone path that's adjacent to the side of the main building I saw when I came in for my landing. "Where are we?" I ask Dev.

"This is what we call City Hall."

I wonder if bringing me here is his way of finally answering all my questions. I can only hope.

As we traverse along the beautifully tree-lined path, the sidewalk eventually opens up to the front of the impressive City Hall. On either side of the building are the illuminated pods I remember seeing before. People stand in a line to either enter or wait for someone to magically exit from the circle. Before I can ask Dev what the pods are, he grabs my hand, and all thought momentarily leaves me. He guides us up the expansive marble stairs toward the main entrance. I feel like I've traveled back in time and am entering a dramatic Roman governmental building.

A row of severe-looking men and women guard the front of the building, wearing the classic black uniform with extra armor adorning them. Every guard holds an impressive Arcus, which I'm starting to understand is used for weaponry as well as transportation. They each sport a black armband on their left wrist, and as we pass, I notice a glowing lightning bolt etched into its surface. My stomach twists with a weird sense of foreboding.

As we walk through the giant open doors, my mind reels from the amount of people hustling by and from everything I'm trying to take in. No one pays me any mind, as I'm merely another citizen dressed in uniform. With Dev's hand still in mine, he tugs me forward to a balcony that's immediately inside the entrance of the building, and my mouth gapes.

The interior of their City Hall is massive. We're standing on a balcony platform that overlooks the entirety of the domed space. On either side are giant stairs traveling down to the floor below. A marble railed balcony wraps around the circumference of the room, level with the landing we're currently on. Doors open and shut on every tier as people go in and out, suggesting that this is only the main center of a much-larger building. The space reminds me of Grand Central Station, except it's a circle and much, much bigger. People walk hurriedly across the atrium while others stand in small groups talking with one another. The most beautiful and realistic image I've ever seen of the earth is painted in the center of the floor like a map. People sidestep around the picture, and a strange, watery sheen appears to move over it. I notice that half of the map is in darkness while the other portion is lit with yellow sunlight, making me believe it must be some sort of world clock.

How strange.

"This place is amazing," I say as Dev guides us down one of the sets of stairs. "Why are we here?"

"We have a meeting about something that has come up," he answers.

Something that has come up.

An image of the glowing, fire-like red light from the last time I was here flashes in my mind. "Does it have to do with what we saw at the canyon?"

He glances at me sideways, scrutinizing every inch of me before answering. "Yes," he finally says.

"*Dev!*" Aveline admonishes. "Shut up! We're already going to be in so much trouble for bringing her here."

"Calm down," he says with an eye roll. "She's probably not going to remember any of this anyway." I frown as I'm tugged along, willing my brain to soak in everything that's happening.

Walking past the strange liquid map on the ground, we travel on toward a giant white door on the other side of the room. Two austere guards flank the entrance, while a group of older men and a woman stand in front, talking. I recognize Tim among the assemblage of people and relax. He's speaking with a shorter and very stocky dark-skinned man who has patches of gray in his closely shaved hair. Each person in the group wears the standard black garb except for one woman who has blonde shoulder-length hair, sun-kissed skin, and intelligent blue eyes that follow me intently the entire time we approach. She has on an elegant, floor-length white robe, similar in fashion to a wrap dress. This is the first time I've seen anyone here in another color, and as I take in her appearance, I find it difficult to look away, but staring hurts my eyes, like I'm looking into the sun. I'm pulled out of her trance by a gruff, rumbling voice.

"What are you thinking, Devlin, bringing her here?" The short man next to Tim pins his eyes on me in shock and anger while his Herculean chest puffs out in agitation.

"I believe she can help us, *Alexander*," Dev says, clearly annoyed at the use of his full name.

The man, Alexander, begins to sputter his protest, but Tim places his hand calmly on the man's shaking shoulder.

"Alex, I supported him in bringing her here. She was going to be in Terra anyway, from previous accounts, and we needed Dev in the meeting today. He wouldn't have come without her."

Alex glances from me to Dev to Tim and then to the lady in white. She nods her head slightly, and he lets out a huff. "Fine, but she's staying out here. This discussion is for Nocturna and Vigil *only*. We'd need another meeting to even *begin* to come to an agreement about letting her inside those doors." He points his short finger toward the large white doors we are standing in front of.

I can hardly register what he's saying because my mind is still stuck on what Tim said. *She was going to be in Terra anyway*? What's Terra? I also try to ignore the happy flutter I got when he mentioned Dev wouldn't have come without me. This isn't the time to evaluate my adolescent swooning.

My thoughts skip forward to the two words that Alex said, and my brow knits in confusion. What in God's name are *Nocturna* and *Vigil*? I'd hoped I would gain answers here, but the list of questions I was mentally writing down has started to bleed off the page. The one thing I do know for certain is I can't ask any of them now in front of these people. I'm observant enough to see that my presence could lead to unknown severities with the wrong move.

"I suggest we go inside before we say anything else that could confuse Molly." The woman in white speaks, not shifting her gaze from me this entire time. Her voice is breathy and soft but has undertones of authority. I can tell that she's the highest ranked among the people standing here, and the omniscient gleam in her eyes takes away any shock I might have felt at her knowing my name.

At her words, the small group makes its way toward the doors while the lady in white stays staring at me for a moment longer. Slightly tilting her head, she gives the impression that she's debating something. I don't seem to possess the power to look away, and after a second longer she quickly shifts her eyes in Dev's direction and then back to me. The side of her mouth twitches before she nods infinitesimally and turns away.

That was weird.

Dev enters my line of sight, and I blink to dispel the enthrallment of the departing form. "Just wait out here," he says. "I'll be out as soon as I can."

"Dev, wait!" I reach for his arm.

He turns back. "Yes?"

"What's a Nocturna?" I lean in and whisper. For some reason it's the one question I decide to ask now. A smirk edges along his mouth as if I asked something amusing, and the only answer he gives is a wink before turning away from my annoyed face and walking through the threshold.

Before the doors completely close, I catch a quick glimpse of the room beyond. It's large with vaulted ceilings, and it has similar characteristics to a grand room one would find in parliament. Both sides are fitted with stadium-style rows of chairs facing toward the center, and a podium resides in the middle of the floor. Directly above the podium, resting in the ceiling, is a giant round orb, producing the majority of light in this space. Blue-white light swirls and glows from within, exactly like the streetlamps and fixtures in Dev's apartment. Looking at the pure substance, a familiar feeling of seeing something I'm not supposed to settles over me.

The room is filled with people clad entirely in black, some wearing pants and T-shirts like Dev and Aveline, with signature quivers on their backs, others in floor-length black robes. There's a smaller group in all white, like the woman I saw earlier—some have wrapped robes, while others are in pants and T-shirts. Almost all of the people in white have golden-blond hair, while the hue of their skin is as diverse as they come.

Right before the doors close, I rest my eyes on an extremely tall, dark-skinned blond man standing with the white group. I take a step forward to gain a better view, but as the figure turns to face me, the doors shut oppressively in my face.

I look sharply between the two guards standing in front of the closed entrance, ignoring my very existence. Their eyes remain forward, unfocused on any one thing. I straighten and move away, knowing there's not a chance I'd ever be able to get in there even if I tried. And boy, do I want to try.

Walking around the expansive hall, I pass other doors that are concealed in the walls—none of which come close to the majestic height of the main door, but still retain their own mysterious allure.

The soft conversations of the people in the atrium bounce around the domed enclosure, making it seem much busier than it actually is. I glance up to the convex ceiling and take in a breath. How did I not see this before? The curved space is completely transparent. Bright shooting stars are visible through the glass as they zip by overhead, exposing the vastness outside these walls. I continue to stare, mesmerized by the humbling view of the sky, when my toe stubs against a solid barrier. Looking down, I realize I'm at the edge of the giant map of the world. An invisible lip keeps me from walking directly onto it.

Seeing it up close, I'm captivated by the details. It's like a real-time satellite projection of the world laid flat. The portion in shadow blinks quickly and sporadically with billions of blue lights, while a few white lights stay burning. The other half of the globe is lit up like the sun is shining on it. This portion has the similar number of blinking lights, but they are white interspersed with some blue.

I walk along the perimeter, dazzled by the watery sheen that sits on top like a protective skin. I don't know how long I stand there watching the shadow slowly move across the map as I try counting the various blinking lights that fill it, but I'm suddenly aware of someone standing by my side.

"This is how I know when you'll be here." Dev's voice is soft and close. He watches the map below impassively. "If you notice, the eastern part of the United States lies in shadow, meaning it's night there." He points to where the part of North America sits under the slow-moving darkness. "The blinking lights represent the number of people either going to sleep or waking up. Blue indicates sleeping and white waking. The number of people asleep is recorded at the top." I shift my gaze to a counter with rapidly changing numbers.

"That's amazing," I say softly, scared that if I speak too loudly, Dev will become aware of his forthrightness. I've seen similar examples of this technology used to show planes landing and taking off, but I don't understand how they could possibly know when someone's going to sleep or waking up. Planes are recorded in a computer system, but not people. "But why would you want to know how many people are sleeping?"

Dev glances around, making sure no one is listening, and I have to lean in to hear his quiet words. "Every sleeping mind gives energy to this place," he says, focusing on the map below. "We would not exist if you did not exist. You could say we are a form of protection for those who dream. We monitor their sleeping minds, persuading the thoughts they dream to come to fruition in waking life if that idea can serve a larger purpose for the world. And often we take inventions we find in dreams and use them for ourselves." He faces me. "That's why we count the people sleeping. You are all important to us," he says, studying me closely and awaiting my reaction.

I stare back, waiting for the same thing—my reaction—but I honestly can't feel anything, and I know it's because I'm in shock. Could such a place exist? No matter how long I stand here, my brain refuses to let what he said sink in, like he's trying to tell me that Santa Claus and unicorns are real. It's just impossible. Isn't it?

"Molly, what are you thinking?" he finally asks.

"So what are you?" I try remaining calm.

Dev's shoulders visibly relax, but his eyes stay hesitant. "I am Nocturna. *We* are Nocturna." He motions around to the other people in the room dressed in black.

"*Nocturna?*" I test the unfamiliar word, remembering Alexander saying it and now getting the answer to my earlier question.

"Protectors, wardens, watchers of the night, of Dreamers," he explains, still gauging how I might be feeling. "Please tell me what you're thinking."

I glance back to the slowly moving map by our feet. "I'm thinking that I have a lot more questions."

Dev nods. "Come, let's get out of here." He laces his fingers with mine, and I hesitate for a second, catching the instant hurt flash across his face. In that moment I decide I'm going to do what I've been fighting all along. I'm going to trust him.

We quickly exit, heading toward the other side of the square where a tall tower stands. I don't ask questions as Dev leads me into an elevator at its base, my mind still resisting the possibility of truth in his earlier words.

As we ascend, I study the other figures dressed in black. They look like humans: two eyes, two ears, a nose, and mouth. How can they possibly be a strange, otherworldly race that monitors my subconscious? Better yet, how can such a race exist? If they looked different than the average human, I might be more ready to believe in this make-believe land that Dev described, but these people look no different than any other person I've seen when I'm awake.

We are silent the whole ride up, and I tuck my hair behind my ear more than once before Dev gently grabs my hand and squeezes. He flashes an understanding smile before the doors open and we are shuffled out of the car.

We wait in a short line as the attendant manning the zipline enters numbers into the keypad, to shift around lines, I suppose, sending groups off to their various destinations. I'm unaware it's our turn to go—still in a daze of incomprehension—when Dev asks, "You ready?" He places his hand on my back. "If you're not up to this, we can travel another way, but this is the fastest."

I turn and blink up to him. "No, no, I'm fine. Do you need to hook me into you?"

He fights a grin. "I thought you could try zipping by yourself again. You seemed like you were enjoying it before." He gently pushes an Arcus into my hands.

"Yeah, I did."

"Good," Dev says. "I'm going to go first so I can catch you on the other side. We can talk about landing techniques later." His spirit seems to be livened by the activity. "See you on the other side, midnight!" he says with a mischievous smile and a wink before jumping onto the line, zooming out of sight.

I stand blinking at the empty space Dev had just filled. *What the... Midnight?*

"Excuse me, miss. You're up," a teenage boy says by my side. Forgetting where I am for a second, I notice the crowd of people waiting for me to traverse the line.

"Oh, sorry."

"Just press that blue button you see next to your foot," the boy instructs. He must know I'm new at this and need to use the sissy way of getting onto the line. I press the button and wait for the platform to rise to the zipline where I connect in. My body begins to thrum with anticipation, and I tell myself to stay calm right before I run and push off the platform.

⋅→▣⊙ ⊙▣←⋅

I make it through the city to join up with Dev, who's standing on a platform on top of the wall at the edge of the city. Even though each of these landing pads looks identical, I'm pretty sure this is the same one that Aveline and I took when I first got here. Dev catches me around my waist, helping me stop.

"You're a quick learner." He beams as he hesitantly removes his hands. I try to ignore the dancing feeling I get in my stomach every time he touches me.

"Thanks." I remove my Arcus from the line, my head much clearer from the ride.

"Here, you don't need that anymore." He takes my Arcus and, punching out, retracts the ends, transforming it into the innocent-looking baton once again.

I take in our surroundings. The endless field extends on the other side of the wall like an untouched world, my solitary elm tree the only element interrupting the gentle hills that roll away into the horizon. The sight of it makes me smile. It's quickly becoming my security here in this unknown place—the one thing that stays consistent and plain.

I turn to see Dev dangling from his Arcus that's connected to the hook at the top of the pole. His arms are taut with his strength, and he watches me with a funny expression.

"What?"

"I like seeing you here," he says, tilting his head to the side. Warmth from his words quickly spreads to my cheeks, and he smiles, beckoning me forward. "We're going to drop down together."

I frown and walk toward him, hating that he can unnerve me so easily. "Aveline taught me how to do this. We don't need to do it together."

"*Need* has nothing to do with it, Molly." Dev reaches out, pulling me into his arms and off the landing. I yip in fright and then hold on for dear life, seeing as we are dangling dangerously high from the ground. "It's all about the *want*," he says in my ear, and the words slide over my body, making the hairs at the nape of my neck stand.

His grip tightens as we lower, and I can't help wrapping my legs around his torso for more security. His breath is hot on my neck, and his chest rises and falls into mine. As soon as he places his feet on the ground, I quickly untangle myself and step away. He stays motionless—one hand still gripping the Arcus attached to the hook, while the other hangs by his side as his intense blue eyes latch on to mine. The overall effect is primal and possessive, and I know I must turn away or I might do something I'll regret...or worse, enjoy.

I start toward the tree, knowing that's why he brought me here—so that I can be somewhere comfortable after everything new I just experienced. The idea that he understands this sets aglow a place deep in my chest despite my greater efforts to remain impassive.

I hear the grappling hook retract and his quiet steps behind me. He lets me walk alone in front of him, gathering and digesting my thoughts. I realize how calm I am. Or at least appear. Somewhere deep inside I know I must be freaking out and running in circles looking for the emergency exit, but a larger part of me is accepting all this knowledge and slowly fitting it into that strange hollow mass that I've been trying to fill for years.

I grow distraught, realizing that I've finally found what I'm looking for in a place that is made up in my mind. Because I know I must be dreaming. Nothing like this could exist. And maybe that's why I'm not spastic, because I actually believe this isn't real, like an addict on a crazy trip, aware that it's only a hallucination.

We settle ourselves by the base of the tree and gaze out at the glowing city. "You said you had more questions?" Dev asks after a few moments of contemplative silence.

I study his face blanketed in apprehension and try to choose my most important questions first. "So what is this place? Does it have a name?"

"It's called Terra Somniorum. Translated, it means Land of Dreams." He watches me closely.

"Terra Somniorum. It's a pretty name," I admit.

He smiles. "It is."

"And you said that meeting was about what we saw at the canyon?"

"Yes." His brows pinch in with concern. "The red glow you saw was a horde of Metus." That word is vaguely familiar, and I try remembering where I've heard it before. "The Metus are parasitic, fear-inducing creatures," Dev explains after seeing my face scrunched in confusion. "At times, they can work their way into someone's dreams and create nightmares. We don't know how long they've been here, probably since the beginning of fear itself. We can only trace them as far back as our most ancient history books allow. We've learned that they're created from the most evil of thoughts and despair in a Dreamer. Demons that haunt a Dreamer in their subconscious are created here, and these demons try to terrorize other sleeping minds so that more of them can spawn. It's a disgusting cycle of evil and fear." He pauses, allowing this all to sink in, while constantly twirling something in his hand. "The meeting was called to discuss some things…concerning the horde, but also concerning you." His eyes shift to me.

"Me? What about me?" How could I be in any way involved in this crazy place?

He doesn't answer for a long time, just keeps twisting the object between his hands. I can't quite make out what it is. "Molly, you're so much more than you think you are," he says almost angrily, and his words send a cold shiver down my spine. How much I want to believe him.

I follow his gaze to the round object he holds, and I'm not sure what comes over me, but I quickly try to grab it. His hand jerks away as he regards me with alarm. I narrow my eyes and don't back down, knowing this is what he was hiding from me the last time I was here. I jump up, draping myself over his shoulders, trying to bring his outstretched arm back in.

"Come on—what's so important that you have to hide it?"

He grunts under me and then is suddenly twirling me to lie on the ground beneath him, pinning my arms above my head. I squirm, trying to get out of his stronghold while acutely aware of his heavy body above mine. The weight of him sends a panic through my senses, but not because I don't want him there.

His body stills, his breathing coming out in ragged breaths, and his blue eyes dilate with a fever that makes my body go limp. I know I'm breathing just as fast as he is. My heart pumps in my ears, my stomach a ball of twisted, aching desire as I stare at his unbelievably gorgeous face inches from mine. His lips part, and I find myself involuntarily moving toward them.

In the blink of an eye, I'm lying there alone, a cold breeze filling the space where Dev was just pressed warmly against me.

Looking up in bewilderment, I find Dev standing at the base of the tree. How did he move so fast? "This isn't a good idea," he says gruffly, the warmth in his eyes iced over.

I gather myself up, feeling hurt and humiliated and definitely confused. *What the...* Could I possibly have been reading his signals wrong? Embarrassment from his rejection quickly turns to anger, and as lame as it is, I've always been the asshat who cries when those two emotions mix. Fortunately, I manage to hold the tears at bay as I ask, "Why?"

"It's just...it's simpler if it didn't."

I turn away, unable to look him in the eye.

"Molly, let me—"

"It's fine," I cut in.

"No, let me explain." He tries again, stepping closer.

"Don't." I snatch my hand away as he is reaching out to touch it. Could he really not see how he was leading me on? God, I just want to be alone. I want to leave before the emotions I have trapped below the surface escape.

As if someone hears my plea, there's a familiar pull of my body drifting away, and I let out a breath of relief. The soft touch of cotton brushes against my cheek, and I swallow the sadness, instead feeling grateful to be waking up to a reprieve from this man.

Chapter 14

L YING MOTIONLESS IN my bed, I stare at my ceiling. I can't ignore the ache in my chest and the tears that gather in my eyes. I go back and forth between being irate at Dev to being depressed that I'm no longer next to him. Then my thoughts come back around to the fact that I'm absolutely without a doubt losing my friggin' mind, feeling sad for a man who *obviously* doesn't exist! Anxiety attacks me.

Could any of what Dev said be real? Is he even real? Is it wrong to want it all to be?

I slap my hands over my face and begin to cry. Frustration and confusion wrack through me with each sob as I lie there, soaking my pillow.

My body eventually loses its energy to act on my sadness, and I sag with exhaustion. This is the first time I've actually cried unabashedly since the accident, and it's a relief to finally let it all out. After a moment more of staring out like a zombie and knowing I need to get up at some point, I shuffle out of bed.

Walking to my bathroom, I open the medicine cabinet to grab the toothpaste.

My hand stills.

The word *Nocterin* flashes out at me. The box of sleeping pills my agency represents sits on a shelf, laughing at me. Is this where I thought up the name for the people in my dreams? Nocturna…they are similar. Maybe my mind did some of its own creative naming in my sleep. But the more I convince myself that it wasn't real, the sadder I feel inside.

Frustrated, I slam my medicine cabinet closed. I don't even know why I took that free sample of pills from work anyway. I've never had issues sleeping. I laugh out loud as I brush my teeth, making some of the paste drip down my chin. I can't miss the irony. Here I am, in that *exact* position—having sleeping problems. I rinse out my mouth and stare at myself in the mirror, thinking of all the mornings I've woken up unrested or in a panic…

No.

I push the thought from my mind. That is *not* a road I need to go down. I'm fine.

After a quick shower, I dress and try to decide what to do today. I'll go out of my mind with boredom if I stay in my apartment one more second. Meeting with Dr. Marshall tomorrow couldn't come soon enough. Hopefully he can give me the go-ahead to return to the office on Wednesday. Dragging my hand down my face, I let out a moan. I can't believe I actually miss work. Becca would die laughing if she knew.

Putting on a light coat, I make my way downstairs, deciding a walk is exactly what I need. It's early afternoon, so most people are on their second coffee run or starting their lunch break. I randomly walk the West Village, seeking new side streets that I normally never go down. My mind continues wandering back to my dreams. How could the Nocturna be something I imagined—something purely in my head? Dev did say that he was a protector of Dreamers, and isn't that just what I am? A Dreamer? At least now I'm dreaming, unlike before when I never remembered a single one. Could there really be a place that exists between the conscious and the subconscious that guides our lives, our decisions? The endless stream of questions wreaks havoc on my brain, and I rub my temple against the small throb that's beginning to grow.

I know next to nothing about the mind and what it can possess, let alone the significance of a dream. Dev's words about me being much more than I think I am keep replaying, and I scoff. Is my life so pathetic that I need to manufacture my importance in a fake one?

And despite my best efforts, my body can't help recalling the feel of Dev on top of me and his sudden rejection. I ball my hands into fists, my stomach clenching in a strange, misplaced anger. How can I be mad at a figment of my imagination? I just want to scream!

I'm so lost in my psychiatric ward–worthy thoughts that I almost trip over a sign on the sidewalk. I grab hold of it to steady myself.

The Village Portal, a Bookstore for the Spirit. Today! 30% Off Everything read the words written in chalk, and I glance up to a small, tucked-away hippie bookstore. Plants hang on either side of the door—which is painted a tacky purple—and dream catchers fill the window while a tabby cat lies curled up in the sill next to a random mixture of health and spiritual books on display.

I've never noticed this store before, but given its contents, it's not a place that would normally draw my attention. Looking around, I wonder what street I'm on as an idea grabs me. This place might have some crazy books on dreams. I study the entrance, deliberating if what I'm about to do falls into the category of normal curiosity or obsession, when I feel a strange heat in my gut. Something in the furthest recesses of my brain is telling me to go in, and before I can stop myself, I'm climbing the steps and pushing open the door.

A tiny bell rings, announcing my entrance, and the scent of incense coats me like an unwanted hug from a stranger. The store is modest in size with floor-to-ceiling books covering its walls and small freestanding shelves in the middle. A kid with dark clothes and more than a dozen piercings in his face sits at the register reading, ignoring the fact that a new patron has walked in.

There are a few other people inside, all stereotypes of the shoppers who would visit here: a little old lady with what appears to be an outfit knitted entirely by hand, a middle-aged man with a beret and a T-shirt that he has probably never taken off, and a younger-looking couple with yoga mats tucked under their arms.

Walking by each section, I look for something that could possibly tell me about my dreams. I read signs that say Metaphysical, Homeopathic, Meditation, and Spiritual. I worry my bottom lip, starting to feel a little foolish for walking in here and am about to make my way out when a sign that says Symbols above a little alcove catches my eye. It's dimly lit in this area save for a single light above the section, giving it an eerie presence. I wonder if they do it on purpose to set the ambiance for the reader. I skim the shelves, immediately seeing dozens of books with the word *Dreams* in the title.

I grab a few off the shelf and read their descriptions. They all look a little ridiculous to me, and the pictures of the authors become my deciding factor for which titles I should probably put back. After a good amount of time perusing certain writings and theories, I begin to feel the ever-present panic in my body dull. The amount of people who have written about dreams and their importance makes me think that my experience might not be that crazy after all…and probably has a logical explanation.

"Molly?" asks a deep voice. I look up to Rae standing at the entrance to this section. The brighter part of the store is behind him, so he's almost completely silhouetted. I can make him out by his unmistakable height and halo-like, illuminated blond hair.

"Rae?"

He steps into the light of the alcove, shifting his dark skin to a deep honey color, shock and slight concern etched on his face. He's wearing a similar black outfit like the night we met. Remembering where I am and what I'm holding, I bring the books closer to my chest, hiding their subject matter.

"What are you doing here?" I ask.

He moves his gaze over the material in this area. "I could ask you the same thing." A small part of his mouth inches up. "I'm grabbing some texts on medicine. This place has good ones on homeopathic remedies."

"Oh," I say, not really sure why I'm surprised by his answer. He definitely looks like the type of guy who's into his health. I shift my weight to my other foot. "I was out on a walk and stumbled onto this place."

Rae squints at what I'm failing to hide in my hands. "Having some interesting dreams lately?"

"No, why would you think that?" I say too quickly.

His eyes search mine for a moment, and then his features relax. "Just assumed from what you're holding."

"Oh, these?" I ask innocently.

"Yes, *those*," he says, amused.

"Yeah, I…uh, I was just curious about some things, I guess." I glance down at my books, not knowing why I'm so embarrassed by them. By the sound of it, Rae shops here frequently. "I hear you're seeing Becca tonight," I say, desperate to find another subject of conversation.

He regards me a second longer before answering. "Yeah, we have dinner. I'm thinking of taking her to this little sushi place in Brooklyn near her apartment. Then maybe to a movie." He slowly turns out of the alcove, and I follow, still clutching the texts. I guess I'll be buying something after all.

"That sounds like a fun night."

"Yeah, I thought so. I remember her saying that she loved sushi." Rae quickly glances at the homeopathic section as we pass it and picks a volume to buy, practically at random. He must really know his stuff.

"She loves a lot of things," I say with a laugh.

"Yes, she does." Rae smiles warmly. "She's quite the force. It's one of the things that captivated me about her." He places his book on the register, and the kid behind the counter huffs at having his reading time interrupted. I smile to myself hearing Rae's honest words about my closest friend and knowing exactly how he feels.

After we make our purchases, Rae and I exit the store. That is, after I almost choked on the total cost of my items. Someone's really profiting here, and I have a feeling it's not me.

"Well, Molly, I would never in a thousand years have thought I would run into you there, but it's always a pleasure," he says genuinely.

"Crazy coincidence." I smile. "Oh, so Becca told me you're in town on business—I hope you aren't planning on leaving soon." I want to gauge how attached Becca should be getting to this out-of-towner.

"Mmm, it might seem that I'll be here more permanently than expected."

"Well, that's good. Work has you here longer?" `

"Yeah, there's a specific contract that needs more attention, so I'm going to be here working until my boss says otherwise."

Good news for Becca. "Well, I'm glad you're staying, even though that doesn't sound so fun." I scrunch up my nose at the prospect of dealing with life insurance contracts for longer than necessary. "I hope your friends in California won't miss you too much."

His smile deepens. "I think they can manage."

"Good. Well, have fun tonight, and I hope to see you again soon. Maybe not in weird bookstores though." I laugh lightly.

"Yes, I'm sure we'll see each other one way or another." He opens his arm to give me a slightly awkward hug good-bye, given his height.

"Okay, have a nice rest of your day," I say as we both go our separate directions.

"You too, Molly."

I actually have to head the same way as Rae but feel like I need to escape what could become another slightly awkward conversation.

⊷≡◉ ◉≡⊶

It's late afternoon when I make it back to my apartment and plop myself on my bed, deciding to dig in to my impromptu purchases.

The first book I open is what I guess is a regular dream dictionary: a plethora of alphabetized symbols and their meanings. I read the opening description.

> Symbols are the language of dreams. A symbol can invoke a feeling or idea, and often has a much more profound meaning that any one word can convey. At the same time, these symbols can leave you confused, wondering what a dream was all about.

I snort at how much that hits home before reading on.

> Having the ability to analyze and understand your dreams is a powerful tool. By doing so, you can learn about your deep secrets and hidden feelings.

Oh geez. My common sense is telling me to stop right there, but let's be honest, who can walk away from the tantalizing prospect of learning about their "deep secrets and hidden feelings"? Obviously not me.

Flipping through the pages, I wonder about what I want to look up. What sticks out most about my dreams?

Black. Everyone is always wearing black. I turn to the *B*s and brush my finger down each word until I find what I'm looking for.

> BLACK: Black symbolizes the unknown, the subconscious, mystery, danger, or death. The color invites you to dig deeper into your subconscious in order to gain a better understanding of yourself. More positively, black represents

potential and possibilities. It can represent a clean or blank slate.

A cold chill tiptoes up my spine despite my earlier doubts. Black symbolizes the subconscious. Is that what Dev and the Nocturna are—my subconscious? Skimming back over the text, my eyes flutter over the words *danger* and *death*, and I quickly look ahead, trying not to dwell on whether they correlate to my dreams.

I peruse randomly through the book, attempting to stay as lighthearted as possible about this whole thing, when I pause on a word that instantly brings up a familiar image. As I read over the definition, my heart rate accelerates.

TREES: Trees in your dream symbolize new hope, growth, desire, knowledge, and life. They also imply strength, safety, and stability. You are concentrating on your own self-development and individualization.

The tree is where I first arrived in my dreams—I fell toward it like a beacon. How many times have I woken up underneath it? When I was still drunk, before Dev pushed me off the cliff? Did I wake up there because it was protecting me, bringing me stability in that strange place? I read the last part again. "You are concentrating on your own self-development and individualization."

Dev's words come back to me fast and hard. *You're so much more than you think.* For a quick moment I question the truth about whether this place could actually be real. But anyone can read meaning into these definitions.

Frustrated and slightly ashamed that I even entertained the idea, I shut the book, yet my mind refuses to stop. It keeps racing forward, turning and weaving through memories of my dreams, flipping over rocks to find something, anything, that will allow me to put this to rest.

Then, like a tractor-trailer, it hits me—the last conversation I had with Dev. The name he said. I quickly grab my laptop and search for the meaning of the word *Terra*. Dozens of search results pop up. *Shit.* I click on the first one. It's a Latin forum, and my heart squeezes when I read one of the posts.

"*Terra* is the Latin word for *land.*"

I hesitate before typing in my next search, guessing on spelling. I swallow as the search results fill the page, and click on the first link. My eyes widen as I read, and I push away from my computer, my hands shaking. I couldn't have made this up. I don't know a lick of Latin! How could I have imagined those words together?

"*Somniorum* is Latin for *of the dreams.*"

The image of Dev sitting with me by the tree hazily materializes. His words, "Terra Somniorum. Translated, it means Land of Dreams."

I fall to my bed, my legs too weak to hold my weight. What's happening? How could I have made that up? I put my head in my hands and push my hair off my face. *I can't breathe. There's no oxygen left for me to breathe.* My eyes scan the room for a way out, and all I see is the door. Grabbing my keys, I hurry to escape, noticing it's becoming hard to swallow, as if I'm experiencing an allergic reaction to my very thoughts. I can't get outside fast enough.

Cold quickly sweeps around my body as I exit my building. I forgot a coat. Despite the discomfort, I suck in a breath, allowing the cool air to clear my head as I descend my stoop, running head-on into someone.

"Oh! I'm so sorry. I—"

"Molly?" Jared steadies me, looking startled and confused, his dark-blond hair swaying in the cold breeze. "Where are you going?"

"Jared! Oh my God. Sorry, I didn't see you." I back up a step. This new situation sends a different shock through my body, and the spiraling thoughts that brought me running outside get forced into a dark corner of my mind. I rub the sides of my arms, attempting to bring heat into them.

"Are you okay?" he asks, pulling me into his warm body, and I welcome the embrace. Smelling his familiar cologne and feeling his strong arms gives me a sense of security that I didn't realize I was craving. "You seem on edge. Did something happen?"

I rest my cheek on his chest. "No, I'm okay. I just needed some fresh air. I was feeling cramped in my apartment." I thought that was a better answer than saying, "I just had a panic attack because I was doing research on dreams I've begun to think are real." Yeah, a much better answer. I take in a deep breath again, clearing away any last remnants of my anxiety attack. "What are you doing here?" I ask.

His brows turn in. "We had plans tonight, remember?"

Shit. It's Monday. I'm getting the days mixed up. This isn't good. "Oh yeah! No, I remember. Sorry, I've been having one of those days and lost track of time."

Jared narrows his eyes. "Are you sure you're okay?"

"Yeah, I'm fine, really. I just needed a little fresh air, that's all." I force a smile.

He only looks slightly convinced. "Okay, well, I was going to suggest we order in again, but if you're feeling cramped, we can go out to eat." He removes his brown leather jacket and drapes it around my shoulders. I must have been shivering more than I thought. The leftover body heat inside his coat wraps around me like a best friend.

I think about being in a restaurant and immediately know I can't handle so many people and all the noise. My nerves are shot. "No, I think ordering in is perfect."

I start to turn into my building, when he grabs my hand, stopping me. "Molly?" he says softly.

"Yeah?" *What have I done now?*

"Hi," he says and brings me in for a kiss.

At first I'm too caught off guard to enjoy it, but once my mind settles, heat expands in my lungs and desire spreads out all the way to my fingertips. A familiar feeling of reacting this way to another man pokes my brain, but I quickly shove it away. Encircling my arms around Jared's neck, I stand on my toes so I can be more level with him. He quickly grabs my waist and places me one step above him on the stairs. His grin is apparent as we kiss, and I can't help but smile back. This man knows exactly what I need. He slowly pulls away, locking his gaze with mine. A pleased expression lights up his face.

"Well, hello," I finally return.

He gives me another quick kiss. "Okay, that's all I needed. We can go in now."

I laugh. "Glad I can be of service."

He gives my butt a little love tap, which gets me scurrying up the stairs.

Once back in my apartment, I quickly shut my laptop that's glaring at me like a possessed demon on my bed and grab a bunch of menus from my menu drawer—an obligatory drawer for every New Yorker. Jared slips his jacket off my shoulders and replaces its warmth with his own by wrapping his arms around me.

"What are you in the mood for?" I display the plethora of takeout options.

"How about pizza?" He nibbles the side of my ear.

I squirm under the ticklish feeling. "I could do pizza."

"Perfect."

Jared walks to the bathroom. "I can do plain or the works, you decide. Oh, but nothing with garlic. I've got plans for you later," he says before closing the door on his mischievous face. I smile but at the same time feel a little nervous. Jared and I haven't been intimate since the accident, and a certain other man enters my mind, filling me with a weird guilt.

Get a grip. Nothing happened with Dev, and even so, he's just a *dream*! Jared is real and handsome and the one I'm dating. More importantly, why the hell am I comparing Jared to someone who doesn't exist?

"So, what do we want to watch?" Jared asks, walking back into the room.

I jump, realizing I've been holding my phone to call the pizza place this entire time, lost in thought. "Uh, I don't really have a preference... anything really." I start to punch in the number to the restaurant.

So far in the action movie we're watching, there have been three explosions and four fight scenes, and I'm pretty sure only forty-five minutes have passed. This is my kind of film.

Jared and I laugh at the amazingly corny one-liners that are uttered before the protagonist beats up his enemies, and I smile as I catch Jared saying the lines along with the movie.

"Only seen this once, eh?" I tease.

"Once in the theater maybe," he admits sheepishly. I begin to laugh but am cut short by Jared pulling me to lie underneath him. "Are *you* laughing at me?" he says in a horrible *Goodfellas* imitation.

"What if I am?"

"Well, I think I can do some things to wipe that smile off your face," he says gruffly before he puts his lips to mine.

"What about the movie?" I mumble between kisses. "Don't you think it's important that I find out how it ends?"

Jared pins both my hands above my head and moves his lips to my neck. "He kills them all and gets the girl."

"You ruined it!"

"I'm pretty sure I know how to make it up to you." He renders me incapable of stringing together any sort of coherent response as he moves his lips with mine. He lets go of my hands, and I hungrily move them to his strong back, digging my nails into his shirt. Moaning, he grips the back of my neck, shifting his body weight down and fully encompassing my form.

All the days and nights of teasing me and the presence of another man ignites a fire in my gut, making any rational thought go out the window. The basic primal instinct of wanting this man floods my senses, and I reach my hands under his shirt, feeling his hard, toned back and warm skin.

He returns my move with his own intrusion of hand to skin and cups his palm around my breast, his tongue sweeping, his lips softly arousing. He rolls me on top, feeling his way across my stomach, and I remove my shirt, delighted in the way Jared's eyes travel over my exposed skin before they go back to me. I hold his gaze as I reach around and unclasp my bra.

He sucks in a breath and bites down on his bottom lip. "I will never get sick of this sight." His hazel eyes mix with lust and a delicate sweetness. I smile down at his handsome face and lean over, kissing him.

Jared and I have had sex before, but for some reason this seems like our first time all over again. I'm not sure if it's because I've felt like a new person ever since my accident or because I'm starting to regard him in a different light. All I know is that I'm starting to like him more than I originally had or intended.

We both lie skin to skin while Jared studies me with adoration and a glimmer of something I know I must hold in my own eyes. He gently bends down, claiming my lips, sending a whole new swirling heat to pass through my brain. As I close my eyes, a weird flash of another man lying on top of me appears. The bluest gaze swimming with a desirous storm and dark features rest just inches from my face. I gasp and move my head to the side. Jared doesn't take notice but instead sees that as a cue to kiss my neck. I stare off into my apartment as Jared warms my body, but another man's face fills my mind.

How can I think about Dev at a time like this? A small anger sweeps through my skin at the fact that he can disrupt me even when I'm the most distracted. I reach for my bedside drawer, finding what I need to return me to the now, and push the foil packet into Jared's hands. I concentrate on his touch, his taste, before relaxing into his body and getting completely lost in his arms.

Jared spoons me perfectly to him, slowly gliding his fingers over my bare arm.

"You're amazing," he whispers in my ear.

I turn, catching his warm hazel eyes, open for me to explore. "So are you." I tip my head up, kissing his lips. Jared suddenly moves from the covers. "Where are you going?" I whine as the absence of his body lets cool air come into the bed. My annoyed face quickly transforms into a grin as I watch his deliciously toned naked rear walking across my apartment.

"I have something for you." He fumbles with his clothes before reaching into his jacket pocket and taking out a small box.

I regard it cautiously as he brings it over, ducking back into the sheets and bringing my body close to his. "What is it?"

"Well, usually when you open a gift, you find out," he says with a laugh.

I shoot him an annoyed glare as I reposition myself to face him and remove the lid. My breath catches. "Jared! You didn't have to do that." I lift a silver charm bracelet out of the box—an exact replica of the one he gave me on my birthday.

"Yes, I did. I think it's a little unfair that you only got to enjoy my gift for an hour before it got destroyed." He picks up my uninjured wrist and clasps the bracelet on.

"You even got the Empire State Building charm." I smile, my heart filling for this man next to me.

"Of course." He takes my newly adorned wrist and kisses the delicate underside.

"Thank you," I whisper.

"You're very welcome."

Lying back down, I steal a glance at the clock on my bedside table. "Shit! It's midnight." *Where the freak did the time go?* Well—I know where part of it went. "What time do you need to wake up for work?" I ask as I scamper out of the sheets and search for my underwear.

Jared chuckles lightly, watching as I search through the mess we made of our clothes. "I don't need to be in until nine." He sits up, resting his back on the headboard.

I throw his underwear at him. "Okay, that's not too bad. I'll set the alarm for eight?"

"That works. I have a change of clothes at the gym, and I can hit it up before I go in." Jared puts on his boxer briefs and walks to where I'm standing in a clean pajama shirt and shorts.

"*Jared,*" I say in warning as he prowls toward me.

"*Molly,*" he returns playfully before pulling me into his arms and kissing me. His lips provoke me to go where I know we'll spend another hour.

"Jared...I know...how grumpy you get...when you don't...get enough sleep," I say between his kisses.

"Mmm" is his only response.

I laugh and gently push him away. "Seriously, the last time this happened, I spent a good hour trying to get you out of bed to make it to work in time."

He lets out a defeated sigh. "Always the responsible one."

Standing side by side brushing our teeth, we eye one another, amused by the paste that escapes our mouths and slides down over our lips. It's so comfortable with Jared. I don't find myself getting any flashes of embarrassment I know I tend to have around some men, like recently with Rae catching me at that bookstore. Why I even decided to go in there is beyond m—

My stomach flips.

My dreams.

I stop midbrush. How could I have forgotten all about what I read today?

"Mols, you're dripping on the floor." Jared laughs at my side. I blink at the paste that is indeed dripping from my chin to the floor. Quickly bending over the sink, I wash off my mouth, my thoughts still centered on the fact that I'm about to go to sleep and, from the track record of all my previous nights, will definitely be dreaming of that land again.

Walking to bed, I attempt to rid myself of my sudden nerves. *It's just sleeping, just dreams*, I repeat.

This is real. I look at Jared waiting for me.

He's real.

I climb into bed and snuggle my back up to Jared's warm chest. He hooks a strong arm around my waist, pulling me closer and kissing my hair.

"Good-night," he says softly.

"Good-night," I whisper back, knowing I probably won't fall asleep any time soon.

This isn't good. I can't be scared every time I need rest. My mind turns in circles, searching for a way to get a decent night's sleep and go back to dreaming of nothing. As soon as I think it, I know it's a lie; I don't want to dream of nothing. A part of me is excited to return to the place that is strangely starting to feel like home just as much as this place does. I wonder if the part of me that's scared is that way only because of a certain person who will be there waiting.

With that last thought, I finally let my eyes close, and the sweet early onset of sleep comes fast.

Chapter 15

THE SILHOUETTED MAN stands alone against the velvet dark, a pillar against the gentle breeze that sways the grass around him. Insects chirp, wind rustles, stars streak by.

Here I am. Again.

I study his familiar outline poised a small distance away, his back to me, as his head's tilted up toward the sky. I was hoping that if I returned to this place, the nervous energy that was rolling around in my stomach would subside, but it has only picked up speed as I remember our last interaction. A wave of guilt accompanies the emotions I'm attempting to push away as I think about Jared, and a small speck of appreciation for what Dev stopped from happening creeps forward. Even though I'm not sure kissing someone else while dreaming constitutes cheating, I decide that avoiding that moral dilemma is in my best interest.

Dev doesn't move when I step next to him—he doesn't even take his gaze from the millions of shooting stars overhead.

"I envy them," he says. His profile rests, smooth and relaxed, allowing a softness to settle over his usually rugged appearance.

"Who?" I ask.

"The Dreamers."

I look toward the sky, a bit confused, but try keeping up with his thoughts. "Why do you envy them?"

"They can dream."

"Do you not dream when you sleep?" I ask, knowing a little of that feeling—well, until recently.

He lowers his gaze to the city that always rests in the distance. Calming pulses of light dance around it like a halo. "Nocturna do not sleep," he says. "Our job is to constantly watch over the Dreamers and our world. We cannot sleep, and have no need." He finally pulls his blue eyes to mine, and I see that they simmer with faraway thoughts. "You *never* sleep?" I say with astonishment, ignoring the hot flutters that dance in my stomach. "Don't you get tired?"

He laughs lightly. "We get tired in a different sense than I think you're used to feeling. We gather our strength from you. From the Dreamers."

How does that *work?*

Before I can ask, he returns with a question of his own. "What is it like? To dream?"

I've never seen Dev like this—so open and vulnerable. He stands exposed, without his usual sarcastic and confident shell, and this has me struggling to keep up the emotional wall that I hastily cobbled together before approaching him. I have a strong urge to hug him.

"I'm probably not the best one to ask." I hardly remembered any of my dreams before I conjured up this place.

He turns away, disappointment apparent.

"But…" I begin to add in haste, strangely not wanting to be the cause of his sadness. "From what I *can* recollect, it can feel like many things and then like nothing you've ever experienced, all at the same time." I try to draw on images and emotions I've had in this world and what I can remember Becca telling me about her dreams.

"Go on," Dev coaxes, his eyes slightly glossy with curiosity.

I watch the sky, figuring out how to describe what he's wanting to hear. "Well, sometimes dreaming is like being submerged underwater. You can feel weightless, and things change and morph all around you. Sometimes colors are vivid, and other times everything is in black and white.

"Sometimes people you know are the star players in your dreams and do the craziest things, but it all feels quite normal at the time." I smile, thinking of some of the dreams Becca has shared with me where I'm behaving bizarrely, but it always seems justifiable in the moment. "Then there are other types of dreams that never really materialize, or maybe they do but you don't quite remember the details. They seem hazy, like they're happening behind a veil.

"There are the bad dreams, the ones that leave you in a cold sweat, and when you finally wake up you're almost certain those nightmares can crawl out and get you." I shiver, remembering the particularly unpleasant experience of being pushed to my death into a canyon.

My gaze roams the field and I breathe in the sweet night air, reveling in the fact that this could all be a dream. I stop on Dev and hold my eyes to his cerulean blue.

"And then there are the dreams that feel as authentic as reality itself, that seem to exist just as your own life does. Where the emotions that you experience there carry over to when you're awake. They are so real, so genuine, that you begin to question your own sanity. And you know that when the day comes that you finally stop dreaming them, you will never stop remembering."

My breathing has grown heavier with each sentence, and I can't find the strength to look away as Dev's gaze sears into mine, his body just as paralyzed.

With his wall slightly down, I see someone strong but tired. Someone who carries too many burdens but will never admit that he needs help. I see secrets he wants desperately to share and a hot energy that's being tied back with a leash, not trusted to be let free. I wonder what he sees when he looks at me.

I find myself taking a step closer and stop short, instantly catching his body stiffen, the mask he dropped once again covering his face. All the things I was able to catch a glimpse of before are gone, vanishing so fast that I'm uncertain if I saw them there in the first place.

He repositions himself away from me. Somewhere during my lecture our bodies must have turned toward each other. I clear my throat, not really understanding what just transpired but desperately looking for a change in conversation. I twist the bottom of my pajama shirt and notice my sleep ensemble and bare feet.

"Uh, do you have any clothes for me to change into?" I ask, suddenly noticing Dev fiddling with something small in one hand. As I speak, he immediately palms it.

"I want to see if something works first." He faces me, and I arch an eyebrow questioningly. "I want you to try and visualize that you're wearing the clothes."

"What?"

He repeats himself.

"Yeah...uh, like I said before, *what?*" Maybe I'm not the only one who's lost their mind.

"Trust me on this. Try to imagine that you're wearing the clothes you had on here last time. Start with the T-shirt and then work your way down."

I glare at him.

"Close your eyes when you do it. It will help you focus."

"How do you know what will help me focus?" I ask, skeptical that he's making me look like a fool and playing some strange joke.

"Molly, *please*," he says, slightly exasperated.

Mumbling under my breath about him being insane and that he better not stick something up my nose, I resign to do as he asks. Once my eyes are shut, Dev tells me to relax and take in a breath. I do but still feel stupid.

"Do it for real this time," he admonishes.

"I *am* doing it for real. How can I fake breathing?"

"You're not taking it seriously. This won't work unless you believe it will. So try again and keep your eyes closed."

I roll my eyes shut and take in a couple of large breaths, feeling myself grow calm.

"Now, imagine the black T-shirt you wore the other day, and then the pants and the boots. Do you remember what they looked like?"

"Yes." It's the only outfit that anyone really wears around here—how could I not remember? I breathe in again and decide to humor him. Picturing the simple black T-shirt, I imagine it being placed over my head and onto my body. As I draw up these images, a strange heat expands in my stomach and travels to my head, cooling as it moves through me. It's only slightly uncomfortable. Once the cold energy is balled up in my brain, the image of the shirt becomes clearer and the fabric on my body slowly shifts, feeling tighter.

"Good! Good, Molly, keep going," Dev coaxes, his voice sounding hollow and distant as I concentrate on maintaining the energy that I've somehow created in my head.

I bring up the black protective pants next, like I'm picking out clothes from my closet. As soon as I imagine wearing them, I have the sensation of my exposed legs being wrapped up and warmed. I desperately want to open my eyes, but I push on, imagining my bare feet encased in black combat boots, and suddenly the grass I'm standing on shifts to something solid.

Unable to wait any longer, I open my eyes. The cool energy that collected in my body instantly swims away like a scared fish. Glancing down, I gasp. No longer am I in my pajamas—instead, I'm in the exact outfit I imagined myself wearing. I pull at the fabric, trying to convince myself that it's real.

"How did this...how did I..." I stutter, turning to Dev, who has on the smuggest and most excited face I've ever seen on another human being.

"Amazing," he says between a wide-lipped grin. "Okay, I want you to imagine you're wearing a quiver just like mine, with the Arcus in it." He speaks quickly, turning around to show me the object on his back.

"But Dev, how could I just *do* that?" My heart beats frantically. This is so strange, like the time that island appeared out of nowhere. I read in one of those books about controlling events and objects in your dreams—the author called it lucid dreaming. Is that what I'm doing now?

"Try to imagine yourself wearing one of these, and then I'll explain everything," Dev says, turning back to face me. "But this time keep your eyes open."

I sense him watching me as I study what he asked me to, imagining what it would feel like if that strap were around my chest and that tube hugged tight to my back. As I hold these thoughts, the heat I felt before expands in my belly, traveling again to my head and cooling down to a near-freezing temperature. My face scrunches at the slight pain, the sensation similar to a brain freeze when you drink something cold too fast.

Something presses between my chest, and a hard surface aligns with my spine. A voice shouts, snapping me back to the present. Once again the energy dissipates in the blink of an eye, traveling back to somewhere inside me.

"This is amazing!" Dev holds my arms, looking like he wants to twirl me around and hug me tight. Peering down, the very strap I was imagining is now wrapped around my body. Dev lets go as I touch the object on my back. A hard, cool cylinder sits securely against me. I know my eyes must be popping out of their sockets, because Dev is chuckling, watching me. My hands frantically and delicately touch the fabric of my clothes and the strap around my chest again and again and again.

"This is insane," I whisper. "*I* did this?" I know I'm dreaming, but it all feels so real.

"You have a gift."

"A gift? What do you mean? Can you do this?"

"No. I can't do that."

"Why not?"

Dev waves his hand dismissively. "I'll explain later. There's one more thing I want to try." He begins to walk away.

"Wait!" I stumble to follow him, aware of how natural this outfit and device feel against my body. "You said you'd explain everything after whatever I just did with this quiver."

Stopping about fifteen paces away, Dev disregards me and bends down, searching for something in the tall grass. Picking up a heavy object, he stands.

I squint at what he now holds. It looks like a rock. It is a rock. I suck in air. "Dev...what are you going to do with that?" Cautiously, I take a few steps back. He displays another one of his crooked grins. I don't like that grin. "Seriously, I need you to explain what's going on."

"I know, but...I really think the best way to test all this is to really push you. Pull the rug out from under you, as they say. See how strong you are without any real instruction first." He throws the nicely sized rock up in the air and catches it again, reminding me of a malicious mobster flicking a quarter over and over, except this quarter could crack my skull.

"Um, I think I have to disagree. I don't know what you're going to do with that, but I truly believe there's a better way of handling this. No, I *guarantee* there's a better way of handling this." I continue to back away, my flight instinct kicking in over my fight.

He takes a couple of steps forward, closing the safe distance I'm attempting to create.

"All you need to do is to think hard that you don't want to get hit by this." He displays his murder weapon.

"I can promise you, I don't need to think *hard* about that one." He's gone crazy. He's going to kill me! This dream has officially turned into a nightmare. "Dev, seriously, let's think about this." I hold my hands up when he moves his shoulder around like he's warming up to throw. *Good Lord.* "You're going to hurt me!"

"No, I don't think I will," he says. "Imagine it's something harmless."

Before I can protest, he launches the rock straight at me.

Chapter 16

I'VE HEARD THERE are three main reactions humans experience in the face of imminent danger. One: the sense to flee. Two: aggravation that they are placed in danger to begin with. And three: becoming motionless with shock. I, unfortunately, am experiencing number three.

Time slows as the rock comes shooting forward, and I stand perfectly, idiotically still as it does. But then something happens—without really thinking about it, I imagine the rock as nothing but sand, no longer joined together but instead scattered into mere grains. Like an urgent prayer, my mind repeats this desire over and over, and in that same moment, a quick heat unfolds and shoots out like a flash to my brain.

When I blink, the rock is gone and small fragments of sand dust my face. Cautiously, I open my eyes, spitting out the debris that found its way into my mouth.

I can't believe he actually threw that rock at me!

Glaring at Dev, I clean myself off before stopping midswipe. The rock never actually hit me. It turned to sand just as I imagined it would. *What the fuck?*

Dev's suddenly by my side, grabbing my hand and pulling me toward the city at a jog. "Come on!" he says, looking like a child who just woke up on Christmas morning. I have no choice but to follow as he tugs me along, my mind trying to wrap itself around what just happened. *I changed that rock to sand.* What does that mean? What kind of gift is this?

Reaching the edge of the city where the fortified wall stands, Dev searches for the platform as I stare at my hands. He says he can't do this, so why can I?

"Dev, what's going on?" I ask again in a whisper.

He shoots out the grapple from his Arcus and it sticks to its target. "That's what we're going to find out," he says as he holds out his hand for me to take.

⊸╌◉ ◉╌⊶

I land on the platform of Dev's apartment building, my heart pumping with adrenaline, but now it's accompanied by the excitement of figuring out what exactly is happening to me.

Unhooking my Arcus from the line, I copy Dev by punching out to retract the sides and fold it back into the baton. Seeing him beam proudly, I coyly smile back.

The excitement that rolls off Dev as we descend in the elevator is palpable, and when we reach his floor, he practically runs down the hall, swinging open the door to his apartment. "Tim!" he calls as he enters.

I take my time walking through the entrance, not quite sure where my sudden calm is coming from—maybe a part of me knows I need to let myself accept this skill, whatever it is, and compartmentalize this new information with all the other facts I've gathered every time I've come to this dream. Dev paces in front of Tim, who's regarding him with concern. Sitting on one of the cream-colored couches in the living room, book in hand, he's obviously taken aback by the sudden intrusion on his peaceful moment. When his gaze finds mine, his features change to that of delight.

"Molly." He stands. "To what do we owe the pleasure?"

"Oh, you know, I thought I'd pop in because I had nothing better to dream up," I say lightly, eyeing Dev from the side. Where's all his usual composure? Shouldn't I be the one acting flustered?

Tim smiles. "Well, I'm glad we were your place of choice." He gestures for me to take a seat in front of the fire.

"No, wait!" Dev says, stopping me midstride.

"What in all of Terra is the matter with you?" Tim turns to him with a frown.

"You need to see this." Dev walks to the opposite side of the room and faces me. He snaps out his Arcus and presses a button so that a string shoots from one end of the arc and attaches to the other, making it into a working bow.

"Dev?" Tim questions with apparent unease.

He goes ignored.

Seeing Dev's expression—one I've begun to recognize—my skin prickles in fear. Whatever he has planned most definitely does not bode well for me. Searching around the room, I look for a place to hide.

"No, Molly. Stand where you are." He reaches behind him, and there's a whooshing sound as an arrow pops out of the quiver and into his hand. As soon as he aligns it to the Arcus, the tip flames to life like a matchstick being struck. The light isn't orange as I'd

expect, but instead a cool, bluish white, the same color that illuminates the lights around this city and apartment. The flame dances
and whips about hypnotically.

My stomach drops out. I know what he has planned.

"Dev!" Tim and I shout simultaneously.

"Concentrate, Molly!" Dev yells as he pulls the arrow back and
releases.

A thousand things happen at once. Tim leaps forward, trying to
knock Dev's aim off just as the arrow is set free. My arms rise protectively as the blazing arrow of death flies straight toward my chest,
and in that same moment, an instinct that comes from somewhere
deep inside me wills a shield in front of my body. My gaze locks on
the arrow, and I push the familiar burning energy that rushes into
my mind down through my arms and out of my hands. A scream,
barely audible to my muffled ears, tears out of my mouth. Don't hit
me! Don't fucking hit me! Over and over it's thought. *Don't hit me*!

As the arrow flies forward, it begins to change course.
Somewhere in the center of my brain, I sense it strike the invisible
barrier I've willed around me. Swiveling to the right, it slams and
explodes into the wall by my side. An ice-cold burst surrounds my
head, the energy quickly escaping me as I fall to the ground. *Oh God,
that hurts*. Panting and clutching my forehead, I wait for the prickling
pain to leave. When it does, I slowly open my eyes.

The sizzling of the demolished wall is amplified by the silence
that fills the room. I carefully pick myself up and brush bits of dust
and drywall off my clothes. Piles of debris cover the floor. I glance
from the huge, gouged-out wall back to Tim and Dev. Tim still has
his hands on the Arcus, frozen in his attempt to knock Dev's arm,

his mouth gaped open and his eyes bulging. Dev, on the other hand, is once again wearing a satisfactory smile.

Looking at him, I'm about to set loose the storm of fury building inside me. A fury that will propel my hands around his neck for attempting something so homicidal, so asinine, so thoughtless—when the front door swings open and Aveline steps into the apartment.

She takes one look at the still-simmering, exploded mess next to me, moves her eyes over to the strange position of Tim next to Dev, and finally rests on my dust-covered self.

"What in all of Terra is going on!?"

Chapter 17

TALKING QUICKLY AMONG themselves, Dev, Aveline, and Tim sit around the dining room table. After Aveline came in, I looked at her in silence for a beat before resuming my plan to kill Dev. Both she and Tim had to help remove my hands from his neck and keep me from punching him right in the privates—the only place I knew I could physically harm him. It didn't help that he wore that irritatingly amused grin the whole time I was trying to fatally maim him.

"That still doesn't explain how you knew she could do this," Aveline says to Dev.

"I had an inkling that something like this was possible the first night I met her. She manipulated the space around her when we were together, but I don't think she had any idea she was the cause."

"This is quite astounding." Tim leans back in his chair, his eyes shifting to me. Still too wound up with anger to be anywhere close to Dev, I stand on the other side of the room by the fireplace, watching and listening to the three of them discuss my "power."

"It actually makes perfect sense if you think about it," Dev continues. "It *is* Dreamers we get the energy from, so why wouldn't a Dreamer be capable of manipulating that energy?"

"I don't know if it's that simple," Aveline counters. "Usually the energy is contained, controllable." She looks to me. "We can't control that energy in the form it's in now. We don't know the strength of it *or* the types of things she can make it do."

I stare into the fire, lost on a lot of what else they say. What I *have* gathered isn't much more than what I already surmised I can do, which is manipulate and change objects and spaces if I think about them hard enough. But is such manipulation really that strange of a thing in a dream?

The strength of it. Aveline's words turn over in my mind. Am I strong? I snort at the idea. I can hardly lift thirty pounds without pulling a muscle. But what I witnessed myself being able to do must have been strength. Maybe not a physical strength, but a mental one? I shake my head. This is so confusing.

Remembering the heat and cold settle in my mind and body when I was changing my clothing, I wonder if that's the power they're talking about. But what did Dev mean when he said that Dreamers are sources of energy? What energy? I desperately want to ask these questions, but I have a strong feeling that no one in this room will answer me. They seem slightly unnerved that I'm even present for their conversation. Well, everyone except Dev.

"I think we should keep this quiet for a bit," Tim says cautiously as I refocus on their conversation.

"Yeah, if the wrong people knew about this, I'm pretty sure they would do everything in their power to stop her from coming back," Aveline agrees. "Not to mention we're already in a lot of trouble for even knowing about this and not going directly to City Hall," she adds sourly.

"They know she comes here, Ave. I mean, we took her to City Hall ourselves," Dev says defensively.

"Yes, they know of her presence, but do they know that she can act just as acutely as the Navitas? If not better?" Tim counters. "If they knew this, I'm pretty certain they would put an end to her visits. Or worse, try to use her for their own gain. There are those in the Council that don't have the best of intentions at heart."

The word *Navitas* is new to me, but I'm still stuck on what Aveline said about blocking me from coming back. "Wait." Every head turns to me. "How can they stop me from coming here? How can they keep me from dreaming?"

No one answers, just as I expected. Aveline casts her eyes down as if that will excuse her from having to respond. Dev looks like he wants to say something, but one glance from Tim keeps him silent.

"Guys, seriously! I think I deserve a bit of an explanation. I mean, I *was* almost killed tonight." I cross my arms over my chest.

Tim sighs. "We're truly sorry, Molly. We can't imagine how confusing this all is, but some issues need to be worked out first, for all of our safety."

"And you were *not* almost killed," Dev adds. "I knew what I was doing."

"Oh, really? So you've launched flaming arrows at someone before without them blowing up?" He purses his lips but remains silent. "Yeah, I didn't think so." I pull out a chair and sit.

"That's not what I meant," he says in a dark, even tone.

"Then why don't you *enlighten* me to your meaning?"

He merely narrows his eyes before turning back to his companions. "Tim, the whole reason I wanted to show you that was because

I really think she could be a huge asset in this…strife we all know is coming."

Tim's brows pinch in. "Aren't you worried about her safety?"

Dev sits back in his chair, regarding me. "No, I'm not worried about that," he says flatly.

"Big surprise there," I mumble while trying hard to suppress the instant anger and hurt that settles over me. He did willingly shoot a flaming arrow at me. And a rock, let's not forget the rock. I can't believe I once wanted to kiss him.

"But, Dev, I'm not only talking about physical harm," Tim continues. "Here we all are, scared about what would happen if our own people found out about her…talents. But what would happen if the Metus learn about what she can do?"

The Metus. I try remembering what Dev told me about them—how they are nightmare-inducing creatures, feeding on the Dreamers like parasites. I shiver. Can't *wait* to run into one of *them*.

"And I don't know exactly what happens if Molly gets hurt here. What that means for her outside of…her dreams." Tim slightly stutters on his last words.

"What do you mean?" I ask, nervousness prickling along my skin.

"I'm sorry. I'm taking this way too seriously. Everything's fine. You have nothing to worry about." Tim leans over and pats my hand reassuringly.

"I don't mean to offend you, Tim, but it sounds like you're the *only* one taking this as seriously as it should be. I don't want to come off like a self-preserving prick," I continue, "but I'd rather not get hurt while I'm here or dreaming or whatever this place is. Or get thrown down another canyon." I flick a glare in Dev's direction, and he raises an eyebrow at my accusatory look. Judging by how concerned Tim is about me getting hurt, I start to really wonder how real this place could possibly be. When I'm here, it feels as real as when I'm awake, but when I'm awake, it's all too easy to make this seem like it was just a dream. *God, this is so frustrating!*

Something touches my wrist, and I glance up to Dev playing with my charm bracelet. I nearly forgot I had it on. His fingers gently graze my skin, and I can't help growing flush. I jerk my arm away, uncomfortable with how my body responds to him.

"Another gift?" he asks.

It takes me a moment to understand that he's asking about my charm bracelet. "Yes," I respond curtly, still upset with him.

"From the same guy that gave you this?" He places his fingertips lightly on my burned wrist.

I slowly move that hand away from his touch as well. "Well, yes, but not exactly."

"Who is he?" he asks.

"Why do you care?" I scoff back.

Dev narrows his eyes before leaning in close. "I *do* care, Molly, despite what you might think."

I lean in just as close, our faces inches apart. "Well, you certainly have a funny way of showing it."

Dev's eyes narrow more.

Tim clears his throat.

I turn away, ignoring the fact that Dev's focus is still pinned on me. I'm so angry! Angry that I don't understand any of this, angry that no one is willing to explain the situation, angry that Dev made me realize that I have some strange power but once *again* won't explain what it means.

"Not that I wouldn't gain a lot of pleasure from watching you two take physical blows at one another," Aveline begins, "but here we are again, at that time in the day where we actually need to work." She stands, officially ending the conversation, and grabs her quiver from the back of her chair.

I feel more than see Dev take his gaze off my face. "I'll do the rounds later. After Molly wakes up."

Oh, yeah...I'll wake up. I can't wake up yet. There are too many questions I still need answered.

"I'm going to take her back to the field and practice some routines."

Tim nods. "All I advise is for you to be careful, in *every* sense of the meaning." They share a look of understanding that communicates more than what was said.

"Is this how it's going to be now?" Aveline asks with pursed lips. "Us always postponing our rounds when *she's* here?"

Dev merely waves her off and places his quiver around his back. Aveline cuts her eyes my way, and I shiver a little at their coldness.

⋅⊷⊷◉ ◉⊷⋅

We make it back to the edge of the city and past the wall. Dev shoulders a big black duffel bag that he brought along from the apartment. I haven't seen what's inside, but whatever it is, I probably won't like it.

"So why aren't there any ziplines that go past the wall?" I ask as we walk in the direction of my tree.

"It's mainly to protect the city. So that it's hard for anyone to enter unannounced. There are guarded platforms spaced along the perimeter that can see anything approaching from miles out," Dev explains, and I realize one of the perks of being alone with him is that he's always more willing to answer my questions. The other perks I try not to think about.

"That will be an advantage then, with whatever this *strife* is you're saying might happen." I watch him carefully for any reaction from my words.

His brows furrow infinitesimally. "Yes, but we hope it won't come down to that." He glances at me from the corner of his eye. "Don't worry about all that now. I'll tell you more when there's more to tell."

"Sure you will," I mumble, studying the closely approaching tree that's become a staple in these dreams.

"Dev, why do I always seem to wake up there, at the tree?" I point to the object in question.

He contemplates for a moment. "I think it's because that's where you first entered this…dream. The tree, I've come to believe, is like a beacon for your mind. A familiar focal point of entry."

Something dawns on me. "Is that why you're always there? Waiting for me?"

He momentarily averts his eyes. "It's one of the reasons, yes."

Hearing his answer, I suppress the fluttering of sensations it creates inside me and decide it's best not to press him on what the other reasons could be.

After a few more minutes Dev stops, dropping the black bag with a heavy thump.

"Molly," he says while scratching the back of his neck, looking as if he's trying to figure out his next words. "I want to clear something up. When I said that I wasn't worried about you getting hurt, it's because I will do *everything* in my power to not let that happen."

"Oh." I blink. "Why didn't you say that earlier?" I ask, gauging how that should make me feel. More importantly, what's the safest thing for me to feel.

Dev merely shrugs, and I shake my head with a frustrated sigh, not understanding this man. When I look back, Dev's whole presence has changed. A devilish smile curves along his mouth, and his eyes glisten with a dangerous anticipation.

"Aww man," I groan, knowing exactly what that face means.

"*Another* way to ensure that nothing bad happens is to practice. See what kinds of latent abilities you have." He bends down and unzips the bag. "Take about fifteen paces back, Mols," he says, and my mouth involuntarily hitches up from hearing him use my nickname. I clear my throat and remove the revealing grin as I walk the proper paces.

Not good…not good.

"I think we've come to understand that you have some sort of power to manipulate physical objects," Dev says as he removes a few innocuous black objects, some which I remember seeing at the apartment. "You can cause their scientific properties to change or materialize with your thoughts," he states like a college professor going over material for his class. He reviews the pieces in front of him, picking up a small black ball as he stands. "Would you say that accurately describes what you've learned you can do?"

I nod, not letting my eyes move from the mysterious ball, trying to figure out all the things it could possibly become. A spiky bludgeon comes to mind. Or maybe it's simply a bomb. Either way,

I highly doubt it will sprout flowers like a Chia Pet and merely tickle me with its amazing fragrance. But I guess a girl can hope.

"Good. Now I'm going to test your reflexes and creativity by not telling you what this is before I activate it." He holds up the ball for me to have a better look. I see no holes for flowers to sprout from. All hope lost.

"Can't we start with the basics…like wax on, wax off?" I joke. He doesn't seem to catch my reference. Go figure—no decent movies in this dreamworld.

"Seeing how well you responded to my earlier tests, I think you'll do fine. Plus, this one wouldn't hurt you even if you weren't able to work around it."

Funny how that does little to reassure me. "But how do I know what to do? I don't even understand how this…*power* works. What's its purpose, what are its limitations, stuff like that?" There are too many unknowns for any of this to go well.

"And we won't know any of that unless we test it, will we?" Dev counters. I sigh in concession, not pleased with the fact that his logic makes sense. He grins. "Okay, let's do this." Immediately I stiffen, terrified of the unknown that's about to launch in my direction. "Remember to access whatever you felt yourself using last time," Dev yells before he presses a button on the side of the ball that makes a powering-on sound.

Pulling his arm back, he launches it into the air as I watch and wait for all hell to burst forth. As it reaches the height of its projected arch, the ball suddenly breaks open to reveal a huge, black net. It soars aggressively toward me, and all I can think of in that millisecond is the whole thing igniting into flames and disintegrating before it hits me.

Just as quickly as I begin to manifest that intense desire, the familiar burning sensation flickers straight from my stomach up my body and cools around my brain. This time I pay attention to the way the energy moves inside. It swirls around my mind like wind, and I don't know if I am imagining it, but if I concentrate hard enough, I notice the energy that I'm holding internally comes off my skin like heat waves.

All these thoughts are taking place as I will the net to burn away before it reaches me (and my guidance counselor said I wasn't good at multitasking). As if on command, it does just that. The black material ignites into fierce orange flames that disappear just as quickly as they begin. Nothing but soot falls from the sky and splatters across my skin, the breeze carrying the majority of it away. My head only slightly hurts from the strain of concentrating on that one.

Dev laughs, and I only have a second to see his beautifully wicked smile before my attention moves to the assembled Arcus in his hands. Two flaming blue arrows sit tightly at the ready. The only thing stopping them is Dev holding the string back.

You've got to be kidding me!

"Don't you think you've advanced a bit too soon!?"

"Nope," he answers and lets go.

Time once again slows as I instinctually recall what worked the last time I was in this position. Concentrating hard, a dull pain seizes my brain as every cell in my body responds, pumping out wave upon wave of energy to create a shield around me. I watch with utter focus as the arrows collide with the invisible bubble, pricking my mind slightly as they curve around the force field to fly past me. They crash into the ground with a loud *BOOM*.

As soon as I think it's safe, I relax, drooping my shoulders. The energy that was swimming in every inch of my brain and body dissipates instantaneously. I breathe in deeply, helping the ache in my head to subside. Once I'm certain that I'm unharmed, the excitement about what just happened spreads over me like tiny shockwaves. *That was so sick!* I grin widely at Dev.

"I think you're having too much fun trying to *test* me," I call to him.

"I wish you could have seen yourself." He beams. "I could almost see the field you made around your body. It was amazing."

My smile widens. I have to admit, this is pretty friggin' cool. The leftover adrenaline from awakening that energy makes me feel invincible, like a superhero. I badly want this all to be real.

My face grows slack. How can I know if it's real?

"Okay, let's try something else," Dev says, bringing me out of my thoughts. "Can you try to create environments? Like you did that first night with the beach?"

I instantly blush, knowing full well what he's referring to and why I must have made that place to begin with. Even at this distance, Dev's cool sapphire eyes hold me just as transfixed as they did that first night, still reminding me of the crystal blue ocean of the tropics.

My body grows warm as these images come to mind, awakening the energy that I need. Without pause, the heat spreads through my head and then cools as the ground under me shifts to a soft surface, and the rhythmic crashing of waves hitting a shoreline reaches my ears. A salty sea breeze passes by.

Dev hollers in excitement and I blink away, taking in the tiny island. The sun beams down like a spotlight in the middle of the dark field, transforming the area where we are standing into a small tropical paradise. The sand crunches under my shoes as elation courses through me.

I did this! I created this with my mind!

Dev laughs and runs toward me, lifting me up in an excited hug. I squeak in shock before grinning at his exuberance. Placing me back on the soft sand, his arms stay securely around my waist, our close proximity making my stomach dance in circles.

"Do you know how amazing you are?" he asks softly. "I don't know why you came here, what wonderful thing brought you here, but my life will never be the same." His eyes burn behind their brilliant blue, rendering me paralyzed. I know I should look away, step away, thinking about what happened the last time he held me this close, but I can't. His strong hands keep me still, his muscular body presses into mine, and the memory of his words still whisper around my ears.

"My life will never be the same either," I say breathlessly, and I know it's the truth. How can it ever go back to the way it was? And if I were being honest with myself, I would never want it to.

Dev suddenly looks conflicted. A fight spins in his features, and it only makes my stomach tighten more. The energy that dances around us is almost painful. Whatever he's trying to decide keeps my whole body on a precipice, waiting to fall, and at this very moment I don't care how much it will hurt if I do.

I lick my lips, trying to cure my nervous dry mouth, and his eyes go to them, his hands pulling me involuntarily closer as he lets out a small moan.

"Molly," he says my name gruffly, like a plea.

And then he brings my lips to his. Our mouths close over each other's as my whole body floods with fever and my ears fill with a loud ringing. His lips are soft and full but hungry and filled with desire. Definitely a kiss I would dream of.

Somewhere in the back of my mind I'm thinking this isn't a good idea, but that voice is immediately silenced by his scruff scratching along my skin, making my lust for him spike higher. I wrap my hands around his neck and try the impossible of bringing our bodies closer, my mouth opening to his, completely accepting what is happening. He hastily removes the quivers from both of us, and with the momentum he creates from bringing our bodies back together, we drop to the ground. Dev's strong arm breaks the fall, and he gently lowers us to the sand. The whole time we stay locked together like starved animals, unable to get enough of the other. This kiss is searing, eclipsing, absolutely terrifying, and I can't stop.

He grazes a hand along the side of my waist and spreads his fingers over my thigh, touching, feeling, exploring. His dark, clean scent consumes me, fills me. The air around us warps and shifts as his mouth moves to my neck, kissing the soft, sensitive skin and sending a shiver down my body. Light dances and flashes behind my eyelids. I gasp and open them. In that fraction of a second, I realize we are back in the dark field, the sandy beach gone. I shut my eyes again as his hand moves under my shirt, deliciously grazing along my stomach and up and up, awakening every nerve ending.

I attempt to rip his shirt from his body and he leans up, easily taking it off in one pull. I take in the sight of his bare chest. It's every inch what I imagined but better, perfect and defined, with a small amount of dark chest hair that makes him look even more masculine and inviting. I move my hands over the hard contours, my thighs inadvertently tightening around his waist from desire. His gaze sears, his blue eyes now dark, and he lifts me to him like the thought of us not touching is painful.

I've never felt like this before. So carnal and frenzied. Never have I craved a touch that all at once burns me and in the same instant cools. I feel outside of myself as Dev whispers my name again, continually kissing every inch of my neck.

And then something's wrong.

I feel kissing on the back of my neck as well, but Dev's in front. I glance around, confused. Dev lifts off by a fraction, noticing my change, and as I stare at him, I know in that moment what is happening. My heart constricts in anguish. I want to reach up and force his body onto mine and never let go. And that's exactly what I attempt to do.

But in a blink of an eye the dark field is gone, replaced by an early morning light. I stiffen and gasp as someone behind me pulls my body tightly against his. Soft kisses caress the back of my neck, sending shivers up my spine. A panic consumes me, and my stomach drops as I grab for my sheets, quickly pushing away from the body.

I turn to see Jared lying in my bed, confusion in his eyes.

Jared?...*oh God, Jared*!

Chapter 18

"Are you okay?" Jared asks, pushing up from my bed.

I SIT ON its edge, looking down at the man who feels like he just materialized out of nowhere. My head still swims with euphoria from the moment…a moment I was just in with one man while sleeping next to another. Suddenly feeling dirty, I pull the sheets wrapped in front of my body closer.

"I'll be right back," I say, surprised I'm able to maintain a level voice as I move swiftly to the bathroom and close the door.

"Molly?" Jared calls out, but I'm already leaning over the sink, splashing cold water on my face, desperately trying to regain my wits. I catch my reflection in the mirror. *What was that?* My cheeks are still stained pink from the fluster I awoke in, and though my breathing has slowed, my mind continues to race forward trying to figure out what exactly just happened. I kissed Dev…Dev kissed me. I would have done much more with Dev, too, if I wasn't woken up by—*wow, this is bad.*

I grip the side of the sink to keep my hands from shaking. I can still see Dev, feel him, and taste him. I realize I want a man who doesn't exist. As soon as I admit this, I feel sick. What about Jared?

Glancing down at the T-shirt I slept in, I'm no longer in the black ensemble I created in my dreams. Remembering my power, I decide to try something. Taking a deep breath, I fix my eyes on my body and imagine wearing those same dark clothes. I go through the same motions I used when making them appear in my sleep.

Nothing.

A quick wave of disappointment and frustration sweeps through me, but when I catch my gaze in the mirror again, I realize what I just did. The laughs start slowly, like fizzy bubbles surging up my belly, until they come cascading out of my mouth in loud guffaws.

I'm insane. This is it—I've officially lost my mind.

Just as quickly as I began to laugh, I switch to tears—behavior that I know is the final stamp on my mental health ward admittance. My emotions pour out of me unchecked. Every thought and feeling is in overdrive, trying to work my way through thoughts of Jared, Dev, this place I constantly go to every night, the powers I desperately want to be real—

There's a tap at the bathroom door.

"Molly, what's going on? Can you open the door?" Jared asks from the other side, the handle jiggling against the lock.

I wipe the tears from my eyes and clear my throat. "Everything's fine. I'll be out in a second." How in the world will I explain this to him?

After trying my best to remove all evidence of my crying, I timidly open the door. Jared sits on the edge of the bed in only his boxer briefs, his gorgeous bare chest exposed. He watches as I approach, concern and a little apprehension in his hazel eyes.

"What happened?" he asks.

I lean against the wall directly in front of him, guilt keeping me from moving closer. I shrug. "I had a really weird dream, and waking up like that startled me."

Jared's eyes narrow slightly. I decide that holding his gaze is what an innocent participant would do, so I try to maintain the connection. I clench my hands into fists to keep from tucking my hair behind my ear in a nervous tick, giving me away. "Then why were you laughing? Was it a funny dream?" Jared asks slowly. I can see his brain mulling over the last few minutes. I have to remember that he's a lawyer.

"Uh, no, not exactly…"

He waits for me to continue.

I need to shake myself out of this and stop being so awkward. "I was laughing because I realized I was panicking over a silly dream, that's all." I force a little smile while taking in the sight of Jared, his muscles taut with worry, hair askew from just waking up, basically looking adorable. He's as good a distraction as any and my fingers flutter, itching to touch him. How can I have feelings for someone else when the perfect man is sitting right in front of me? It was just a dream, right? Innocent enough. Even though somewhere deep down I know it was more than that. I push that feeling far away, like I've begun to do on so many mornings.

Jared's expression softens as he sees me assessing him. "Come here." He lifts a hand to me. I hesitate a moment before allowing him to take me in his arms, his touch now reassuring instead of panic inducing. "I'm sorry I startled you. That wasn't my intent…I was obviously looking for a different reaction." He gently kisses my shoulder.

"It's okay." My guilt expands. "I should be apologizing to you. I'm not really sure what all that was. You probably think I'm crazy."

"No, not *crazy*." He grins against my skin. "But you are a strange one."

You are a strange one. Someone else said similar things to me, someone I was willingly kissing moments ago. I study Jared, seeing the care in his eyes. How much he's quick to forgive of my growing manic ways. I lean up and kiss him softly, removing any phantom sensations that still linger from Dev, replacing my memories with Jared, with lips that are right, that are real. His body responds instantly to my touch, and he rolls us to lie on the bed, keeping his arms around me.

He's gentle, caring, and hesitant to go any further, probably considering how I acted when I woke up, and I'm grateful for it. My mind still wavers between what I'm convincing myself is real and what I must have dreamt. Glancing quickly at my clock, I remember I have an appointment with Dr. Marshall today. It couldn't have come at a better time.

⋅→⇒ ⇐←⋅

The hospital doors glide open as I enter for my follow-up tests, and I drop my cell in my bag, just ending a call with my mom where I promised to tell her immediately how the results turn out. I check myself in and take a seat.

"Ms. Spero?" A larger older woman in scrubs announces after hours of me zoning out to daytime TV in the waiting area. I follow the nurse, resigned never to know if Hillary's evil twin sister, Mallory, steals Hillary's man as she lies in a coma. *Sigh.*

I'm shown into a room where a nurse takes my blood and checks my vitals, and I change into a gown to do another MRI.

After all the poking and prodding, I sit in Dr. Marshall's office, waiting for him to come in and tell me how everything looks. My legs bounce with restlessness as I take in his office. It has no real character to garner what kind of man he is. The walls are bare except for his medical and scholastic achievements. No family photos, no pictures of a girlfriend or boyfriend, not even a plant. His desk is immaculate. Save for a sleek desktop computer and penholder, nothing else clutters its surface. How boring to be in the only doctor's office that can't be snooped in—what else are patients supposed to do while they wait?

I've already texted Becca about her successful date with Rae, happy from reading her gushy messages about how sweet he is. She asked to come over tonight, but I need a night alone. I want some time to sort through my thoughts and, if all goes well with my tests, a plan to go into work tomorrow. I need my life to get back to normal, with the hope that it might help in other areas.

The door opens and Dr. Marshall steps in. He holds a big folder that must contain my scans and a smaller one that I'm assuming has all my other information. "Molly," he says cheerfully while showcasing his very white teeth, taking my hand in his. "How are we feeling today?" He moves around to sit at his desk, placing the manila folders neatly in front of him.

"Okay."

"Just okay?" He tilts his head to the side but doesn't move the smile from his face. Why does it bother me so much that he's so chipper? "You look a little high strung." He glances at my bouncing knees, and I steady them instantly.

"Oh, no, I'm fine. I guess a little antsy for my results."

"Understandable." He leans back in his chair. "Before we get to that, is there anything you would like to talk about first? Anything new or unusual happening since the accident?" I tuck my hair behind my ear, mulling over if I should discuss my dreams. He *is* a doctor. Who better to talk to about it?

"Well..." I begin. "I've been having these weird dreams."

"Yes?" he coos in the form of a question. "Well, that can happen after something so traumatic. Are they nightmares?"

"No, not really. They're just...vivid, and they're almost the same ones every night." I don't really know how to describe the fact that they are playing out like I'm living a second life without sounding crazy. Dr. Marshall looks at me curiously.

"Can you remember what they are about?" he asks after a moment.

"Sorta," I lie. "They're just of this place, this field, but none of it really makes any sense." I don't know why, but I get a sense that I shouldn't talk about them anymore. "It's probably all stupid, right?"

Dr. Marshall studies me, his face unreadable. He moves forward in his chair and places his hands on his desk. "Getting struck by lightning can cause all sorts of strange things to occur, especially mentally. You'd be surprised at the rewiring that can take place. What you're describing isn't uncommon. I would try not to worry about it too much."

"Oh" is all I manage to say. *It isn't uncommon?* I'm a little disappointed. Could other people be dreaming the same thing as me?

"My only concern from this is whether or not it's leaving you well rested. Are you having a good night's sleep despite these dreams?"

His question brings up images of Dev—Dev shirtless, Dev's lips on mine. "Yes, yes, I'm having a fine night's sleep." I concentrate on my hands, catching the charm bracelet around my wrist. *Jared.* Guilty, guilty, guilty. *Ugh.*

"Good. Well, everything sounds like it's in a positive place, considering." He stands and picks up my scans from the folder. Flicking on a light board that's mounted on the wall, he clips them in place. Alien-looking images light up with what I'm guessing are scans of my brain.

"None of this should make any sense to you, but this is a picture of a perfectly healthy brain." He points to the multicolored images. I let out a sigh of relief and then quickly frown. If my brain isn't the problem…then what is?

"All your tests came back with shiny gold stars, just like this scan. You are a healthy woman, Molly, and a very lucky one at that." He smiles and I weakly smile back, running my fingers over my scarred wrist. *My wrist.*

"Doctor," I interject, "is there a new kind of medicine the hospital is using for burns?" I lift my wrist for him to see. "Because mine practically healed overnight."

He steps forward, taking my wrist gingerly in his hands. His features grow serious for a second as he studies my skin. He lightly touches the newly formed flesh and then looks back at me. He holds me there for a moment more before smiling again. Something passes through his features, but I'm not sure what.

"You were putting that ointment on and following directions like I gave you?" I nod. "Yes, well, that would explain it. Medicine, when used correctly, is pretty magical. This healed up very nicely and still has a way to go, but I think the scar won't be too off-putting in the end." The annoyingly jovial tone is back in his voice.

"Good," I manage to say, not really sure what I was expecting, but I don't think that was it. "So do you think I can go back to work tomorrow?"

"Hmm." He mulls it over for a second. "Well, I'm very happy with what I've seen here today, and I think that a few more days of rest wouldn't hurt, *but* if you feel you're up to it, then yes, I would be comfortable with you going back to work."

I grin, a little shocked that I could be so happy to actually go into the office. Is he really sure nothing's wrong with my head?

"But if you feel like you've overdone it, you must rest," he says with all seriousness, and I nod like a child who will agree to anything just so she can go outside and play. "Is there anything else I can help you with? Any questions you might have forgotten to ask?" His sandy-blond hair glistens from the ceiling lights in his office as he waits for my response.

"No, I think that's it." I stand. "Thank you so much for your help, Dr. Marshall." I give him another genuine smile. Even though his unusual, happy disposition unnerves me, he does seem to only be trying to help.

"Good, good." He opens his office door for me. "And remember, just call if you need anything. Again, very happy that you're healthy." He gives me one last big grin before I turn away and head toward the exit.

Grabbing a cab back to my apartment, I text my mom, Jared, Becca, and my boss, Jim. My mom and Jared are glad that everything checked out okay, and I make plans to see Jared on Wednesday. Jim is extremely happy to hear I'm coming back to work, and Becca calls me crazy for not riding this out longer, but she's excited to finally have her lunch partner back.

The rest of my day passes by in a blur. I have a newfound energy from the news that I'm shipshape and healthy. When memories of my dreams creep back up, I immediately turn away from them and find a task that will keep me mentally occupied. Analyzing them any more than I already have will only lead to a headache and more confusion. I'm fine. The doctor said my brain was a picture of health; the vivid dreams are not uncommon.

There's doubt with every breath I take to believe this.

After making dinner and picking out my clothes for work tomorrow (yes, I still do this like a twelve-year-old), I climb into bed and flick on the TV to an old spy movie. I cuddle up close to my pillow as I relax and watch the black-and-white actors on the screen. Small butterflies fill my stomach when I begin drifting off, and I tell myself it's merely nerves to go back into work tomorrow, that it has nothing to do with what might or might not happen once my eyes shut...nope, nothing at all. With that last whisper of a thought, my lids droop to a close and the butterflies dash away, instantly replaced by something all too familiar.

Chapter 19

I STRETCH MY legs and roll over. Blades of grass brush against my skin. I open my eyes and sigh at the image that surrounds me. I'm back.

Not uncommon, my ass.

Sitting up, I search for Dev, nervous to finally be next to him after suppressing what happened while I was awake. Will he remember? How do I tell him that it can't happen again? I know it's just a dream—a crazy, real-feeling dream—but I will not be a cheater in my subconscious or conscious state. No matter how I feel when I'm around him. Plus, keeping our relationship purely platonic will, no doubt, help how I act around Jared.

I continue my pep talk as I walk around my tree looking for Dev. He's not here. He's always here. Should I be worried?

A cool breeze brushes over my exposed skin and I shiver, glancing down at my pajamas. Studying their pattern, I chew on my bottom lip. *Okay, I'll try it once, and if it doesn't work, I won't try it again.* But this time when I quickly bring up the images I want, I feel the energy that was missing when I was in my bathroom. I smile down at my newly adorned black clothes. Looking around in excitement, I realize I'm expecting to find Dev, but once more I'm alone. I frown. Where is he?

After sitting under my tree for a few minutes, I decide to make my way toward the city in search of Dev. Maybe he's at the apartment or City Hall. I'm not really sure how to get there, but once I'm inside, I can always ask.

As I walk up to the wall, I conjure an Arcus to scale it. Imagining the object that seems to be permanently imprinted in my mind, I feel the quiver rest securely on my back almost instantaneously, the leather strap wrapping around my chest. A cool energy prickles in my head before it disappears once more into the center of my body. I wish desperately that this were something I could do when I was awake. Letting out another sigh, I continue forward.

I've only taken a couple of steps when I hear a strange guttural sound nearby, and the most disgustingly foul smell I've ever encountered touches my nose. It's like the oldest, rankest garbage, the kind that has sat in the sun for too long. The gargling noise draws closer, and a desperate sensation of fear creeps into my skin, making the hairs on the back of my neck rise. I slowly turn around and set eyes on the ugliest creature I've ever seen in my life.

It looks like it's made up of dense mucus, like a hot liquid of reds and browns, with glowing, empty orange eyes that are locked on to mine. The form stands at least seven feet tall and has a body that is indescribable except for the fact that it's constantly in motion, shifting its stinking lava-filled core to mirror what a human form could look like if it had no bones or skin to hold it together. It's a creature that could come from the very pits of hell, and the combination of its smell and sight threatens to make my stomach hurl. I suck in a terrified, muffled scream and do the only thing my weakened mind can manage to make me do—I run as fast as I can toward the city wall.

I smell and hear, more than see, the mutant creature chase after me. It lets out a horrible, unearthly high-pitched scream as I draw closer to the fortification. The sound alone wants to paralyze every cell in my body. I reach up behind my back, feeling the Arcus holder jump into my hand. *What am I going to do? What am I going to do?*

A hot substance moves past my body and lands with a grass-singeing thump in front of me. *Shit! This thing is spewing something at me!* I scream as another hot ball of mucus brushes over my left arm, searing the skin like a hot iron. Falling forward from shock, I drop the Arcus and grab my scalded skin, tears streaking down my face. I turn and with blurred vision look behind me, trying to push up off the ground. *Why haven't I woken up?* I want to sob and fold into a ball, certain that I'm about to die, but something keeps me from doing that. Something new that awakens inside me. Dev's words come rushing back, reminding me of the power I have here, the things I can do. An internal flame flickers on.

I watch the grotesque burning form move closer, and my hatred for it gathers inside of me. I wipe at my eyes as the hellish creature stops a few paces away. It moves one of its ligaments into its gel-like stomach. Everything inside me wants to look away, but I can't stop watching this self-mutilation as the creature grabs hold of its abdomen and wrenches flesh free. The mass in its hand ignites into a fireball, and the hollowed area in its body fills back up. My jaw grows slack with shock, and another wave of fear hurtles through me at what I just witnessed. *What is this thing?!* The creature holds the chunk of flaming mass up, and if it had a mouth, I can almost imagine it smiling before it cocks its arm back and hurls the burning mass toward me.

Time slows as I take in a panicked breath and quickly imagine the one thing that I know puts out a fire like this: water. I hold out my hands, feeling the energy that I call up in my mind flow fast and hard through my fingers at the creature. I think over and over again about water—strong, blasting, cool water. My head swirls with the ice-cold sensation of power as my fingers flex out, shooting rivulets of liquid through each tip. My arms surge with flowing energy, my hands starting to cramp with the force of holding them straight. The blast quickly consumes the oncoming fiery bulk and douses it into nothingness. I let my hands fall to my sides, exhausted from what I just accomplished, my mind aching.

The creature has moved farther away out of my blasting range and tilts its head back and forth with animal curiosity. Even from where I sit, I can see its gleaming orange eyes, eyes that hold a sudden understanding. It cocks its head back and lets out a bone-chilling scream before it locks its attention back on me and lunges.

I hardly have a moment to think about protecting myself when three blue-and-white flaming arrows smack right into its chest. The momentum of the impact pushes the monster back, and I watch wide eyed as the cool light travels within and fills the creature's entire body. Before the thing can let out another scream, it explodes into millions of slimy pieces, leaving nothing but its stink in its place.

I shift quickly around to see Dev at the top of the wall, Arcus in hand. Aveline stands next to him, stupefied. Turning back to where the nightmarish creature was standing moments ago, I finally let out what I was pushing away—I start to cry.

"Shhh. It's okay. It's gone now." Dev speaks softly as he holds me in his arms.

"What was that thing?" I ask, pushing away from him and taking in calming breaths to stop the tears.

"*That* was a Metus. A creature made of pure fear and evil."

"I don't understand what it was doing all the way out here, by itself," Aveline says as she scans the field around us. "Look there!" she exclaims and takes out her Arcus. In the distance are a group of glowing forms. More Metus. Noticing that we've spotted them, their brightness suddenly winks out, and the field plunges into darkness once more.

"Colló," Dev mutters, a strange-sounding curse. "They had to have seen what Molly can do. We have to tell the Council." He looks back to me. "That's where we just were and why I wasn't at the tree earlier. There's something happening…something that hasn't happened in a long time."

I'm too much in shock to take in all of what he's saying. Those are the things that enter people's dreams to create nightmares? My stomach twists.

"Can you stand?" he asks, and I nod. "Molly, you're not going to like what I'm about to say." I brace myself. "But I'm going to need you to leave. It's not safe. You have to wake up."

"You're right. I don't like what you have to say."

"*Molly*," Dev says impatiently.

"I'm coming with you. I just got attacked by one of those things, for Christ's sake! I think I deserve some answers now." I stare resolutely at him. "Plus, there's no canyon close by for you to push me into this time."

His jaw clenches. "You won't let that go, will you?"

"Let it—" I choke on the words. "On what planet would *anyone* let that go?"

"It doesn't matter," he says dismissively. "You'll be waking up soon anyway." He walks back to the wall.

"If that's true, then just take me with you until then." I grab my left arm gently as I follow him, not backing down.

He abruptly turns, his blue eyes severe. "You. Can. Not. Come."

"WHY!?" I snap. I'm a little startled at my outburst, but the combination of leftover adrenaline coursing through me and the constant frustration of being left in the dark has put me on edge.

His eyes cut to where I'm holding my injured arm, softening a fraction. Something passes over his face: A memory, an image? Whatever it is leaves a deep sorrow on Dev's features before he schools them back into a scowl. "Look at yourself." He gestures toward my arm. "This is too dangerous for you."

I narrow my eyes. "Whatever happened to me *being the key*? The one *you* said could help out in all of this? Whatever *this* is." I throw out my noninjured arm to our surroundings.

"She has a point," Aveline finally says. She's been silently watching our exchange while scanning the perimeter.

"Stay out of this, Aveline," Dev counters in a dark, hard voice, not moving his gaze from mine.

"Fine, but I'm going to set up the line. Whatever you're trying to do, do it fast. We need to get out of here." She turns and runs toward the platform. Dev and I are left glaring at each other.

"I'm going to follow you even if you don't want to take me with you," I say definitively, happy I've come to learn how to use the zipline. I need to know what all this is, whether he's willing to tell me or not.

Dev sighs and roughly brushes his hand over his head, frustration evident in every tense muscle in his body. "I think this was a mistake," he says softly.

My chest tightens at his words. What's a mistake? Which part of all this does he think was a mistake? There are too many variables that fit into that category for me to be certain. If this was about our kiss, then I agree and am a little pissed off that I wasn't the first one to say it. That was supposed to be my line. If it's about me coming here and being taught that I have some strange power that no one else in this place possesses, then tough shit! It's too late now.

"What do you mean?" I ask, hardness in my tone.

"I *mean*, this was a mistake!" He throws his hands toward me. "I should never have gotten you involved. This isn't going to work. Look at your arm! And that was just *one* of them. I said I wouldn't let anything happen to you, and I've already failed at that. This is not your fight to fight. Wake up, Molly! Go back to where you belong."

His words burn into my skin. "I CAN'T!" I yell, tears breaking free. I know I can't go back. Even if I wanted to, I'd only fall asleep and end up here. The frustration of knowing this makes me want to scream and break something. I suddenly understand why people smash things in movies when they are fuming mad. If I just had a desk in front of me I could topple over...

But I don't.

I have Dev.

Both of us are breathing heavily as we stand off, his face hard and gorgeous and insufferable. My arm throbs from the burn, but I refuse to assess the damage or admit that it's causing me pain. "The only reason this is dangerous is because *you're* keeping things from me. If I knew what was going on, knew what 'dark' thing you say is happening, I could be better prepared to help. I may not know how to shoot a bow and arrow, but I've certainly got a few tricks up my sleeve, or did you not see how I took out that fireball?"

He's quiet a moment, studying me. His eyes jump back and forth between mine, searching for something that I can't decipher. They grow sad, sorrowful again, and then morph back into hard stone.

"Just go home," he says in a low tone. "I don't want you here."

All the air leaves my lungs. *Don't want me here...* Is it really possible to hurt any more than I do? Why is his rejection this potent? Why is he saying these things? More tears prick my eyes, but I keep them back. *Just a little longer.* I bite down on my lip to keep it from trembling. Dev gives me one last mixed look before turning and heading in the direction of the platform.

"Dev," I manage to choke out. Is this really happening? Where's the Dev that was playful? Annoying, yes, but never this mean. What was the point of teaching me all those things when now he's saying I'm not good enough to use them? What about saying his life will never be the same since I've come into it? What about the kiss? *What about all of it*?!

I unknowingly move forward, following him toward the wall. "Dev," I call out again. He doesn't turn. "God damn it. Look at me!" I reach out and pull on his arm just as he attaches his grapple to the platform. He slowly gazes down at me. The Dev I know is nowhere in this face—his jaw is tight, his eyes cold. He gently removes his arm from my grip.

"Why are you doing this?" I plead.

"Do us all a favor, Molly, and wake up."

As if on command, I begin to hear an obnoxious buzzing sound. I scrunch my eyes, concentrating on where I am, trying to push the blaring noise into the background of my mind.

"No." I reach to grab hold of him again, but then he presses the button on his Arcus and flies up. Away from me, away from everything I had come to rely on here. Dev has left me.

And I am pissed.

I open my eyes to the morning light, the incessant buzzing of my alarm clock a harsh reminder of what pulled me back. My face is damp from unchecked tears. My stomach is in knots and I want to cry, kick, scream, and do anything else that can rid me of this horrible feeling of anger and despair.

I slap off my alarm, restraining myself from throwing it across the room. *This isn't fair!* I don't care if it is just a dream and means nothing. I need to find answers. I have to get back.

I close my eyes. My mind races with everything that just happened, making the task of falling back asleep pointless. Dev's words stab at my chest. *I don't want you here.* Tears brim my eyes again. Why do those words hurt me? I'm not supposed to care about him. But the heart is a notorious rule breaker and logic its worst enemy.

Glancing out my window, I decide it's too bright in my room. Grabbing my drapes, I feel a tingle on my left arm and gaze down to flawless skin. No evidence that I was hit by a burning mass. There *might* be the slightest tinge of pink, but that could merely be me trying to convince myself.

That pain felt so real. I need to get back there. I need answers.

Over the next couple of minutes, I try everything to bring my mind to unconsciousness. I listen to calming music. I make myself chamomile tea. Nothing works. Lying restless in my bed, I stare up at the ceiling, my eyes burning. Unrest shifts in the back of my mind like I'm forgetting something, some detail that's possibly important, but I'm too distracted to care. With each passing second, my mind moves farther and farther away from reason. I've never felt so determined yet so helpless.

And that's when it hits me.

I jump from my bed and run into my bathroom, opening my medicine cabinet. I move my eyes over the contents on the shelves until I find what only desperation and lack of reason has brought me to. I stare straight at the box of sleeping pills.

Chapter 20

THE SLEEPING PILLS are small in my hand, nonthreatening and white, but my forearm aches from the weight of them. Bad decisions can be surprisingly heavy.

Glancing into the mirror, I study sunken eyes rimmed with dark shadows and hair that falls disheveled and knotted. I don't know this girl.

Pinching away another wave of frustration that threatens tears, I search back in my mind, disoriented between what is now and what was then. The only certainty I hold on to is that I've begun to hate it here.

Have I gone crazy? Is any of this even real?

As I gaze at the face in the glass, I know there's only one way to answer my questions.

I pop the pills into my mouth and swallow.

⋆⟫⟨⋆

When I open my eyes again, my familiar tree is not what greets me. Instead, I find myself standing on the edge of a giant city square, the impressive City Hall building looming at the other end. My body swells with satisfaction, and a strange tension in my chest evaporates. *It worked!* Did I wake up here because I was so determined to get to this location?

I don't have long to ponder this, because I realize the passing pedestrians are all regarding me with confusion. I look down at my pajamas. *Shit.*

Speed-walking to hide under the canopy of trees circling the square's edge, I quickly switch my clothes, now easily camouflaging into the rest of the crowd. *I can definitely get used to this trick.* I turn in the direction of City Hall and meander my way through the swarm of people. Everyone is hustling and bustling, not taking a second glance at just another girl in black.

Walking up the marble stairs, I tip my head down as I pass the armed guards lining the front of the building. Just like the people in the crowd, they pay no mind. I stop inside the front landing of the open rotunda, finding myself in awe once again. Nothing has changed. The giant map on the floor still slowly moves just as the earth must spin. People mill about, shuffling into doors that line the circular space. If anything, City Hall seems busier than ever. I search for one door in particular, remembering how Dev said he needed to talk to the Council right before I woke up. If I had to go on any of my hunches, it would be that the room they all entered the last time I was here is where they are now. Gazing across the room, I zero in on what I'm searching for. More impressive than any other entrance here, this door sits at the exact opposite end from where I stand. My heart skips a beat in anticipation. I have absolutely no idea what I'm going to do once inside, but I'll figure that out when I'm there.

Upon my approach, I take in the four men standing in front of the door, two on either side. Each holds an Arcus and wears the black armbands with a glowing lightning bolt. My stomach twists in nervousness as I try my best to appear like I belong and walk past them.

Two of the men step in front of me as I reach the threshold.

"What is the state of your business?" one asks in a hard tone. My hands grow clammy as my mind races for a correct answer.

"I'm supposed to be in the Council meeting," I say evenly, regarding the man who spoke. He has reddish-brown hair and a clean-shaven face. His beady green eyes move to his companion, where they share a look before coming back to rest on me.

"We've never seen you in a Council meeting before. What is your position?" Despite my terror of not knowing how to answer, I can at least have solace in the fact that I chose the right door.

I open and close my mouth a few times, trying to dig myself out of this hole. With my telling expression, the two men stand straighter, gripping their Arcuses tighter. *This isn't good.*

"I need to speak with Dev," I finally say. At least this shows I know someone on the Council.

The men glance at each other again, and the two guards who were standing farther off move closer. "What is your business with him?" asks the brown-haired guard.

"It's just that, *my* business." I hold my eyes to his, and they both stiffen at my brazen tone.

This is ridiculous. I try to see if I can move them apart with my mind—I could move other objects here, why not people too? As I stare at their forms, all my thoughts focus on them moving so I can pass. My head swims and prickles with the energy, but nothing happens. *Why didn't that work?*

"What are you doing?" asks the redhead again, eyes narrowed. In my panicked state, I decide to do something desperate. I try as best as I can to slip past them and grab one of the door handles. They both clasp onto my shoulders and have me pinned to my knees with my arms shoved behind my back before I even have a second to reach the doors. *Damn, they're fast!*

"Get off me!" I wriggle and roll under their grasp, but it only causes the two other guards to come to their aid and hold me down as well.

Something binds my wrists together and fear washes over me. *What have I done? What will I do?* I shift my wrists, touching the material that pins my arms back. It feels like plastic. The guards stand me up and begin to shuffle me to another side of the hall.

"What did I do?" I ask the redhead, who is holding one of my arms as they drag me away. He doesn't even give me a cursory glance. "Am I to believe it's against the *law* to need to talk to someone?"

Still nothing.

I want to scream in frustration. I didn't come all this way to be stopped now! I feel the material around my wrists again.

Plastic…I can work with plastic.

I imagine the binds as thin pieces of string, easily breakable thread. After the icy-cold energy leaves my body, I know it's worked, feeling a slackness around my wrists. Elation courses through me. I can't move people, but this will do just fine. I furtively glance to each guard at my side, gauging their grips on my arms and smile to myself. Not tight enough.

Easily and silently I snap my wrists free and in one quick movement plant my feet and reverse backward out of their hold. Those self-defense classes I took with Becca came in handy after all. Each man is caught off guard, and I'm able to turn and run back toward the doors. My heart pumps fast in my chest. There's yelling from every direction, but I dare not look around for fear of losing momentum.

Fifty paces away.

Ten paces away.

I can almost feel the handles around my fingers when my body gets thrown to the ground. I scream and flail about as two guards pin me down, and my face presses securely against the cool marble floor. My body aches from where it smacked against the hard stone. Finally, defeated in my last heroic attempt to reach the doors, I stop struggling.

This time, four guards drag me out of the hall, and from the silence that fills it, I don't have to look around to know everyone has stopped and is watching me.

We walk down generic white hallway after white hallway while anger and embarrassment burn hot in my chest. My arms feel bruised from the guards' grip, and if I wasn't so irate, I know I would break down in tears.

Eventually, we stop in front of a middle-aged woman behind a large white desk that sits at the very end of one of the hallways. She wears the common black threads and has pitch-black, chin-length hair and charcoal-gray eyes. Her skin is as white as Aveline's, and if it wasn't for her hawkish nose and sour-shaped mouth, she could pass as pretty.

"She was caught trying to trespass into a Council meeting unauthorized," the redhead reports, and I want to roll my eyes.

When he says it like that, it makes it sound so much worse than it was.

The woman keeps her gaze level with mine, assessing and categorizing whatever she sees. "What is her name?" she asks in a voice that matches her tight demeanor. She moves to tap something into a tablet in front of her.

"We did not acquire it," Red answers. The woman snaps her eyes up to his, annoyance flashing. "She broke free of our binds before we could do so much as drag her from the area," he states in a way of an explanation.

"Broke *free* of your binds?" the woman says in astonishment, eyes widening as they return to me.

I can't help myself. I smile smugly.

"Yes, ma'am, but we were able to restrain her again." Red stands tall and straight like a soldier. All the men do, actually. They must run a tight ship around here. I wonder if Dev acts like this when he's not around me. My smile widens at the thought.

"*Obviously*," the hawk woman exclaims coolly as she scrutinizes my grinning face. I don't know what's come over me, but I hold my expression. I'm not one to usually defy someone older than myself, but as of late I've been doing a lot of things that aren't like me. Why stop now? Plus, I have a feeling I wouldn't like this woman anyway.

She leans forward, crossing her arms over her tablet. "What is your name?" she asks slowly, frigidly.

I want to say something smart, something obnoxious, something someone would say in a movie that would make the crowd laugh, but my newborn rebellion seems to have only taken me so far.

"Molly," I answer with unoriginality.

"Molly," she repeats like she's tasting the name in her mouth. Leaning back over her screen, she types something in. "Cell A12," she replies curtly with disinterest, not looking back up as they drag me away.

⋅→▭ ▭←⋅

I'm in a stark white holding cell. The entire space is empty except for the bench I sit on that's attached to the far wall. Opposite me is the door I came through, with a tiny window leading out to the hallway. The light in the room is eerily depressing, even with the bright swirling of the blue-white light that hangs in strips across the ceiling. This place reminds me a little of where they might operate on aliens in a sci-fi flick.

I've wrung my hands red waiting for a fate I'm uncertain of. The anger I felt when I was first brought here has subsided a bit, but I know it can easily surface at the first presence of a confrontation. I told the guards over and over as they ushered me here that they needed to get Dev, that he would explain everything. I have no idea if they were even listening—no one responded or showed the smallest reaction to my words.

I stare at the white door, thinking of how empty it is, how it's void of anything original, when the familiar warmth of energy moves through my veins. My curiosity piques at what my mind picks up on subconsciously. I hold on to my thoughts, not moving my eyes from the entrance.

Excitement travels over my scalp as I watch the door flicker and disappear. Suddenly, it's no longer there. I stand and slowly walk forward, staring at the open space. I can leave. *But where would I go?* I'm pretty certain this is some sort of jail, and if these people are anything like us humans, they have guards at every turn. My heart sinks. I can't possibly escape from here. I sit back down, deciding the best plan is to bide my time and see what happens. If anything, I'll eventually wake up and escape that way. The anger I'm holding down bubbles with the thought of going through all this and still not getting any answers. Quickly imagining the door back in its place, I watch it materialize, closing me in once more.

I'm studying my black combat boots when my cell finally opens and two new guards walk in. Dev enters behind them, his face frozen in a fierce glare. My stomach flips at the sight of him, and I stand. He doesn't even look at me before he turns toward the men.

"Please leave us," he says in a tone that's not a request. The two men glance between one another and then back to me. "*Now,*" Dev says terrifyingly soft. At this, the guards don't hesitate. The cell door closes with an oppressive click and I brace myself, preparing for the wrath that's surely to come.

Dev slowly turns, fixing his chillingly hard blue eyes on me. "What are you doing here?" His voice is firm and low, void of any friendliness.

"Hi to you, too."

"It's morning where you are, so I'll ask again. What are you doing here?" I've never seen him so angry before and never directed specifically at me. I have to admit, it threatens to knock down my wall of composure, but luckily this thought only fuels my anger. I narrow my eyes and decide to use a tactic that he's used on me: diversion.

"You know I can get out of this cell easily," I say, sitting back on the bench, faking a casual demeanor. At least I hope it looks that way.

He waits a breath, his eyes probing as he regards me. "Yes, I know."

"What else do you know?" I demand as I cross my arms over my chest.

Dev ignores my question. "How are you here right now? What have you done?" His tone is hard, yet he seems to be fighting with another emotion. I remain silent, staring at him indignantly. I can practically see his mind churning and then stopping on some sort of conclusion that brings worry to his face.

"Molly, what did you *do*?" he asks, his voice laced with concern rather than anger.

I decide to tell the truth. "I took sleeping pills."

"*What?*" His eyes widen and he takes a step closer. His reaction for some reason makes me feel smug.

"I think you heard me just fine."

"Why would you do that?"

"Why won't *you* tell *me* what's going on?!" I edge forward on the bench, my hands in fists by my side.

"How many did you take?" he continues, obviously sticking with the argument he'd rather have.

"Don't worry about it," I return curtly and stand, walking to the other side of the room.

"*Molly.*" Dev says my name like he's reprimanding a child. I bristle.

"Let's stop with the evasion, *Devlin.*" His eyes narrow at the use of his full name. "Tell me what's going on," I continue. "I would never have taken the sleeping pills to get back here if you would just let me know what's happening. Why does this place feel so real? Why can't I stop dreaming of it? And why do I have these powers?"

"Inquisitive, aren't you?" he responds dryly. Despite his attempt at humor, I remain silent, glaring at him. He lets out a sigh. "I should never have brought you into this."

"INTO WHAT!?" The frustration bursts through the very center of my body. It's so strong that it feels like lightning is flashing inside every vein, and I can almost hear the thunder. The lights in the room seem to flicker with my palpable anger.

Dev's eyes whip to mine, and I'm shocked to see they look a little scared. "Did you just do that?"

"Do what?" He watches me carefully. I cross my arms and turn away from him, not understanding what he's talking about. "So, are you going to answer me? Or just do what you always do and avoid my questions?" I push our conversation back to where I need it to be, my anger still white hot.

Dev puts more distance between us by walking to the wall furthest from me and leaning against it.

"After meeting today with the Council, I've come to realize this is too dangerous for you, and there's too much at stake. Especially after I saw you up against one of them."

"What's too dangerous? The Metus? Are you talking about what happened earlier?" I take a step closer to him. "I was caught off guard, Dev! If I had known what that thing was, I could have taken it down. But once again, because *someone* keeps me in the dark, I'm left to my own devices when it comes to this place. And while we're on the topic, why does it really matter? You guys keep telling me it's all just a dream, right? So then what's the big secret?" I pause to see if he'll respond to any of this. He doesn't. He merely keeps his eyes level to mine, his jaw clenched. I can feel the pull of energy between our bodies, heightened by our anger.

"You know what I am beginning to think?" I continue after a moment, securing my feet to the ground so I don't respond to the urge to move closer. "I'm beginning to think this is way more than that. This place is *too* real, *too* organized and functional. I looked up the words *Terra Somniorum*, and guess what? It means just what you said, but the funny thing is, I don't *know* Latin, Dev, so how could I imagine a place with that name?" His eyes spark, and knowing I hit a nerve, I push on. "You guys have names for what you are, and a city that you say is fueled by *Dreamers*. Each person here seems to have an occupation and a purpose. You and Aveline go on your so-called *rounds* to protect this place, from what I've gathered. You tell me some things that you deem innocent enough to let me in on but stay close-mouthed about others. If this weren't more than a stupid twenty-four-year-old's dream, I don't think everyone would be so secretive. And you want to know what makes me believe more than ever that this place is more than you're letting on?" I ask rhetorically, unable to keep my body from moving toward his, leaving a mere foot between us.

"It's the fact that I *don't* dream, Dev. That's right," I say, seeing his eyes widen a little. "I've never remembered a dream my whole life and then suddenly, *bam!*" I slap my hands together for emphasis. "I get hit by lightning and I'm here every night? And I know what excuse you're going to give," I say, putting my hand up when I see him about to respond. "I've been telling myself the same excuse up until yesterday. You're going to say that the lightning caused me to finally remember my dreams, that it messed up my brain. Well,

I have news for you. I just had my follow-up with the hospital, and everything checked out. There's *nothing* wrong with me!"

Throughout my ramble, Dev hasn't moved a muscle, and he still doesn't once I've finished. We both stand glaring at each other in silence, each of our bodies pulsing with frustration. His eyes are hard and all consuming. Both of our breathing is ragged, and one of his hands twitches at his side as if he wants to move it toward me, but he stops before that can happen.

My body sways in his direction, yearning to close the distance and touch him, spread my hand against a chest I know is solid muscle. By some miracle I don't. Which is definitely, *definitely* a good thing, because in this moment I hate him.

Dev takes in a breath and leans his body away from mine, his face emptying of anything it might have held before. He now regards me with a cool, calculated measure. I take a staggering step back. *Say something, damn it!*

"Prior to coming here, I was informed that some of my peers want to speak with you. They are called the Vigil. I'm to bring you to them." His voice holds no evidence that he heard a word of what I just said or that he felt the mind-aching heat crackling between us.

"Are you serious right now?" I can't help my mouth gaping open in astonishment. "Are you really going to *ignore* everything I just said!?" *For the love of everything holy!* I can't believe this! I just can't believe it. Turning away, I try to rein in all the frustrated rage I have balled up inside. I take in a few deep breaths, trying to calm myself. "Who are the Vigil and what do they want to talk about?"

"I honestly don't know what they want," he says, not seeming too pleased by this. "And I'm sure they'll tell you who they are once I bring you to them."

"Well, I'm not going anywhere until you answer my questions. I've had enough of this, Dev! Are you going to do that? Are you going to answer me?" I ask in a way that's more a desperate plea than an angry question. He looks into my eyes, and for the first time I see an emotion other than cold resolve. I see pain.

My stomach tightens as I watch him shake his head. "No, I'm not. At least not yet."

With those words, the tears I held back with all my might brim my eyes. "I hate you," I whisper and turn away so he can't see me cry.

"Molly." Dev moves to put his arms around me.

"Don't touch me!" I scream and shove him away. He moves back, shocked. Were we really just entangled in each other's arms two nights ago?

I don't know why I thought he'd finally give me answers, but in the pit of my stomach I'm certain that there *was* truth in the things I said to him. I know this place isn't just a dream, and I feel betrayed at whatever friendship he made me believe we had. I need to get out of here. I need to be alone.

The walls seem to close in on me, and my chest squeezes with each second I try to hold back the breakdown that will inevitably overtake my body. I search the room in desperation.

"What are you doing?" Dev moves closer in concern, this time not attempting to touch me. "I need you to calm down. We need to talk to the Vigil."

"Screw you!" I need to get out of here, and fast. I know I'm being irrational and stubborn and impulsive, and for the first time in my life, I don't care.

I look at the only exit to my cell and wonder if what I'm about to do will work.

Letting the familiar energy wash quickly through me, I stare at the door. My heart races, and I let out a breath of relief when it melts away, revealing a darkened field beyond. Without another thought or glance at Dev, I run forward and through the portal, instantly feeling the fresh night air settle over me.

I turn when Dev calls my name and watch him rush forward. I hardly have to think it before the opened space to the room on the other side quickly closes with a snap, shutting him in and leaving me standing in the field next to my tree, my sanctuary.

Utterly alone.

I'm on my knees, letting the tears course out of my body, when the world around me rocks back and forth. Gasping, I dig my fingers into the dirt to balance myself. *What's going on?* Looking around in panic, I feel the ground beneath me shudder like an earthquake. Then instantly, without any warning, my body is viciously immersed in a pool of freezing water. My mind screams with the sensation of drowning. Right before I'm about to suffocate, I wake with a gasp.

Spluttering and greedily taking oxygen into my lungs, I lay in my bed. My clothes are soaked, as are the sheets around me. I stare in fear at the form that hovers over me, empty cooking pot in hand, before I notice it's Becca.

It takes me more than a moment to realize that I'm back in my apartment. The room is pitch black save for the ghoulish glow of the TV I left on before I fell asleep, and the sound of the evening news is muffled in my ears. Becca glares down, pinning me with an array of heightened emotions: anger, fear, uncertainty, panic. Her eyes are puffy and rimmed red from crying. She drops the metal pot on the floor with a *thud* and picks something up from my nightstand, thrusting it in my face.

"You better have one *HELL* of an explanation for this." Her voice seethes and wavers like she's going to cry again. Shoved in my face is the box of sleeping pills.

Chapter 21

I STARE FROM the box back to Becca back to the box. I try to say something, but all that escapes is a whimper before I put my hands over my face and cry, something I seem to be doing a lot lately.

Whatever rage Becca felt clearly melts as she holds me in her arms. Maternally rocking me back and forth, she rubs my back and makes calming *shushing* sounds. I lie there unmoving, and like all great cries, the emotions that brought on the pain and tears settle into a dull fog in my chest. Staring into my depressingly dark apartment, I feel almost nothing. A*lmost*, because a new wave of emotions prickle up my spine as I take in the knowledge that all of this—waking up in my apartment after taking sleeping pills, feeling a need to take sleeping pills in the first place to go to an imaginary land, and the fact that I still have a strong belief that this imaginary land is real—can only mean one thing.

I'm officially deranged.

"Babe," Becca whispers softly to me. "I'm really going to need you to explain this to me. Saying this probably won't help, but I'm freaking out here."

"I know." My voice is hoarse from crying. I also now know why I had that strange feeling like I was forgetting something before I went to sleep. I completely forgot it was my first day back at work. How could I forget that? I'm never that irresponsible—at least, I wasn't in the past. Could I mess up my life any more? My throat tightens with the desire to bawl all over again.

"I mean, all day I've been out of my mind." Becca rakes her hand through her hair. "You didn't show up to work, and Jim came over at lunch saying he'd been trying to reach you since ten, that you weren't answering any e-mails or calls. I tried calling you over and over and you didn't pick up. At first I thought maybe you decided not to come in, but I knew you'd let me know if that was the case. Then I reached out to Jared after work to see if maybe you guys played hooky or something, but he told me that he hadn't heard from you all day either, and he'd also reached out because you guys had plans for tonight, but you never responded...I started getting really worried. I kept trying to come up with a logical reason for why you just went MIA, but after a while I couldn't take it anymore. I came over, buzzed at your door for a good thirty minutes, and finally let myself in with the spare keys you gave me." She lets out a shaky breath. "And then I saw you...just lying in your bed, with no lights on. I kept calling your name but you didn't wake up..." She pauses and I can hear her holding back tears. I tighten my grip on her.

"You were just *laying* there, Mols. You looked like you were dead, and then I saw the sleeping pills next to your bed and I lost it. I tried shaking you awake and nothing worked. I've never been so fucking scared in my life. That's when I got a pot of water and threw it on you. Thank God the movies taught me that trick." She tries to laugh, but the fear is still there.

I can't believe I put her through all this. And Jared—I completely forgot we had plans tonight. Does he still expect us to hang out? I couldn't possibly entertain that idea right now. The very real fact that I'll have to explain myself to him makes me want to change my name and move out of the country.

I prop up from Becca's lap and look into her frightened, worry-stained green eyes.

"I don't think saying I'm sorry would even cover this in the slightest. But I am—I'm *really* sorry for making you worry." More tears push on the back of my eyes, but I don't let them escape. The sooner I can convince her I'm not actually losing my mind, the better. If only I could convince myself.

"Just tell me what's going on. Why did you take sleeping pills? Were you…did you take them to…"

"No, no." I grab her hand.

"Then what?"

I regard Becca, my friend, my sister. The one person in the whole world who knows I still keep my childhood blankie tucked under my mattress, knows the exact combination of food and movies to bring me when I'm mending a broken heart, the girl who let me play my favorite song on repeat for a week in college, who probably knows more about myself than I do. I look at her and for once have no idea what to say.

"You're going to think I'm crazy." My voice sounds small after mustering up the courage to tell the truth.

"Shhh, no I won't." She places her arm on my shoulder, eyes troubled.

"Trust me…you will."

"Molly," Becca admonishes.

I take in a breath, trying to figure out how to begin telling her all that has happened without condemning me to a mental hospital. "Ever since the accident...I've been having these dreams." I watch Becca carefully, fearfully. She stares back reassuringly and inclines her head for me to continue. I swallow. "These dreams that...you're going to think I'm nuts. But they feel so *real.*"

"Are these the same ones you were telling me about before?" she asks, and I nod. "What do you mean they feel real?"

"I mean they feel *real,* Becca, as in, when I go to sleep, it's like I'm waking up and living another life. Like I have *two* lives. It's just so...confusing."

She stays silent a moment. "So you—so you took sleeping pills so you could go to sleep and be back in...that life?" Extreme concern is etched on her face now, and I can't blame her.

"I don't really know why I took them." *Yes I do.* I make a frustrated sound. "I knew you'd think I was crazy."

Because I am.

"Molly, I'm sorry. I'm just...I'm trying to understand this, that's all. It's not like you to act like this." She shifts her weight on the bed. "Why did you want to go back...to sleep?" Her face is impassive again.

"To see him," I say without thinking.

"Him?"

We're interrupted by the buzzing of my door. Becca curses under her breath.

"What?"

She stands, moving toward the buzzer. "I completely forgot I told Jared I was coming over to see if you were here and that he said he was going to meet me."

I think I'm going to vomit. "Well don't let him in!" My mind spins in circles. I can't begin to deal with seeing Jared right now on top of everything else.

"I have to let him know you're okay."

"Don't answer the door. Pretend like I'm not here." I'm grasping at straw after desperate straw. The buzzer rings out again. *Shit!*

"Molly, I can't do that. He was crazy worried about you, and you guys *did* have plans tonight. But I'll figure out a way to get rid of him." She buzzes him up.

I glance around my apartment and down at my soaked clothes. *Shit, shit, shit!*

"How are we going to explain why I'm all wet?!" I get up, searching for any clothes nearby I can throw on. Before I get too far, my door bursts open and Jared strides in. He looks edible, wearing his perfectly tailored skinny gray suit and tie. His cheeks are flushed red from rushing up my stairs, and his hazel eyes are wide with worry. They find me and hold still.

My stomach drops out, and I have absolutely no idea how to handle this situation. Jared's gaze flickers around my apartment, taking in the closed-in, dark space, Becca standing in the middle of the room looking awkward and still concerned, and then back to me in what I can only imagine is a disheveled state of matted-down hair and drenched pajamas.

"What happened?" Panicked confusion is heavy in each word. He walks forward but seems hesitant to touch me. Pain hits between my ribs.

"It was a false alarm," Becca says, covering up her worry with a well-crafted casual air. "She had a bad case of the stomach bug and was out of it all day." I couldn't have thought of a better lie, given the fact that I truly feel like I'm about to be sick.

Jared eyes me shrewdly. "Why are you all wet?"

Becca laughs lightly behind us. "I was bringing Molly a glass of water and tripped. You should have seen her face. If she wasn't recovering from puking all day, I might still have been laughing when you walked in."

"Why is there a cooking pot on the ground?" he asks, not buying any of it.

Crap! I have to remember he's a lawyer and lives in the details. Becca gives me helpless wide eyes behind Jared.

"Oh, I put that there in case I couldn't make it to the bathroom," I say matter-of-factly. Becca quietly lets out a breath and gives me a quick thumbs-up. Despite the situation, I smile.

Seeing my grin, Jared's whole mood instantly lightens, and he wraps an arm around my shoulder. The pain I felt from his hesitation to touch me subsides. Even though I can't blame him—I would have been running for the Holland Tunnel by now.

"You look awful," he says gently.

"Gee, thanks," I say dryly, and he laughs. So does Becca, except hers seems forced. I give her a hard look.

"You know what I mean." He places a warm kiss on the top of my head. "Are you feeling any better? I had no idea what was going on. I didn't know why you weren't returning my calls and texts. If I knew you were sick, I would have been here earlier."

I'm slow to answer, my mind still all over the place, and being this close to Jared, I'm distracted by the smell of his familiar cologne.

Luckily Becca is there, once again, to save me. "She put her phone on silent. That's why she didn't get any of our calls. She said she was literally living in the bathroom all day."

"Babe." Jared hooks me under his chin. I feel horrible lying to him.

"Yeah, not pretty. In fact, you should probably go. We don't want you to get contaminated by her nasty illness." Becca walks to the door, getting ready to open it. She's acting a little too rushed, and Jared watches her questioningly.

"I'm not going anywhere. I know how to take care of a sick person like the best of them, and I'm sure you're not as inclined to rub her feet as I am?" He raises an eyebrow at Becca, asking her to prove him wrong.

"All right, that's not fair." She places a hand on her hip. "I might not be down to oiling up our dear Molly here, but I think she'd rather have a friend that's not going to lose a boner over seeing her this sick and indisposed."

"Becca!" I shriek in embarrassment. Who knew I could still blush with everything going on?

Jared laughs and rubs my shoulder. "It's okay, Mols. I *am* a grown man—I've heard worse." He turns back to Becca. "As for your fear of my attraction to Molly being altered by this, you couldn't be farther from the truth. There's nothing cuter than a little sickling for me to take care of. Plus, I think we're at the point in our relationship where we're past all that."

We are?

Guilt dances the fox-trot in my belly at what I'm about to do. "Jared, Becca's right."

"What?" He gently moves me to face him. "But we had plans to hang out tonight. I don't mind staying in and taking care of you."

"I know. It's just...I do feel really gross. I mean, look at me." I showcase my saggy wet clothes and limp hair.

"I don't care about that."

"I know, but *I* do." I try tucking my disheveled hair behind my ear. The room is silent for a moment.

"So you want me to leave?" Jared says low, just to me. I can hear the hurt in his voice.

"Yes, but not because I don't want you here!" I rush to explain when his body stiffens. "I still really don't feel well, and I'm a mess, and I just want to sleep, and..." I don't know what else to say. I need him to leave. I need both of them to leave actually, but I know Becca is a way harder nut to crack than Jared. I concentrate on the floor, unable to meet his eyes. To see the sadness there.

"Okay...I get it." Jared stands a little taller now, his voice laced with something I've never heard in it before. Anger? Bitterness? Whatever it is, I don't like it.

"I'm *really* sorry. It has nothing to do with you." I rest my hand on his arm, taking a step closer. "I appreciate the gesture of you wanting to stay, I really do. And I'm sorry...I'm sorry me getting sick ruined our plans for tonight." My guilt grows fatter with each lie. "I just think Becca is better for this...at least for the moment. Please, don't be mad?"

Jared holds my gaze, searching, and then lets out a sigh. "I'm not mad at you." He says the words, but they don't sound believable. "I'm just...disappointed."

The air is snatched from my lungs. "What?" Becca and I both say in unison.

Jared shifts his eyes to Becca, realizing that she's still there, and then back to me. "I thought we were more than this." There's an edge to his voice.

"That's not fair and you know it," Becca says with a frown. "She's *sick*. You can't get mad at her for not wanting to be around the guy she's dating after she just—"

"Becca," I interrupt. She closes her mouth but doesn't stop glaring at Jared.

"I'm not doing this to hurt you," I say to him. "I just want to be alone right now. Is that wrong of me?"

"You're not alone if Becca's here."

"You know what I mean."

"No, I don't. But you know what, never mind." He takes a step back. "Call me when you decide you don't want to be *alone* anymore." Jared turns and stalks toward the door. I call out his name, stopping him before he walks through the threshold.

He looks back, and for a brief moment the wall he pulled up dips down and hurt shines through.

I feel like a shit sandwich.

He lets out a frustrated breath before he gently says, "Feel better."

And with that, my door shuts and Jared's gone.

"Well, that went well," Becca says from my side.

I glare at her.

"I'm sorry"—she puts up her hands in reprieve—"but if you want to know my opinion, he's being a little sensitive. That was ridiculous."

I don't respond, still in shock. Did Jared and I just break up? Or was that our first fight? I've never seen him get mad before. My stomach somersaults into more knots, and my head throbs from the sheer amount of emotions that spin through me. My whole life is falling apart. What's happened to me? I'm lying to the one guy in my life that I'm starting to care about in a much-bigger way—and for what? To fake an illness to cover up the fact that I took sleeping pills and skipped out on work to go back to sleep? To go back to a place that only exists in my imagination?

My body rocks in panic, realizing what I've done. What I was willing to do. I stare at my hands—they shake with the adrenaline that's pouring into my veins from fear. Fear of what I've become.

"Hey, hey." Becca has her arms around me and is calmly speaking into my ear. "Everything will be okay, sweetie—I promise. Let's get you a bath." She guides me into the bathroom. "Nothing like steamy hot water to work out all this…stuff."

"I'm okay, I'm okay," I say more to myself than to her. "I think I can take it from here. You don't need to stay."

"I'm going to ignore that you said that because if I don't, I'm pretty sure nothing will stop me from slapping you across the face."

Like I said, harder nut to crack.

⋯⟾ ⟽⋯

After Becca fills up my tub with hot water, she leaves me to soak—and perhaps more accurately, to sulk. As much as I want to be alone, I'm thankful that she's here. Having an able mind around allows me to relax into my unable one.

I lie there, loosening my muscles, and try to make sense of what's going on inside my head. I took sleeping pills to go back to sleep—to try to finally force Dev to answer my questions. Yet here I am, with no questions answered. Instead, I have one best friend who most likely thinks I've gone off the deep end, and one man I care about who thinks I don't feel the same way about him. Then there's Dev.

I blow bubbles in the water with my mouth.

Could I really have chosen to go back to that place when I have a life to live here? This is what scares me the most. Did I really choose sleep over being awake? To be fair, I only wanted answers. Is it so wrong of me to want answers?

I stare at my toes that break the surface of the water. The familiar panic attack jumps with each rapid beat of my heart, and I splash water over my face to clear away the threat.

I can't do this again. I can't go back to that place and see Dev again, be in Terra again. I need a break. I need more time to get my life in order. More importantly, I need to get my mind in order. I need to stop being a blubbering mess who's constantly in tears. I need to get back to being the Molly from before the lightning—the Molly who had a simple life, if a bit boring, with nothing that threatened her mental state.

I sigh.

I need a lot of things.

After a while of staring off at nothing, an idea floats in front of me. One that I was playing around with before but never took too seriously, probably for good reason. But after everything that's transpired, of course this is the right thing to do. It all makes sense now. As soon as I make the decision, my chest relaxes and my vision clears.

I can't go back to sleep.

Walking out of my bathroom, I find that Becca has put fresh sheets on the bed and made me some tea. "Here you go, little fish." She hands me the mug, and I smile at another one of her ridiculous names. "You feeling better?"

"Yeah, actually." My answer is hardly a lie this time. With my new decision firmly in place and the hot bath working its way through my tight muscles, I feel reborn.

I eye the drink warily as I grab new pajamas. This will definitely make me sleepy. Going to the bathroom to change, I dump a good amount of the tea down the sink. I'm not too worried about staying awake tonight given that I did just sleep for a solid sixteen hours. I'll just need something to distract me.

With the TV on, Becca and I settle under the covers and watch in silence.

"I was thinking…maybe you should go see Dr. Marshall again."

I glance at Becca, her eyes still trained on the TV.

"Yeah, I was thinking about it too." *Doesn't mean I'm going to though.* "But I really think I had a bad couple nights of sleep. I'm actually feeling much better."

She carefully probes me with her shrewd green eyes. "Yeah, well, having someone look into it never hurts. We all know I'm in therapy and am much better for it." She turns back to the TV. She must really be concerned if she's mentioning her therapist—something she rarely does.

"Yeah, I know."

Car horns honk below. "Are you nervous to go to sleep?"

"No." *Because I'm not going to sleep.*

"Good," she says with a little relief. "You'll be okay. Don't worry too much about it. Every interesting person I know has had a mental breakdown at least once in their life. Just think of this as your initiation," she says with a grin while snuggling down into her pillow.

Silence.

"Mols?"

"Yeah?"

"You can always talk to me. You know that, right?"

"Yeah, I know."

Silence.

"And that I love you?"

I smile. "Yeah, I know that too."

Becca falls asleep.

I do not.

Chapter 22

IT'S MIDDAY FRIDAY, two nights since I've slept. Yes, that's my version of a sane fix to this insane situation—two nights where I've stayed wide awake. Too scared to shut my eyes and relax into a place that, for most of my life, has been a comfort.

It's also been two days since I've heard from Jared. And I hate it.

After the night Becca slept over, we went into work together. She didn't really say anything but watched me get ready for the day. There was no more mention of that night or of the things I admitted to her. But I knew she hadn't forgotten. She stopped by my desk more often than usual, and I caught her more than once watching me when she thought I wasn't paying attention.

The first day after going without sleep wasn't as hard as I initially thought it would be. Having slept through most of Wednesday probably gave me enough energy to run on empty at work on Thursday. Jim was extremely happy to see me back, and I picked up my usual account to find it in a similar state as when I left it. Seeing the sleeping pills that caused a rift in my life did set me a little on edge every time I looked at them, but other than that, I easily filtered into the agency like I was a normal, functional adult. I almost felt like myself again. *Almost* being the key word.

By Thursday night, my body definitely wanted to shut down and rest, but I refused. Becca practically forced her way into my apartment to stay the night again until, thank his sweet blond locks, Rae called her and asked that she play hooky with him on Friday to go to Coney Island for the day. With the promise of that early morning, it didn't take much convincing to make her stay at her apartment instead, since she needed to pull together her perfectly casual but cute boardwalk outfit.

Now that it's the second day of not closing my eyes, I'm definitely feeling the effects of my sleep protest. Jim has come by more than once to ask how I'm doing, probably because even I've caught myself in an unresponsive stare, like someone stole the brain from my head. Each time he asks about it, I just shrug it off, saying I'm still trying to get back into the swing of things. He politely smiles but gives me the same sideways glance that I've caught Becca doing.

It's awesome.

While I sip my maybe twelfth cup of coffee, I think about the past two zombie-like nights and the lessons I've learned from them. The first being that I now despise the taste of coffee. Even as I currently drink it, I loathe every minute. I actually think it's begun to reverse the effects of keeping me awake. I've also learned that QVC really does sell the most amazing products at 4 a.m., a couple of which are making their way to my apartment right now. I've had the awesome realization that no amount of eye drops can keep your eyes from burning with the knowledge that they haven't been shut in a good forty-eight hours. And maybe, just *maybe*, the most important thing I've learned is that yes, people really *do* need their sleep to maintain a sound mind.

Come Friday, my head has had a dull throb since lunch, and I rub my temples while I stare down a stack of papers that sits on my desk. After all those crazy escapades in my dreams, my normal waking life seems even duller than I remember. Each time I sit through another mind-numbing status meeting, my resolve to try to stay awake weakens. To add to that, every second I stay awake is another second that I think about my dreams—everything reminds me of them, of *him*, of the things I could do there and absolutely without a doubt *cannot* do here. As pathetic as it sounds, I miss it; I miss my dreams that brought me to Terra. I miss how I felt there, the self-awareness and control that I find myself lacking here. Most of all, I miss Dev. I miss a man I only see in my sleep, his annoying confidence and wry smile, and yes, I even miss the way he can all too easily piss me off. I miss someone who doesn't exist.

I catch myself going back and forth with various feelings of heartache, from thoughts of Dev to thoughts of Jared, both taking up equal space in my mind. Space, which I know for one, shouldn't even be there.

I'm not going to be able to keep this up much longer, and that terrifies me. Everything terrifies me, actually. *I* terrify me.

The whole reason for not going to sleep was to get the old Molly back, but the person who sits at my desk is no one I like or recognize. She definitely looks worse than the Molly that wanted to believe her dreams were real. All these thoughts make me more and more scared to think about tonight and how I'll make myself stay awake.

Again.

⋆⇒◉ ◉⇐⋆

It's early afternoon when I make my way back to my apartment. Jim told me to go home early and rest, seeing that I was unable to do anything productive. I thanked him and blamed my tiredness on the accident. And really, I guess in a way, all of this is because of that night. That night that has somehow transformed me into this *thing*.

Dropping my keys on my kitchen counter, I check my phone—nothing from Jared. I don't know what's stopping me from reaching out to him, but I feel like I can't until I have whatever is going on with me under control. And something tells me that won't be any time soon. I know from the silence on his end that what happened the other night wasn't something small. It's very unlike Jared to keep quiet for so long, and this knowledge has my hands itching to dial his number. I want him to tell me everything will be fine, for him to do what he's always able to do—make me feel like someone worth caring for. Someone who matters.

If that sounds pathetic, then it probably is, but hell if it's not true.

The buzzer to my apartment rings and I drop my cell, saved from what I was about to do. That is, unless that's Jared right now...

Shit.

"Yes?" I ask into the intercom.

"It's me, sunshine! Oh, and Rae. Let us up!" Becca calls out on the other side.

Unsure if these two are much better, I glance down at my slightly disheveled work outfit, wondering if I look how I feel.

"Oh Molly, you look horrible," Becca chimes as she walks in the door.

"Thanks."

She drops her purse on the chair near the door and flips her fiery hair over her shoulders. She's wearing a light-gray sweater and thin forest-green chino pants that only her legs can pull off.

"I'm serious. You're like a homeless dog after a rain storm. Are you feeling okay?" She walks up to me in the kitchen as I try to imagine exactly what she that would look like.

Rae enters through the door and practically has to duck his head so that he doesn't hit the frame. He's wearing a light navy wind jacket over a white tee and black jeans, all of which flatter him nicely. I immediately want them both to leave when his eyes go wide as they find me. *Man, am I really that bad?*

"Hey, Rae," I say with a small smile.

"Hey," he answers, still a bit stunned.

I try not to roll my eyes as I open the fridge to get out the Brita. "I'm feeling fine," I answer Becca's earlier question, and she gives me a knowing look. "Okay, maybe not *fine*," I admit.

Becca opens her mouth to speak, and then remembering Rae, does something I've never witnessed before: she closes her mouth and indicates that we'll talk about it later.

Wow. She must really be worried to not want to discuss this in front of Rae. *This isn't good.*

"We just got back from our day of playing hooky, and we thought we'd see if you were here." Becca changes the subject and practically skips to put her arms around Rae's waist, a huge puppy-dog grin on her face.

"You guys have fun?" I ask as I pour myself some water. Pretending to be peppy is currently proving difficult.

"It was so much fun! I wish you could have been there. Well, kind of wish." Becca gives me a suggestive wink.

I flick my gaze to Rae, perplexed by his slightly angry glare. *What's his problem?*

Turning away, I walk to the open area of my studio as Becca fills me in on their adventures at Coney Island, and I find myself tuning in and out of her story, my eyes feeling like they weigh a thousand pounds. If I could just close them for a second...just hold one of my blinks a little longer...

"Becca, why don't you show Molly what we brought her?" Rae's voice snaps my eyes open. How long did I have them closed?

"Oh, yeah!" Becca jumps up to retrieve her purse.

I feel Rae watching me, and I use whatever small amount of energy I have left to not bring my attention back to him. Something about the way he's acting unnerves me. I try swallowing the sleep-deprived taste in my mouth.

"We were walking on the beach and Rae found it. It's so crazy to see something like this there—mostly trash washes up on that beach," she says while wrinkling her nose.

I look to her outstretched hand, and my whole body seizes up. My scalp prickles with unchecked shock, and my legs threaten to give out from beneath me. There in her palm is a shell.

The shell.

The perfectly round spiral design probes a memory of Dev sitting on a beach, lifting up a shell and tracing the lines around with his finger. Tracing *this* shell with his finger.

This isn't possible.

All those moments he was holding something in his hand, something small, out of my immediate view come flooding forward. Was it this? Did he keep it since that first night? Could this really be *that* shell?

Oh my God.

A quick wave of relief floods me that I might not be insane, that my dreams aren't *just* dreams. But how? What does this mean? The shell, my dreams, Dev, this being here in her hands while I'm not asleep…

I'm going to pass out.

"I know how much you like to collect small things from places you visit, and we thought this would be perfect on your trinket shelf," Becca says, bringing me out of my internal paralysis. She pushes her palm forward again for me to take the object.

I watch my arm move of its own accord, reaching for what's in her hand, and try to keep it from visibly shaking as I grasp the shell between my fingers, rubbing the cool surface as I continue to search for what this means.

My eyes involuntarily go to Rae. He holds my gaze intently, and I'm not sure if I imagine it, but I think I see him nod ever so slightly.

What the fu—

"Molly, are you okay? Do you not like it?" Becca asks, shifting her gaze between Rae and me.

"Uh…yeah, yes, I love it. Thank you. It's perfect." I know I sound off—my voice fluctuates unnaturally high in all the wrong parts.

Becca's brows pinch in. "What's going on?"

"Huh? What?" I ask back. My mind whirls, staring at the object and then back at Rae, making it impossible to focus on anything that's happening in front of me.

"Molly, what's up? You're acting so strange."

Before I can answer, Rae pushes off from the wall and drapes an arm around Becca's shoulder. "I think Molly needs to get some rest. I'm not trying to be presumptuous"—his gaze travels over my form—"but it seems like you're not feeling so well and probably need to get some sleep. We'll get out of your hair."

Sleep...

Becca regards me with renewed concern. "Are you okay?" She touches my shoulder, and I meet her eyes. "No." I hear myself say, shocked that I said it out loud.

"*No?*" She steps closer. "Molly, what is it?"

Rae's grip slightly tightens on her, and she scowls at him. He shoots me an expression I can't decipher, and I swallow. Who is this guy? Is this really happening?

"No, I mean—I do need to get some rest. I think I'm coming down with something. I haven't felt well all day."

"Do you want me to stay?"

"No, I think Rae's right. I need to sleep."

Really, I need to be alone so I can freak out properly. And what am I supposed to say to her? *I actually think these dreams I'm having every night are real and your new beau might be a bigger out-of-towner than we thought.*

"Are you sure? I mean, you don't look well at all. You have no color in your face. And after what happened the other night...I can stay and make sure you have everything you need. I won't even bother you when you're sleeping. I can, like, read a magazine or something in the corner, really quietly."

I manage a small smile at my friend. She's so good to me.

"No, you two finish your day together. I'll call you if I need anything, but I really think I just need to lay down." To emphasize this, I sit on the edge of my bed, clasping the shell tightly in my hand.

"Okay, well, I'm going to check on you later tonight, if not in the morning when you wake up." Becca regards me like she doesn't enjoy the idea of leaving me alone one bit.

"Let's let her rest," Rae says, gently guiding her toward the door. "We'll find a place to eat, and you can give me pointers on how you got more rings on the bottles than me."

Becca grins at him, distracted for a second before giving me another once-over. Seeming satisfied, she smiles. "You feel better, jelly bean." She hugs me tight.

"I will, thanks. And I'll call you in the morning."

My nerves flutter anxiously, waiting for them to leave. Will I go to sleep? Should I? I need to talk to Rae somehow. Could he really have found this shell on the beach? Something in his demeanor makes me think otherwise.

Who is this guy? There are too many questions!

Studying the shell again, fear mingles with the perspiration that dews across my skin. Am I hallucinating from lack of sleep?

"Later, Mols," Becca calls from the door.

"Bye," I say absently.

Rae guides them out, and I stand to close the door. I'm about to shut it when he gently turns around and holds his hand out, stopping it. He bends down, his hazel eyes oddly shining bright in the dim light of my stairwell.

"It's real," he whispers, and I blink up at him. Unable to move, to speak, to breathe. "Do you hear what I'm saying Molly? *He's* real."

And with that, Rae continues to do what I suddenly cannot. He closes the door behind him and leaves.

Chapter 23

I BLINK ONCE. Twice.

What?

He's real? *Holy Shit*! *And what the hell?*! My mind screams, but I haven't moved, still staring at my closed door.

He's real? It's real?

Slowly, I remember to breathe, and as soon as I do, I find myself gasping, desperately taking oxygen into my lungs, attempting to douse the extreme freak-out I'm about to have. Did Rae really say that and leave?

Crap, he left!

I rush from my apartment and out of the building. The last nip of winter hangs in the air and splashes against my nerve endings. Wrapping my arms around myself, I frantically look up and down the street.

No sign of them. How long was I standing there staring at nothing? This is crazy. What am I going to do, call his name as I run down the street? It wouldn't be the oddest thing done in New York, but still…

Walking back up to my apartment, my mind bounces all over the place like a rodent on speed. I could call Becca and ask to talk to Rae, but how would I explain that to her?

Was he talking about what I think he was talking about? I mean, what else could it have been? But what does that make him? How is he here? Can Nocturna travel between places?

I find myself sitting back on my bed, eyes fixed forward while these questions race through my head. I *knew* something was off about him. Okay, maybe not totally off, but now thinking about Rae does bring to mind the people in white I saw every now and then in City Hall, like they were born from the sun. And his coloring is so unique, the dark skin and blond hair.

How could he just say that and *leave*?!

I shift my weight, and something falls from my bed to the floor. The shell.

Peering down at the delicate object, I practically hear it laughing at me, threatening to snap the last strings that hold my sanity together.

I know what I need to do.

I need to sleep.

The endeavor proves all too easy. After getting ready for bed, even though it's only five in the afternoon, I climb under my covers and nearly cry with joy. All I want to do is close my eyes and finally, *finally*, sleep.

Although I might be *just* as excited to find out that I'm not really losing my mind after all. Instead, I might be finding out that everything I've ever believed is about to be blown to pieces.

Holding the shell in my hand like a penny I'm about to wish on, I shut my eyes. The darkness falls fast, and I am gone.

⋅⊶⫳⊷ ⊶⫳⊷⋅

Unknown time passes, and the sound of crickets chirping rises around me. My eyes remain closed. Wind rustles over my body. Grass softly whispers. This is nice, sleeping. I want to lie here, asleep, in the darkness forever.

"Molly!" A man's frantic voice interrupts my slumber. I squeeze my eyes shut even tighter.

No, I don't want to get up yet.

"Molly, look at me." Someone touches my shoulder and shakes my body when I don't respond.

Why can't they leave me alone?

"What's wrong with you? *Molly*! Open your eyes. Please open your eyes!"

Slowly, hesitantly, I do. A man in black is crouched next to me. His worried blue gaze peers down as his jaw is set with tension against an unmistakably gorgeous face. Dev.

"Oh," I squeak out.

"In all of Terra—" he says in a rush, bringing my body up to his, hugging me tightly. My arms are trapped against my sides, rendering me unable to hug him back.

"What happened? Where did you go? I was so worried!" The words come out pained and broken. I begin to relax against him, taking in his familiar smell and feel, the soft shirt, strong arms, rough scruff against my neck, hot breath on my skin—all of this melts away the painful days that I forced myself awake. It's so nice to be held again, supported again. I haven't been touched like this since…Jared.

Lightly, I separate us. This does nothing to keep Dev from touching me. He moves his hands down my arms, then brushes his fingers against my cheek, like he's trying to convince himself that I'm here, sitting in front of him. With each touch my stomach churns with butterflies and my head grows flushed. I was not prepared to meet this version of Dev. I thought I'd be coming back, guns-a-blazing, to face Mr. Hyde. Instead I've been bombarded with the sweet Dr. Jekyll. Where's the mood-altering potion when you need it?

"Dev." I gently grasp the hands that are cupping both my cheeks and lower them.

Something flashes across his eyes at hearing the timbre in my voice. "Molly?"

Remembering why I'm here, I gather up my thoughts that were easily scattered. "We need to talk."

"I know"—he lets out a sigh—"I know." He settles down next to me, his hand still holding mine. I can't seem to bring myself to remove it.

How do I start?

Luckily, I don't have to figure it out, because Dev speaks first. "Ever since you left through that door, I knew—I knew I should have told you everything right then." He squeezes my hand tighter, forcing me to meet his gaze, and I blink in wonder.

This man in front of me is real. Rae said so himself. So why am I still having a hard time believing it? Deep, deep down, I know it's because that means there are actual decisions that need to be made, and no part of me is wanting or ready to make them.

"Is this real?" I ask for the umpteenth time since I've come here. I hold my breath and wait.

Dev's face softens for the first time, and the corner of his mouth tugs up. "Yes."

My breath hitches, and I want to scream, do my version of the jig, punch him in the face, and cry all at the same time. Instead, I let out the longest sigh and slump my shoulders, suddenly feeling exhausted. The weight of that uncertainty was like an earth strapped to my back, and I was Atlas, trying desperately to keep its weight from crushing me.

"Moll—"

"It took you long enough!" I shove him slightly. How many nights have I been agonizing over this question? I took sleeping pills, for Christ's sake! And *then*, desperate woman that I was, I didn't sleep for two days. I know that being angry isn't the best option at the moment, but I can't stop my annoyance from flaring as I think about everything that could have been avoided if he had just told me the truth.

Dev's reaction to my short-fused attitude is predictable: he smiles like he's watching a kitten trying to intimidate a lion.

"You don't understand," he begins. "I was trying to protect you. There's so much that I wasn't sure I was able to tell you. I didn't want to get you in trouble for knowing, and then when you got attacked by the Metus...I just knew I couldn't risk losing another— couldn't risk losing *you*." He takes in a breath. "I was stupid when I said I wasn't worried about your safety because I thought I'd always be around. I should have known...I should have known there would be times like those. I *do* know there'll be times like those."

He turns from me, hiding his brilliant eyes under his dark lashes. I can't help feeling that this guilt is not just stemming from me, but that this revelation means something even greater to him. I can also tell he's not used to talking like this, admitting so much.

At first I stay silent, taking in his words. My heart gives away how I really feel by its quickening rhythm. "Do you know someone named Rae?" I ask after a while, finally getting to the reason why I came back. Well, *one* of the reasons.

He smiles. "Yes."

"He gave me the shell."

"I know. I asked him to give it to you. When you didn't show up the first night and then the next, I knew you were trying something rash to stay away. I needed to give you proof. Proof beyond my words."

"You kept that shell since that first time…on the beach?"

He doesn't answer my question, but his face says it all. The way he's staring at me nearly melts my core. *Geez, pull yourself together.* A couple of days without this guy and my tolerance seems to have been thrown out the window.

"But how did it not disappear with the beach?"

He shakes his head. "It just didn't."

"So…it's true—you're real? Rae's real? What is he? How can he be where I'm awake? Can you do that?" The thought of Dev in the city, in my apartment, in my bed…nope, don't go there.

His eyes sparkle with amusement. "So inquisitive, aren't y—"

"Don't start," I warn, and he fights another smile.

"Yes, I'm real. Rae's real. The other stuff…is complicated."

I narrow my eyes. "Explain."

He sighs. "Do you remember the night you came to our apartment, and we explained to you what your name meant? Star of Hope?"

I nod.

Dev points to the sky. "See all those shooting stars? Those are people, Molly." I gaze at the lit expansion, watching millions of stars zip past overhead, one of the things that has always amazed me here. They are people—but how?

"They're unconscious minds going to their dream landscape." He answers my unasked question. "This place"—he motions around us—"Terra Somniorum, it's the in-between place. The space between your reality and your dream landscape. I guess you could kind of look at it as a purgatory, but it's not so depressing and terrible to be stuck here. We monitor the Dreamers."

I remain expressionless, totally in awe of his words. I remember what he told me in City Hall—that was all real.

"The night you came, the very first night we found you lying under the tree, Aveline and I were out making our rounds, and we saw one of those stars fall from the sky. Like a meteor, it lit up everything and crashed into the ground. We ran to it, unable to understand what it was or what it could mean. When we got to where the star landed, we found you."

"Whoa" is my college-degree response.

Dev tucks my hair behind my ear. "Yeah—whoa." I clear my throat and sit up straighter. Somehow I managed to lean in rather close as he was talking. "The weird thing was," he continues, "where we found you, under this tree, is where I'd go anytime I wanted to be alone. I would come here to think and get out of the city. And that's where you landed. Sometimes, I think..."

"What do you think?" I nudge him to finish.

He delicately plays with the top of my hand. "Sometimes I think that you were sent to me, that someone knew I would find you."

These words jar my memory, and I recall a vision of Dev alone under the tree, watching him from a distance, unable to call out or for him to see me. That first night in the hospital, I dreamt of Dev, right after I got hit by lightning.

He turns his face skyward, and his eyes glisten under the soft light. His sincerely fierce countenance breaks apart any strength I had to keep him at arm's length. As the saying goes, I'm absolute putty in his hands.

This is not good.

Chapter 24

I LISTEN TO Dev talk about Terra Somniorum, the Nocturna that inhabit it, and how this city is the main hub for a few smaller ones. I learn that this place works like a small country—there's a governing council with representatives from each part of the society acting as a Speaker. Dev takes up a seat on their military board—for lack of a better word—securing the citizens against their only real threat, the Metus. How someone so young could advance to such an esteemed position, I'm still unsure. The additional seats that take up the Council are that of technology, transportation, health, and a dozen others that are quickly lost to my lingering shock. This is all still surreal, as if I'm dreaming within a dream.

Dev explains that Rae is part of a race called the Vigil, a name I realize I've heard many times. The Vigil are the exact opposite of the Nocturna: they deal with humans in their *awakened* state, acting like guardians to particular people while they are conscious, and helping to carry out dreams they feel have potential. This is how most of our technologies have been developed, ideas have been established, and movements have been made. From the short description Dev gives, I learn that the Nocturna monitor people's dreams, and when certain thoughts become of interest, the Council sends out a Vigil to help guide that Dreamer, silently or directly. That's why the Vigil can travel between this place and the next—something about their molecular makeup allows them to physically move between worlds. I learn that most of the Vigil live in another city and seem to be revered as the more superior race—or at least are treated as such.

All of this is mind blowing. The very thought that most inventions and advances in society came to fruition thanks to these races scares the Scooby-Doo underwear off me.

Shit, I'm wearing Scooby-Doo—

"Are you okay?" Dev absently brushes his fingertips against my palm.

"Uh, yeah, I'm just, you know, trying to convince myself that this is happening. That there's a world floating somewhere inside my mind."

"Well, technically, we're located in an entirely different dimension, not really inside your—"

"Yes, thank you. I got it. I'd rather not try to fit the idea of multiple dimensions *as well* as a world that controls the outcome of my own into my overly stimulated brain at the moment. We can save that lesson for day two."

Mirth crinkles Dev's eyes. "Okay."

"I still don't understand how I'm able to be here, though…"

"Yes, it's something I've been trying to figure out too. But you did say that you were hit by lightning, right?" I nod. "I think that somehow enabled you to travel here—maybe not in a purely physical sense, but mentally at least. I'm still not positive, but I know that has something to do with it." He flicks his gaze toward the city and mutters what sounds like "colló" under his breath, frowning.

"What? What is it?" I ask, not understanding that word and thinking he's spotted some of those slimy, evil Metus.

"I forgot that I needed to take you to see someone."

"Who?" I ask, slightly shocked. Who would want to see me? More importantly, who *knows* about me?

"Her name is Elena." Dev stands, helping me with him.

"What does she want?"

He shrugs but doesn't take the look of displeasure off his face. "I'm sure we'll find out."

⋅⊷⚏ ⚏⊶⋅

As we make our way into the city, I change out of my pajamas and into the black uniform using my thoughts—something that I ask Dev about again. His only response is that he thinks I'm about to get the answers to a lot of my questions.

We maneuver around people as we make our way to City Hall. I pay little attention as we pass certain checkpoints, Dev not needing to show any ID as we go. I guess he's well known around here. I follow him into the building like a child accompanying a parent in an office supply store, disregarding my surroundings. My mind's still furiously taking in everything that was just thrown at me—that this all exists in another dimension. I mean, *holy cow*! There are other dimensions! The Matrix had something going for it. I wonder how many other universes or beings exist out there that we humans have no idea about and if the Nocturna know them all.

"Well, well, if it isn't the elusive Devlin." A sweet, womanly voice chimes from behind us, echoing down the empty hallway.

Dev abruptly stops in front of me, his shoulders tightening. He's slow to turn around, but when he does, he's smiling. Intrigued by who could elicit such a reaction from Dev, I search out the source of the voice.

Boy, do I regret that.

The prettiest and perkiest—in all the right places—strawberry blonde leans casually against one of the walls that lead into another hallway. The quiver strap across her chest calls attention to her ample womanly features, and her legs remind me of Becca's long, graceful stems. Even though she wears the black garb of the Nocturna, something seems off about her, like she doesn't quite fit in here.

She's with another guy about my age who has dark skin, curly brown hair, and model-like features—of course. His height is close to Dev's, but I pay little attention to him, as I'm still transfixed on this gorgeous girl in front of us. I can hear every Victoria's Secret model crying in shame just looking at her. Her almost-iridescent honey-pink hair falls in waves past her shoulders, and her delicate face has a feline quality to it, with almond-shaped eyes and pouty lips. Her emerald-green eyes approvingly appraise Dev and then light up in a strangely seductive way when they land on me. I have to admit, even I'm turned on by her.

"So this is what has our dear Dev rearranging his schedule and skipping his rounds," she croons, circling me like a panther assessing its prey. "The notorious *Dreamer.*"

"Play nice, Aurora," Dev says, his devilish grin spreading—a grin I thought he only reserved for me. Something hot inside my gut flickers on.

"You above anyone know how nice I like to play," she practically purrs in his ear as she circles back around to his side. *Sweet mothers of virgins everywhere*, no man could resist this temptress—and judging by how Dev is looking at her, he hasn't.

My stomach does a strange flip-flop again, and the blood drains from my face. Is this jealousy? Watching Dev and Aurora practically eye-fuck each other, I want to make the ceiling fall on them. Before I have a chance to rein in my inventive revenge, a familiar prickle of heat zooms to my head and cools.

"Shit," I whisper as I stare at the cracks that have already gathered in the ceiling. A strange rumbling sound shakes the hall. Dev breaks eye contact from his flirty friend, glances to me, and seeing my face, stares straight to the area above his head. Without losing a beat, he grabs Aurora and moves them both out of the way with lightning speed while parts of the ceiling crash onto the exact place they were once standing. When the dust settles, the four of us exchange glances.

"What in all of Terra was that?" Aurora says in shock. I have to admit, I'm rather pleased to be the reason she's lost her goddesslike coolness. I guess she's human after all—well, as human as the Nocturna can be.

Dev catches me in my moment of triumph, and for an instant, a weird, wicked gleam passes over his features. *Great, now he'll think I was jealous.* I take in the broken ceiling and the huge chunk of it that sits on the floor.

Yeah, okay, maybe I was.

But, holy Toledo, good to know these powers have that sort of benefit. If every woman had this gift, I don't think there would be a man left alive.

As we walk on, leaving little miss sex kitten and her tall, hunky friend to do whatever it is they do, I can practically feel Dev's smug expression.

"I guess you're not too fond of Aurora." It's not a question.

"I don't know what you're talking about."

Dev chuckles. "Whatever you say, midnight."

My breath catches. That name again. He gives me a wink without breaking stride. How did he... *Rae.* He was there that night at the bar with those popped-collar idiots. He must have told Dev. Something about the fact that Dev asked Rae to keep tabs on me makes me feel warm and tingly inside. I almost forget about sex kitten. Almost.

After a while, we make it down another stark corridor. Two guards—this time all in white and rocking the blond locks that seem to go hand in hand with most of the Vigil—stand outside a door. This area reminds me of the holding place I was put in; maybe it's the same. I search around for my hawk-nosed bestie.

"Molly Spero, requested to be seen by Elena," Dev says to the two guards, placing his hand on my shoulder. They nod, and one opens the door for us. Dev extends his hand for me to enter first, a gesture that will always remind me of Jared.

God, Jared. What would he make of all this? I know I could never tell him—he'd never believe me. Hell, I hardly believe it and I'm standing here. The thought that I could never confide in him, or really anyone when I'm awake, makes me sad.

When I enter the room, I immediately notice Tim sitting in one of the chairs around a plain chrome table. He's a little on edge but manages a smile as I walk in. Aveline stands behind him, her expression growing more severe as our eyes lock.

There's another Vigil in the room that I've never seen before who stands behind a lady who is seated at the same table with Tim, his face impassive. The woman wears an all-white wrap dress and has immaculate, shoulder-length dirty-blonde hair and blue eyes that are as intense in color as Dev's. A strange energy radiates off her, and if I didn't know better, I would think she was glowing. I recognize her immediately as the lady in white I saw that day in City Hall.

She smiles genuinely and rises with the grace of a queen. "Molly, so happy you could join us," she says, her voice breathy but authoritative. "I'm Elena." She holds out both of her hands, taking them in mine. A little jolt goes through me, and I stare at her in a trance. There's a familiar pull between her hands and the strange energy that hides in my abdomen, coaxing it awake.

She lets go, and the sensation immediately disappears.

Before I have a chance to take in what happened, Rae walks in, giving me a lopsided grin. Seeing him here still doesn't douse the shock that he's actually a part of all this. What a sneaky son of a—

"I see you took the hint," he says in his deep baritone voice, settling an arm around me for a half hug.

"Yeah, thanks for sticking around to explain all that."

He laughs by my side. "I wish I took a picture of your face when I told you this was real. Well, that, and I wish I could have shown you how horrible you looked—"

"Thank you, Rae. I think Molly would like us to get started. Our time with her is ticking, as we all know," Elena interrupts with a smile.

"Of course." He steps back, but not before giving me a wink. I smile up at him. I don't know Rae all that well, but having him here is a strange comfort. He's the one connection to my normal existence beyond this world. Even though he's from Terra, just looking at him reminds me of home, and that eases me a bit. I wonder what this means for him and Becca? Probably nothing good. My heart sinks.

"Shall we all sit?" Elena gestures to the seats around the table.

Dev pulls out my chair for me, wolfish smile present when he sees my suspicious glare. Only Dev can make a gentlemanly gesture seem like an amusing joke. But it's easier to keep him at arm's length like this, and the Molly that's back in her bed sleeping knows that's where he needs to stay. She really does.

"I'm sure you are all wondering why I have called you together," Elena begins. Tim, Aveline, and Dev share a look. "First, I would like to say that none of you are in any sort of trouble."

Tim softly exhales, and his reaction raises my suspicions that Elena must be the head of the household around here. I shift uncomfortably in my chair.

"Molly, I'm not sure how much you have learned since you've been here, or how much you've come to understand about your capabilities, but I would like you to please inform me of everything you know before we get into the details of why you are here."

I instinctively glance at Dev, not knowing if I'll get him in any trouble by telling her the things I've learned. His expression is guarded, but he nods.

I recount to Elena all that I know—or at least all that I think I know: what Dev has told me about Terra, the things that I've learned I can control with my mind, what I've learned about the Vigil and the Nocturna and their duty, and about the Metus and the time one attacked me. I leave out some small details, like the teeny tiny one regarding Dev and me making out. No one really needs to know about that.

She asks me what happened prior to the nights I found myself waking up here, and when I tell her about the lightning, she doesn't so much as blink. Throughout my whole spiel she remains expressionless but genuinely interested. I feel like I'm talking to a therapist. And just like a therapy session, I'm drained and in need of a nap by the end of it.

All eyes go back to Elena when I'm finished, expectantly waiting for her to yell at us or put us in some weird other-dimensional prison for all of eternity. I'm convinced she'll at least tell the guard behind her that he must now cut off my head.

Instead, she smiles. A real, reaching-the-eyes smile. Then she turns to the room.

"I have called you all here because each of you now plays a part in what is about to happen. Normally, Nocturna are not involved, but because of the way Molly entered Terra, each of you deserves to know what's going on." Elena pauses a moment, letting her words sink in. "There is no easy or correct way to say this, and frankly, I've never had to explain this before in front of such a large group, so please refrain from any comments until I am done." She looks each of us in the eye before turning her attention to me, like a doctor about to give her patient test results. My stomach tightens. "Molly, we've been waiting for you. You're the Dreamer that has been sent to help us fight the war against the Metus."

Chapter 25

I MENTIONED ONCE before about that time I got stuck in advanced calculus trying to understand differential equations, failing to decipher whatever alien math mumbo jumbo my teacher was spitting at me.

This is nothing like that time.

This I hear loud and well-polished-crystal clear. Like Elena spoke the words inside my brain instead of to my face. Which is why I have left my body and am mentally sucking my thumb in the corner.

Everyone in the room remains silent. Tense and silent.

"In all of Terra..." Tim whispers.

After letting the echo of her words die down in my brain, I feel a bubble of laughter coming up my throat, forcing its escape. What I thought would be a huge belly laugh ends up sounding nervous and crazy. "Are you kidding?" I ask.

Elena ignores my reaction and continues to speak. "We are about to begin a battle against the Metus—an enemy that we have been fighting, as many of you know, for longer than time can recount. We don't know what the initial catalyst is for their numbers to grow, but they do, and they now have grown to a dangerously high figure."

I steal a glance at Dev, who is sitting next to me. He seems unfazed by the information about the Metus, which means this must have been what he found out in the last Council meeting that got him scared for my safety. *This* doesn't shock him, but he does look absolutely furious about the other information Elena continues to provide. That would be the news that I'm some sort of Dreamer prophecy. He doesn't acknowledge my gaze, fixed on a spot straight ahead. A muscle along his jaw pops.

"When this happens, it affects your conscious world," Elena says to me. "War in Terra means war on earth. Our worlds are one in the same, connected in ways that we still don't fully understand. As the Metus numbers grow, we find need to balance them. To do this, we are sent a Dreamer, someone to help us stop the potential war making its way from our land to yours. That is what your presence means, Molly—there is a threat of war reaching your conscious world through the overpowering number of Metus invading Dreamers' minds."

She stares at me intently, making sure she holds my attention. She holds a lot more than that—I think I see my sanity and my metaphorical balls in the palm of her hand.

"However, war is not an imminent or even guaranteed outcome for earth. It takes much longer to gain the full momentum of the conscious mind. If we defeat the Metus fast enough, this outbreak of evil won't be seen on earth—we can stop a possible world war. This is the Dreamer's destiny, their duty, to help stop the war before it's begun."

Nothing internally seems to work. I stare at Elena, transfixed, like a fish in a bowl staring up at the surface of the water, trying to make out the blurry form above. All I know is that if I get the courage to stick my little fish head out, I can never go back to swimming around innocently, oblivious to what's outside my bowl. I can never go back to pretending it's not there. If I peek out, I'll have to acknowledge it, deal with it, and possibly change all that I am because of it.

"This story has a long history," Elena continues in her soft, powerful voice. "A Dreamer is chosen, specifically selected by Destiny to break our dimensional barrier and help us defend against the Metus using the power that we harness here in small doses. This is the one force that assures their permanent demise."

"Hold on," Dev says. "What do you mean there's been a long history of this? Dreamers have come here before?"

"Dev," Tim reprimands, but I can tell he wants to know the answer as well. In fact, each of the Nocturna appears just as dumbfounded.

"It's fine, Timon," Elena reassures. "We can now open this up to a discussion."

"How courteous," Dev mumbles under this breath.

If Elena heard his blatant rudeness, she has chosen to ignore it and continues her speech. "Yes, Dreamers have been present at every major battle in our history. That is their purpose, to stop such catastrophes from happening. They take care of the threat in Terra before it reaches their conscious world. You yourself, Devlin, have seen a fraction of the power Molly possesses here in Terra. You were quick to pick up on it and test it yourself."

Dev stands and begins to pace the room. "So there was a Dreamer present in World War II?"

"Precisely. There has been a Dreamer present at every war ever fought between mankind. They have also been present in wars that have just been fought here in Terra. The Dreamers are the main reason we win those battles."

Holy shit! How am I supposed to fight all of those things? *War*? I can't fight a war! I can hardly win an argument against my mom.

"But I fought in that, helped with battle plans and security. How was I never informed that we had this kind of"—he flicks his gaze quickly to mine—"of arsenal at our disposal?"

"Hold up." I raise my hand. "You were around during the *Second World War*?"

He stops pacing. "Yes."

"But then you'd be, like…really old."

The corner of Dev's mouth twitches.

"We don't age as humans do," Elena explains. "We age, but slower."

Of course they do. "How much slower?"

"Five to ten years for a human can act like a year to us. Time here moves faster than in your world, but not in the process of aging." This is unbelievable. "Our young grow into themselves quickly, but once they hit maturity, they age slowly."

Speaking of children, I haven't seen any around this place. "So where are they? The kids, I mean."

"They are held in a different location until they come of age. Terra can be too dangerous at times to grow our young here. Because this city houses a large quantity of the *Navitas*, it's too risky a target."

The way she says "grow our young" creeps me out, like they are born from eggs. But hey, maybe they are. I'm not quite ready to dive into all the magic behind Vigil and Nocturna procreation. But what in all of creation is the Navitas? I think I've heard it before, but I put the thought in my pocket for now.

I turn toward Dev. "So, how old are you exactly?"

He seems to think it over. Which isn't to say he's thinking of whether or not to tell me—he seems to be trying to count. Not a good sign. "I would say I'm around one hundred and forty years of age to your standards of counting."

"One hundred and forty..." Well, that explains why his position on the Council is so high. He's not so young after all. Far from it. Should this gross me out? I take in his perfect physique, chiseled jaw hiding under manly scruff, perfectly kissable lips, piercing blue eyes, and thickly cropped raven hair. No, I would say I'm not grossed out at all.

"Shouldn't you act more mature, then?"

Everyone in the room chokes back their laughter. I, on the other hand, am 100 percent serious, and by the way Dev regards me with his wry grin, he knows it too.

"I can act *very* mature when need be." His eyes grow dark as they pin me to my seat. My breathing hitches. Did he really just pull a sexual innuendo right now?

Elena lightly clears her throat, bringing our attention back to her. Dev's cocky half smile is the last thing I see before I turn around. I have a strange urge to smack it off his face. When did I become so violent? Probably around the same time I learned I'm destined to fight a multidimensional battle.

"As I was saying, when the Dreamers come to us, they are kept separate from the rest of the population, and when they do fight, they are placed in an area where not many can see them. They have always been kept a secret, and for good reason, which I will explain in a moment." She places her delicate hands on the table, interlocking her fingers. "The manipulated energy Molly holds inside her, or as we call it, the Navitas, is in every human on earth, which you all know is what we harness here in Terra to power and create most everything we use."

"I certainly didn't know this," I say, unable to keep the indignation out of my voice.

"Of course, I'm sorry. Let me explain." She turns her full attention to me. "You have energy inside your mind that we call the Navitas. It's the Latin word for energy. You will soon find that most of our names here derive from Latin origin," she says with a gentle smile before continuing. "The passing Dreamers you see in our skies radiate with this energy as well, giving us strength and life through the very air we breathe. The same energy is used to power our world much like electricity is used to power your own. The Navitas in your kind is powerful, and it is the very essence of what we live on. It has always been this way."

Whoa...

"Think of it as malleable energy," she continues. "With the proper guidance and motivation, this energy can be molded and made into practically anything." Elena pauses for a second, noticing my glazed-over look. She leans in, smiling with understanding as she tries to explain again. "Did you know that your ability to connect thoughts and allow motor functions to be carried out is achieved with the help of millions of chemical and electrical synapses in your brain?"

I nod slowly, remembering some of this from school.

"Well, to put it very simply, the Navitas, your power, is like the synapse itself—that electrical energy. And this place"—she motions around with her hand—"is like a giant open brain for you to play with and create just about anything." My jaw drops so fast it practically bruises itself on the table. She nods, seeing that I understand. Or at least understand enough to be completely overwhelmed. "We are able to harness the Navitas from Dreamers' unconscious minds, and we use it to create and power things in our own world. It's pure creative energy at its core," she says with an awed pride.

I think about the strange glowing lights around the city. That's the energy from someone's brain? It's a little creepy.

"We even thrive on that energy, allowing the Navitas to grant us certain abilities and talents that humans do not possess." I'm about to ask her what exactly those are, but she doesn't give me an opening. "Now, only one Dreamer in particular is allowed access to our world where their energy can be used for themselves. From the almost infinite amount of power they wield, you can understand why only one is ever present here at a time. This is also the reason a Dreamer's presence is, up until this particular case, kept secret."

"Wait, wait, wait…" I raise my hand for her to pause. "I hold an infinite amount of power?" Even in my completely and utterly disbelieving state, I notice a strange excitement building in my gut. I wonder for a moment what that says about me.

Everyone, and I mean absolutely everyone in the room, has stopped breathing. Well, except for the Vigil—they seem to be taking this all in stride.

"Yes. *You*, Molly, are this Dreamer and have the energy inside you, ready and willing to do your bidding. You can manipulate everything around you in this world. It is what will help us keep the Metus from growing enough in number to infiltrate minds and cause all-out chaos and violence.

"There's always a Dreamer ready to be activated, but they are only summoned when there's a legitimate threat. Some Dreamers come and go in your world without ever knowing who they were destined to become. Peace will extend through their activation period, never calling them to Terra. And, believe it or not, some wars on earth are not always the outcome of Metus activity. The Vietnam War, for example, was purely of human doing, but this is not to say that more Metus were not created because of such malice. They were in abundance, but a Dreamer was never called to us for one reason or another." She frowns slightly. "In most cases though, violence in your world is due to more Metus being created in ours. And the creation of higher numbers of Metus in our world is due in some respects to unhappy or disturbed minds in yours. It's a cyclical genesis of anger and despair."

Everything Elena is saying blows my mind apart bit by bit. More Metus mean more violence? I think of all the crazy news stories that have been popping up over the past few days. Could that all really be because of some hoard of dreamworld boogeymen? And could those actions create even more of them? Following this logic, my mind reels faster than it already was.

Then there's the fact that I have magic mental energy inside me, which I can't really deny, given that I've seen this put to use firsthand, but still…an infinite amount? I don't feel like I have an infinite amount of anything. And what's this about my world enabling the existence of this one and vice versa? Talk about extreme symbiotic relationships.

Movement draws my attention to Dev leaning against the wall. His face is unreadable, but he's regarding me with such fierceness that I wonder if he can see through my clothes.

I glance down just in case.

He turns his stony eyes back to Elena. "So, you knew what Molly was doing here all along?"

She nods.

"Then why wait so long to intervene?"

"The way Molly came here was...unusual. Every Dreamer has come directly to the Vigil, which has always been done with the intention of keeping them secret and thus safe from the population at large. If everyone knew the capabilities a Dreamer possesses in this world, it would put that human in great danger. Not too many would welcome such uncontrollable power willingly. When you brought up Molly's presence at the last Council meeting, and her potential ability to help us against the Metus, that was my cue to finally intervene. Your knowledge of her strengths—even the small amount you revealed in front of the entire Council before we were able to take Molly under our protective guise—could have had irreversible consequences. We feel that most minds are safest when ignorant and, with this specific case, kept ignorant until we can fully assess what exactly we possess."

I want to ask Elena what she means by "this specific case," but Tim speaks before I get the chance. "Do all the Vigil know this history of the Dreamers?" he asks. Through this discussion, Aveline hasn't said one word. She seems to be having an internal battle of her own, not really looking anyone in the eyes.

"A small number of us have always known of their presence, yes. It has been our duty to guide them," Elena explains.

"So what you meant to say is that the *Nocturna* are safest when kept ignorant," Dev adds.

"That is not what I meant—"

"No, but is it not suggested?" Tim's expression is the angriest I've ever seen it, which makes it all the more terrifying. "I can understand, Elena, why some would not be safe with this information, but to keep such a large thing secret from the very people the Vigil have worked with for centuries..." Tim stops, unable to go on.

"Did you know what she was?" Dev turns to Rae, who remained standing throughout.

He gives his friend a guilty look. "Yes."

"You knew and never told me?" Dev's face falls in disappointment. "All the times I confided in you about her, even sent you out to watch her... Wait—" Dev's eyes narrow. "Were you watching her because I asked or because you had other intentions?"

Rae's clearly torn between his duty and preserving his friend's feelings.

"Rae was given orders to watch the Dreamer while she was awake. It isn't much different from when a Vigil is sent out to watch over a human. This just happened to coincide with a request issued by you," Elena explains plainly.

"I couldn't tell you, Dev. You have to understand," Rae adds. "Think for a second if our roles were reversed. Would you have told me?" He seems genuinely saddened that he might have angered Dev.

Dev obviously rolls this around in his mind a bit before he nods to his friend, easily accepting his excuse. *Really, that's it?* I roll my eyes. Boys.

Turning back to Elena, he says, "I still don't understand why you knew what was going on but didn't try to stop us from making contact with Molly."

"Honestly, I was intrigued by the fact that she had been pulled to somewhere—or more specifically, someone—else." She looks at Dev and he shifts, slightly uncomfortable with her meaning.

I find myself blushing. I was drawn to Dev?

"I wanted to see why that happened. You must understand— every Dreamer that has come here has had a specific purpose. Yes, they have all come to help us fight against the Metus, but each has left their own individual mark on our society. Whether it's changing the infrastructure of our weaponry or our educational system, or affecting something as simple as how we view one another, each Dreamer has left their mark on this world. Very similar to how they leave their mark and inventions in their own."

Whoa. Extremely heavy stuff. What could I possibly influence here, besides how to properly organize an Excel spreadsheet? I don't really have any valuable talents. At least not back home.

"So the fact that Molly came to you three"—she glances to Dev, Aveline, and Tim—"intrigues me greatly. Something I hope we will discover more about soon."

"Okay, okay, let me get this straight." I finally find my voice and try to remain calm. "Because the Metus are somehow growing in number, more of them are getting into the minds of Dreamers, which influences their behavior when they are awake." Elena nods reassuringly, so I continue. "When this starts to get out of hand and it's predicted that DEFCON One will be going down in the immediate future, a Dreamer, who has been selected since they were born, gets brought here to help fight off these melting parasitic mutants and save all mankind from possible war?"

"Yes, that's correct. The Dreamers are activated," Elena states.

I think I'm going to be sick. "What exactly do you mean by *activated*?" I ask hesitantly, surmising I may already know the answer.

She takes in a breath. I can tell this isn't her first rodeo. "When you were struck by lightning, you were able to connect with our world. That's why you are brought here when you sleep. A Dreamer's mind is easily tapped into when it's least busy. Once your mind is open to our dimension, you are easily channeled here in the form of a dream."

"So is everyone that gets hit by lightning able to travel here?" I ask.

"No. You need to have access on our side as well as yours."

"This is absolutely nuts!" I start to laugh and glance around the room. Everyone wears the same expression, like they just woke up with a nasty hangover. Except for the Vigil—once again, they look fine. "I mean, I'm just Molly. *Just* Molly, the girl who sleeps in late and would sit in her pajamas all day if she could help it." Finally I feel it. Panic. "I can't be some crazy person destined to come and fight a war here to keep peace in my own. I hardly like killing spiders! Plus, I don't even know anything about war! I practically failed history in high school and didn't even take it in college. I mean, really, tell me this isn't crazy?"

"Something's crazy, all right," Aveline mutters across the table.

Chapter 26

"I NEED TO stress to everyone that what we have just discussed *cannot* leave this room." Elena addresses the group. "I'm aware that a few of your companions and members of the Council know of Molly's presence, but her powers are still not public knowledge—and it would be best to keep it that way. I trust you all understand the reason for this discretion."

I numbly observe the slight nods from my fellow companions. Even though I've heard it straight from the horse's mouth more than once, I still can't quite come to grips with what Elena is saying about me. There are a million questions I need to ask, but she assures me I'll have plenty of time for that later, asserting that Rae will debrief us on the rest of the details.

Satisfied with the group's consent, Elena stands to leave. Before she gracefully floats out of the room, she turns and clasps my hands in hers. Again, the familiar electrical pull tugs at my abdomen.

"Molly, I'm very excited to have met you. There is much to be done, and I have a feeling you will be a Dreamer to remember."

"Uh...thanks."

Elena smiles her refined yet genuine smile and releases our connection. The tugging sensation disappears. Saying her farewells to the rest of the room, she is ushered out by her bodyguard and followed by two other men who are waiting outside the door.

A large, warm hand rests on my shoulder, and I crane my neck up to see Rae. "How are you doing?" I can't mistake the amusement in his voice.

How is he finding this funny? "On a scale from one to ten? I'm negative a thousand."

His laughter is deep and rumbling. "Then it will be my job to make you positive a thousand."

⇥⇤

The five of us sit in the room a little longer, listening to Rae explain how, since I didn't come straight to the Vigil when I first arrived, there are a lot of lessons I'm behind on. I learn that Dreamers must go through thorough training for combat and extensively study their powers. If being given the task of stopping a large-scale war wasn't enough, I also have Dreamer homework to catch up on. A lot of which sounds extremely difficult and out of my wheelhouse.

Just peachy.

Rae also explains that, because of my lost time, I'll need to make plans in my "awake-state," as he calls it, to allow myself to be in Terra for a longer stretch of time.

"What does that mean?" I ask.

"It means you will need to make up an excuse for why no one will be seeing you for a couple of days. There is a way to keep you asleep within a form of controlled lucid dreaming, so that you can be here with us for more than just one night at a time."

"Is that safe?" Dev steals the question right from my mouth. He's been oddly quiet, and I'm desperate to know what he's thinking.

"It's perfectly safe," Rae replies. "Tim, I would like to talk to you about the possibility of housing Molly in your apartment for the duration of her first extended visit."

First? How many long-ass naps will I be taking? Dev seems to be thinking the same thing, and his brows pinch together.

"Of course, of course. We'd be happy to have her," Tim replies.

"Speak for yourself," Aveline mutters from her side of the table. I completely forgot she was there. "Am I needed anymore? Because I really could not care less about the rest of this meeting."

"*Aveline.*" Tim frowns.

"It's okay, Tim. Aveline, you can go," Rae says.

She smoothly stands and straps her quiver around her back. Without a parting glance or good-bye, she stomps out of the room and closes the door. *What did I ever do to her?* I look at Dev questioningly, and he gives me a tight-lipped smile before turning away again. Is he mad at me too?

"How will we explain Molly's constant presence to the rest of the Nocturna?" Tim asks, continuing the conversation.

"This is going to sound strange, but Molly will actually have to sleep while she's here. So there will be times when she's out of sight from the rest of the population, and we can easily cover by saying that she has woken up in her own world. If she does travel around Terra, she'll be in the standard Nocturna garb, which should easily blend her in. But honestly, with all her training, she won't have time to stroll around. She'll be in a secured containment center that we have for Dreamers when they train."

"You have a Dreamer training facility here in Terra and we've never known?" Tim asks, his surprise unchanging.

"Yes. Most of it is underground in areas the Nocturna have never needed to go."

"Unbelievable," Dev mutters sourly. The room grows awkwardly quiet. The hurt and anger from the Vigil's deception shows across both men's faces and tense bodies.

I clear my throat. "Rae, how can I sleep…well, while I'm asleep?"

He smiles graciously. "At first, you'll still be tired here. To you, it will feel like a normal day has passed. Your brain will be active in a similar capacity to when you're awake. Eventually, if you're ever here for a longer period of time, you'll find that you won't get as tired as you normally would."

"What exactly is a longer period of time?"

"That's nothing to worry about right now. First, I'll need you to figure out how to get away for two days." He pulls a small folded piece of paper from his pocket. "When you wake up, it will be Saturday. I need you to meet me at this location Saturday night at eleven. We've always used this place for moving between our worlds." He hands me the paper. "You won't be awake again until Tuesday morning, so make whatever excuses you need to about being out of town and why you won't be returning any calls or texts."

How the hell will I manage that? I'm going to have to take off work? I almost laugh—work seems like the least of my problems.

"Who will be training her?" Dev asks.

"We have certain Vigil in charge of different parts of her training. But I mainly will."

For the first time I feel some of the weight lift off my shoulders, knowing that Rae will be there throughout this process.

"I'll help in Molly's training as well," Dev says in a tone that leaves little room for dispute.

Rae and Dev lock eyes, a silent conversation taking place. Eventually, one side of Rae's mouth slowly slips up.

"Of course."

The weight that was lifted from my shoulders drops into my stomach. Dev training me? In what?

"I hate to cut this short, because I know you have plenty of questions, but we're running out of time, and I have a feeling there are some people in this room that would probably like to discuss some things with you, Molly." Rae pointedly looks at Dev.

⋅⇥▣ ▣⇤⋅

We walk away from the city toward my tree in silence. The breeze stirs my hair, easing the ache that has settled in my temples. I like that Dev knows how this place calms me.

Rae was absolutely right about having more questions. I have so many that I can't keep track, still reeling from everything Elena said about how strong my powers are and what I'm meant to do here. It doesn't even seem like it's that bad right now in my world—I mean, there's violence, but is it any more than the usual? Maybe I haven't been paying that much attention.

I steal a glance at Dev. He's studying the grass, features stiff and brows furrowed. His angry scowl makes him look more intimidating than usual.

"You were rather quiet during that debriefing." I decide to speak first.

He shoots me a look. "What was I supposed to say?" he asks with a small laugh that sounds empty. "Nothing I wanted to say could have changed the situation."

"What do you mean?"

He stops and turns, bright-blue eyes latching on to mine. "Do you think I like the idea of you being this person that has to bear the weight of the world on their shoulders? The whole thing's ridiculous."

I find myself actually agreeing with him—which means somewhere pigs must be flying—but what am I supposed to do about it? It's not like any of us are left with much of a choice in the matter, myself above all. Whatever I am, whatever my duty, it's been this way for centuries. I'm quickly learning that anything is possible at this point.

Brushing a hand through his hair, Dev lets out a frustrated sigh and looks in the direction of my tree. "When I knew—when I decided that you needed to know about all this, I never intended for you to have to be this heavily involved. I don't want you to be." He holds my gaze. The weighted emotion that sits in his eyes leaves me with no words. I don't really want to be responsible either.

For most of the silent stretch of our walk, all I was thinking about was how I could get out of meeting Rae, but the fact is, I'd eventually fall asleep no matter what. And if I am completely honest with myself, there's a sick part of me that's curious—what exactly *are* my "limitless powers" here? How could I possibly gather the courage to eventually fight in combat? All of this feels like something out of a crazy movie, and I don't know when my head will truly accept it as a reality.

"It doesn't seem like any of us have a choice," I finally say.

Dev takes a step closer and brushes back a loose hair from my face. "I know," he says in a low voice as he drops his hand. "I'm an ass for not asking this sooner, but how are you feeling?"

Man, what a loaded question. How am I feeling? I'm freaked out, my stomach feels like it shriveled up and died, a part of my brain definitely must have run off with the rest of my sanity, but then...but then I'm also calm, which scares me the most.

"I'm freaked out. But doing okay, considering."

A half smile tugs at his mouth. "Why am I not surprised? You're tougher than you look."

I snort out a laugh, turning away. "I don't know about that."

"No, you are. And I think you know it too."

I stay silent, unsure how to respond.

"Molly." He says my name so that I look up at him again. His eyes are bright and magnetic—I can never get enough of them, like they're glowing from within. "I'll be there with you," he says, making sure I see the sincerity in his face. "I'll be there through the whole thing. I'm not going to let anything happen to you."

"You can't promise that."

"No," he says thoughtfully, "but I can do everything in my power to try."

It's moments like these that make me realize that the Dev behind the arrogant and pompous exterior is actually sweet and kind and sincere. This is the Dev who has me questioning my relationship with Jared—and now that I know he's real, it's the Dev who has me trying desperately to backpedal away from a mountain of confusing feelings.

"Have you figured out what you're going to do about getting away for two days?" he asks, bringing me out of my internal thoughts. I take a step back.

"Yeah…I think I'm going to tell people that I still need some rest after the whole lightning fiasco. Say that I'm going to my parents'."

"What will you tell your parents you're doing?"

"Uh, I guess I'll tell them I'm going on a trip with Jared or something." I say the words without thinking.

Dev stiffens. "Jared?" He says the name in a low voice, like he's filing it away for later use. "Is this the one that likes to give you presents?" His tone shifts to feigned lightness as his gaze drifts to my wrist.

I absentmindedly touch the thin charm bracelet. Even though I'm not quite sure what's going on with Jared, I haven't taken it off. "I guess you could say that."

Dev's face remains expressionless, but his eyes hold a thousand thoughts. He seems to settle on one, and when he looks back at me, I see an intense resolve. "Do you love him?"

"What?"

"Do you love him?"

"What kind of question is that?"

"A normal kind of question," he says smoothly, folding his arms over his chest.

"I don't think that's a normal kind of question." I copy his move and fold my arms over my chest. He shrugs and I bristle. The wicked Dev is back.

"Well?" He raises a brow.

"*Well*, I'm not going to answer that."

"You just did."

What the—

"I did not!" I straighten my arms to my side.

"Yes, you did. If you loved him, you would have easily said it."

He has a point, but it's none of his business. "So what are you insinuating?"

"That you don't." His face is King Smug.

"And..."

He leans in close. "*And*, that's good for me to know."

I'm shocked into silence, which seems to please him further. A slow, sardonic smile grows from the corner of his mouth, and his eyes gleam with thoughts I'm too scared to ask about. Our faces are so close that if I tipped my chin up a little more, our lips would touch. Not that I want them to be touching...

"You know, I often think about how sweet your lips tasted against mine," he says in a deep, velvety voice, raising the hairs at the nape of my neck.

Dear Lord. Can he read my thoughts?

"What a thing to say," I reply, disgusted, taking a step back. I can't believe he was making me all gushy seconds ago with his talk of "being there for me." What nonsense.

"It's true." He compensates for my retreat with a step forward. "I bet you think about it as well."

"You couldn't be more wrong."

"Really?" He practically purrs as he grabs my waist and brings my body tight against his.

Breathe. I need to breathe.

"Dev, let go!" I push against him and he chuckles, the vibrations in his chest pulsing into mine. Heat spreads everywhere. "You...disgust me," I manage to pant out. My brain hates where this is going, but my body wants so much more of it.

"I disgust you, do I?" He leans in closer, looking lascivious. His warm breath touches my lips, and his intoxicating scent fills my brain, making me dizzy.

"Yes, I can't stand even—"

Dev's mouth pressing hard against mine cuts off my words, and my head goes up in flames. I'm only aware of our lips moving together and his soft tongue brushing against my own. I'm barely able to remind myself that I should hate this, should be stopping this. That I shouldn't find my hands raking through his hair as I let him push our bodies tightly together. He lets out a low growl, and I can't tell if we are standing or lying down, that's how much my head is spinning. Bursts of light and dark flash behind my eyelids, and my body feels weightless in his arms. All too soon, Dev is gently pushing me back, away from his mouth. Our foreheads stay touched together as we both pant, trying to catch our breath.

"*See*, I don't disgust you in the least." He releases his hold.

Wha—what? His eyes brim with beguilement.

"You dick!" I shove at his chest. He hardly moves—instead, his attention is drawn to something behind me and his posture stiffens.

"I can't believe I let you kiss me!" I shout. I feel like such an idiot.

"Molly, I need you to stop yelling and get behind me," Dev says in a low, tense voice.

I sputter and squawk unattractively at his demand. "Get behind you? Are you mental? I have every reason to slap you right about now."

"You can slap me all you want *after* you get behind me," he says, still staring past me and slowly taking out his Arcus.

"I really don't see how—" Dev swings me around so that I'm at his back, lurching me out of my sentence.

"Ow!" I rub my arm and move to the side. I stop dead when I spot what's occupying his attention, and all the blood drains from my face. "Oh," I breathe.

"Yeah, *oh*," Dev says and readies his stance.

About fifty yards away and circling us are three Metus.

Chapter 27

"WHAT SHOULD WE do?" I whisper, scrunching up my nose as a gust of wind sends the assaulting odor of the Metus our way. I have no idea how we didn't notice their approach, but then I remember what we were both preoccupied with moments ago. Add this to the reasons of why that can't happen again.

The nightmare creatures croon their eerie clicking sounds as they wait for one of us to make the first move. Their lava flesh melts down and then up again like a constant suction is needed to keep their forms in place. I hold back a gag. I will never get used to these monsters. Which is probably a good thing.

"*We* are going to do nothing," Dev says. "You're going to stay where you are while I take care of this."

"Were we not just in the same meeting? Didn't Elena say *I* was the one sent to save all your butts from these things?" I now hold an Arcus in my hand, which I easily conjured up while I spoke. Dev glances at my new equipment.

"Do you even know how to use that for combat?"

I hold it out awkwardly. "Yeah, of course."

"You're a bad liar." Dev takes out an arrow as the Metus in the middle of the pack shifts closer. The tension between them and us is pulled tight, ready to snap. "You haven't had any training. Once you have, we can reopen this discussion."

"Oh, *can we?*" I'm aware of how childish that sounded even before Dev arches one of his brows at me.

I'm about to apologize, when his attention whips forward and in a flash he's released a blazing arrow into the guts of the Metus that began to charge toward us. In mere seconds the Navitas consumes it from the inside out and it bursts apart. Burning bits fly in every direction, and the air erupts in an onslaught of foul smells to which no one in the entire universe should be exposed.

I bend down, coughing. "Oh my *God*, that's horrible."

"Just another way they can weaken your guard." Dev has a new arrow notched.

In one moment, the two remaining Metus are howling in unison, and in the next they are nothing but fiery liquid puddles that are lapping toward us like possessed scorching blobs.

What the f—

"Colló!" Dev breathes in panic. "Get to the tree!"

He doesn't have to tell me twice. We both run.

I glance behind me as the orange flaming masses begin to gain on us. The ground lies black and singed in their wake. *This isn't good! This isn't good!*

"What do you do...when they...do that?" I pant out in a panic. Dev is right beside me, not a hitch out of breath. "They don't normally do that." He swivels around and shoots an arrow at one. Its flexible form dodges just in time.

Shit! *Shit*! *Shit*!

We reach the tree. "Now what?" I glance around helplessly. So much for being the one to save anyone's butt.

"Climb!" Dev yells as he quickly circles the tree, dragging one end of his Arcus into the grass. A faint glowing mark is left ringing us.

"I don't think climbing will stop them." I back up and bump against the trunk as the blistering puddles close in.

"No, but it will keep you a safe distance away from what I'm about to do."

"What are you about to do?"

He answers by releasing a flaming arrow into the ground near the freshly drawn mark. Instantly, like a lit fuse, a tall blaze of Navitas rises and circles us. We stand surrounded by a protective wall of lapping blue-white fire, and something in me surges with the nearness of such power. I stagger, lightheaded, and place a hand on the tree for support. Dev paces a few feet away, gazing beyond the blaze to our enemies that have now regained their more-solid forms——well, as solid as lava-filled masses can be. One of the Metus emits a frustrated, bone-chilling shriek and mirrors Dev's pacing with its own. Its towering seven-foot body barely meets the top of our protective barrier, but its orange, glowing form is easy to discern through the blue-white wall of Navitas.

"Come on, friends. Why don't you step on over?" Dev taunts as he positions a new arrow into his Arcus.

As fast as my dizzy spell hit me, it just as quickly leaves, and in its wake a rush of vitality slaps me in the face. It's like I downed a full tray of espresso shots. My body trembles with barely contained energy, and my breathing comes out in short, quick bursts. I feel really off, but a good off——an indestructible, anything-is-possible off.

"Dev…" I call out, unsure of what's happening to me.

He glances behind him and, seeing my state, rushes over. "Are you okay?" he asks, balancing his attention between the Metus and me, which is becoming tricky because they have split up—one on either side of the circle.

"I don't know…I feel…I feel really good. *Too* good."

"Um…" Dev furrows his brows, confused. "Okay?"

"I think it's all the Navitas." I gesture to the blazing ring around us. "I don't know how to be around so much. I don't know how to explain it——except that I want it."

"You *want* it?"

"Yes." I squeeze my eyes shut as another surge of strange euphoria courses through me. Why didn't they mention this in the debriefing?

"I'd put out the barrier, but then it would let in the Metus. I need to take care of them first."

In that moment, one of the creatures leaps over the flames. It doesn't clear it completely, but nicks its left foot, singing it away. Luckily, it doesn't grow back. Stumbling for only a second, it continues toward us. With its useless limb dragging behind and its open, pining mouth, the Metus takes on a zombie-like quality. If I wasn't metaphorically crapping my pants at this moment, I might actually be laughing for preferring zombies right now.

"They're getting braver." Dev steps forward, shielding me with his body. "That, or stupider."

He takes his time walking forward to engage the monster. "Molly, don't move from that spot," he says as the Metus begins to throw bits of its flesh in our direction. Dev easily whacks them down with his Arcus.

I feel pathetic just standing here. I should be doing something, helping in some way. But I have no idea what I can possibly do, and the fact that my focus feels all over the place might be a bit of a hindrance. Sounds are more prominent...movements around me seem sluggish and then too fast. My senses are jumping from normal to heightened sporadically, and it's discombobulating. To add to that, I think the spike in adrenaline is starting to make me wake up—my body is experiencing that lightness it gets during such occasions. But I *cannot* wake up now. Trying to shake off the sensation, I concentrate harder on where I am.

"Is that all you've got?" Dev goads as he slashes out with the deadly sharp end of his Arcus. The Metus growls in anger. Why is Dev playing around?

"Dev, hurry!" I shout moments before a bright-orange form charges over the wall closest to me. "Oh *shit*!" I stand there like an idiot, waiting for my life to flash before my eyes because I know Dev won't be able to take care of both Metus in time. In that instant, I experience another wave of intense sensation, causing my knees to buckle and my eyes to roll back. *This is* so *not helping right now.*

"Molly!" Dev yells as he finally sees the new threat. The creature, sensing its time running out, charges toward me with a howl. I scream and quickly backpedal. I hear the gooey pop of the other Metus being destroyed and the horrid smell that follows. Took him long enough!

With the monster a few steps away and Dev quickly moving in, I reach the Navitas wall, trapped within our own safety circle. This close to the Navitas, the strength I was using to keep the overwhelming amount of energy from overtaking me slips. Like two magnets rejoining, the entire barrier channels into my back. My body arches painfully and my mouth opens in a silent scream as my hair and clothes whip about as if in a windstorm. My skin heats to an unnatural degree as the last of the Navitas is sharply swallowed through my spine, and I feel trapped within myself, my body now solely a vessel for the all-consuming energy. Perfection and euphoria heats me to the core, and I become disconnected from this world, from any world.

I calmly look out through crystal-clear vision as time slows. The Metus's fiery claw stalls midair. Dev's face freezes in anguished panic, and the sky above appears normal as the shooting stars pause in flight. It's peaceful in this space between seconds. Between actions and reactions. Where everything just is. This is when I find my hands rising of their own accord, pulling at the energy that just gathered in my body. Like tugging on a thick cord, the Navitas is removed from my core and condenses into a swirling blue-white ball in my palms. It curls and flutters and caresses my skin. It's the most beautiful thing I've ever seen, and holding it out, I feel a strange affinity for the energy. The Navitas is life and hope and creation, and I desperately, achingly love it. But then, before I can stop myself, and as if I'm merely throwing it away, I lob the Navitas at the Metus.

From the precise moment it touches the tip of the creature's finger, time returns to normal, and like an atom bomb detonating, the creature bursts into shimmering dust, and we are all blown back by blinding-white light and the powerful wave of an explosion.

All is quiet. No cricket chirps, no grass rustles in the wind.

Slowly I feel a hand brushing the side of my face. "Molly?"

I open my eyes with a groan to Dev hovering above me, cradling me in his arms. "Where are you hurt? I don't see any bleeding. Is it internal?" Dev gently wipes my hair that is plastered with sweat away from my face, and his eyes scan every inch of me in worry.

"So much for trying your hardest to protect me," I rasp, my throat dry. I'm a bit surprised I haven't woken up yet, but maybe that Navitas energy boost allowed me to stay here longer. Interesting.

"You're making a joke right now?"

"It would seem so."

Dev reluctantly lets me sit up, and I stretch the crick out of my neck. Besides a sore backside, I don't feel too bad.

"Well, I'm not laughing," Dev says with a glare, which I return.

"It would seem not."

"How can you joke?"

"How could *you* have played around with killing them? For the love of Terra, Dev! You don't have to worry about impressing me. I'm impressed! I will always be impressed!"

His scowl drops as a huge grin spreads across his face.

"*What?*"

"There are a few things. First, you used a Terra phrase." His eyes grow warm with his smile. "Second, you said you'll always be impressed with me."

I roll my eyes. Men.

"But seriously, you're okay?" he asks again.

"Yeah, I think so." I test the movement of my limbs––a little stiff but not at all like I would expect after being hurtled hundreds of feet. My tree now stands a good distance away, and there are patches of singed grass here and there, but nothing that would signify that a fight with lava blobs, fire rings, and explosions just occurred. "That was crazy." I let out a breath of relief, finally letting it all sink in.

"Yes," Dev agrees and sits, taking in our surroundings. After a moment he asks, "What happened back there?"

"I'm not really sure." I gently rub at the hollow feeling that's been left in my chest. "As soon as you put the barrier up, all I wanted was to be joined with it. It was weird, like an intense craving. I felt a little out of control." I recall my shaking hands and the strange waves of euphoria. "But then when I got closer to the wall, something in me snapped. I let go of whatever I was holding on to, and that's when I felt the Navitas enter me."

Dev nods. "I saw that. I thought it was hurting you. Then it was like time jumped and suddenly the Metus burst apart, and we all got blown back."

"Yeah...I...I can't really explain what I did or why it happened. It didn't hurt though. Well, not in a bad way. It just felt...strange, like I was a bystander in my own body and the energy knew more of what to do than I did."

"Well, hopefully we'll get some answers once you've started your sessions with Elena."

I rub my chest again, the bereft sensation ebbing. "Yeah, that would be nice."

"I'm really glad you're okay," he says softly while placing his hand on my leg, his gaze contrite. "I didn't think the Metus were a threat once we were behind the Navitas. I would have never...if I knew they could..."

"I know." I cover his hand with my own. "But it all worked out in the end, didn't it?" I give him a small smile. "Just *don't* do it again."

He lets out a relieved laugh. "Never."

It grows a little awkward—and possibly too familiar—with us touching and staring into each other's eyes, so I clear my throat while removing my hand and ask, "You said they haven't turned into those liquid blobs before?"

Dev leans back on his elbows, looking more exhausted than usual. "That definitely isn't their normal style. The last time they got like this was before the war. When their numbers grow, it makes them stronger and can sometimes give them new abilities."

I blink in shock. "So every time there's a war with them, you're not completely certain of what you're going up against?" How can anyone prepare to fight an enemy like that?

"It's not as bad as it sounds. Their ability mutations tend to not be too drastically different from their normal behavior. And once we know their new skill, we can adapt accordingly. If we want to gain anything positive from what just happened, at least we now know one of their new abilities. We'll figure out a better way to attack them in that form."

I can see his security and military experience coming out as he breaks down what just transpired, but *for real*—only *one* of their new abilities?

"That's the ultimate glass half-full perspective I've ever heard."

"One of us needs to stay positive." Dev bites back a grin.

"And here I thought that role was exclusively Rae's."

"No, I like to think his is more of the court jester but without the juggling skills."

I lean back chuckling, picturing Rae dropping colored balls, knives, flaming batons… It's rather priceless. With him still in my mind, I bolt upright, "The piece of paper!" I gasp and fumble in my pockets.

"What? What is it?"

"I never checked to see where I was supposed to meet Rae tomorrow." Finding the note that was thoroughly crammed in my pocket, I carefully unfold it. What's scrawled across the paper has me drawing in a shocked breath, muttering a curse, and then breaking into a fit of laughter from the irony of it all.

Dev takes the slip from my fingers, his brows pinching in with confusion. "What's the Village Portal Bookstore?"

Chapter 28

WAKING UP TO the sounds and soft light of a Manhattan morning is, to say the least, surreal. I find myself lying in bed for a few hours, running over all the new information I learned while I slept: how events in another dimension are affecting my own, how I'm the Dreamer destined to fix it all, and how I have some crazy unlimited powers in Terra and absolutely none here.

Then there's this small matter that keeps nagging at me that, in the larger scheme of things, shouldn't be a concern at all. That small matter being that the man I convinced myself was a dream just so happens to be a real person. I'm not even sure what this means—or if it should mean anything at all. I'd like to think that kiss didn't, and I'm going to stand by that belief for as long as I can.

Right before I woke up, Dev promised that he'd be waiting for me later tonight. After seeing the concern on my face—and despite my best efforts to stop him—he had hooked me into his side and whispered that everything would be okay. As annoying as it is to admit, it made me feel better, hearing him say those words and knowing he'd be there waiting.

The fact that just a few weeks ago I was sitting on my window-sill feeling like my life wasn't all that I wanted it to be, and now I'm lying in my bed having learned that it's *way* more than I think I can handle, seems like a cruel dose of karma. The expression "be careful what you wish for" comes to mind, and I can't help but laugh at the absurdity of it all.

I could easily stay in bed all day ignoring the responsibility that's been thrust upon me. A large part of me wants to, given that I still haven't come to grips with what this means for my life. And that scrape with the Metus wasn't exactly reassuring of what's to come. I suppress a shiver as the assaulting smell and visual of their dripping skin still reaches me here.

Eventually, after a few more moments of staring out my window, I find myself getting up and ready for the day, knowing I have a lot to do and not a lot of time to do it in.

Before I can get far, my cell phone beeps and Jared's name lights up the screen with a message. My stomach drops.

We need to talk.

⊷⊷⊷ ⊶⊶⊶

Sitting in a coffee shop close to my apartment, I wait for Becca. I asked her to meet me here for a quick bite and to take care of my alibi face-to-face. I also have a weird desire to see her before whatever happens tonight. There's something extremely daunting about being put to sleep for two days straight. Besides my comatose state at the hospital earlier this month, I've never gone under for surgery, never been given anesthesia, so I really have no idea what to expect.

There's also a weird, foreboding feeling that's been building in my chest—I worry that when, and if, I wake up from this whole ordeal, I most certainly will not be the same person as the girl who went to sleep. These thoughts have me wanting to see my best friend before it happens. Even if I can't tell her the truth.

I nervously pick at my napkin as I flip through the morning paper, searching for any reports dealing with violence. An activity I would have desperately tried to avoid in the past, I now find myself disgustingly curious about, though I'm still having trouble believing they're happening because of lava-filled mutants in another dimension.

I've already read through four stories and can't seem to finish the last bite of my croissant, when Becca flops down in the chair across from me.

"Hey there, ladybug. You're looking better. I guess the sleep helped?"

"Tremendously," I say, pushing the cup of coffee I ordered in her direction. She smiles like a child getting a new toy.

"You're the best." She picks it up, taking a sip.

I smile. "I try."

"Read anything interesting?" She nods to the paper in my hand.

Folding it up, I shake my head. "No, nothing interesting in the least. So, how was the rest of your day with Rae?" I ask, wanting to gauge how attached my dear friend actually is. I'm a little nervous about what Rae being from another dimension means for their relationship. I know how bizarre that sounds, but hell if it isn't the truth.

"Oh, you know…it was divine," Becca replies, getting all doe eyed as she recounts the rest of their evening. By the end of her account, I'm smiling, but internally I'm making a huge underlined note to talk to Rae about what exactly he has planned for Becca. If there's even the smallest threat that he will hurt her, I will make sure we are back in Terra where I can deal with him properly. *Creatively.*

"So, what did you want to talk about?" Becca asks, popping the last piece of my croissant in her mouth.

"Oh, I wanted to let you know that I think I'm going home for a couple of days. Well—I *am* going home for a couple of days."

Becca tilts her head to the side. "Why?"

Let the lying commence. "Well, I mean, you've seen how crazy I've been these past few days. I think I haven't been able to properly relax and recover from the accident, and I need some Mom and Dad R & R. You know, get away from the city." The lies flow easily, a talent I never possessed in the past. Guilt sits heavy in my stomach.

Becca nods in agreement. "That makes sense. I thought for sure you would have done that as soon as you got out of the hospital, but you *are* stubborn when it comes to relying on others."

"I am not!" I say defensively, and then after a moment ask, "Am I?"

Becca laughs. "Mols, you're the *worst* with that. But don't worry"—she pats my hand—"I still love you anyway."

"Thanks," I say dryly.

"So, how long will you be gone?"

"Uh—I leave tonight, and think I'll probably be back sometime on Tuesday." I already e-mailed Jim, who understood my request for more time off.

"Tonight?" Becca eyes widen. "Will you see Jared before you go?"

My stomach tightens again as a weird dread settles in, thinking about his text from earlier.

"Yeah, we're supposed to meet after this, actually."

"But…"

"But…nothing."

"Mols, please, I can tell you're nervous about something. I know you guys haven't talked since…that night."

I hope I'm not that transparent, or this whole lying gig will not work out. "Yeah…I just didn't know what to say to him after that."

"Understandable," Becca says with certainty. "And *you* shouldn't be the one to apologize. I think he was completely out of line that night. Yes, you might not have *actually* been sick, but honestly, if you were, he should've understood and left you alone, not acted all sensitive about you not needing him. What was that about anyway?"

I shrug, even though I probably know where that came from. I've been a little out of it when it comes to communicating with Jared, for obvious reasons. I know he's looked at me more than once like I've been keeping secrets from him, but I've never wanted to explain myself—and now, more than ever, I can't.

Still, something inside me wants to be with Jared. As wrong as it might sound, I need something normal here to keep me balanced with what I'm dealing with in Terra. And I can't deny that a stubborn part of me wants to know where our relationship could go. Right before all this became real, I was beginning to find a place for him in my heart. And while I don't think I love him, I have a strong feeling that I could. So despite this enormous stick-in-my-spokes revelation that Terra and the oh-so-mercurial Dev are real, I still want a life here, and I want Jared in it.

That is, if he still wants to be.

"*Hello?*" Becca waves her hand in front of my face, and I blink back to her. "Wow, what crazy math problem did you just solve in your head?" She laughs. "I've never seen you so concentrated before."

"Sorry." I smile weakly. "Just have a lot on my mind."

"Clearly," she says while picking at the leftover crumbs on my plate. "So you don't know what's up with you two?"

I shake my head. "No, but I don't want to lose him, Bec."

"Aw, babe. You won't lose him. I actually think you've got him tied around your little finger."

I let out a sarcastic laugh. "The two days of silence from his end says differently."

"Well, he contacted you first, right? To see you later today?" She takes a sip of her coffee.

"Yeah, but his text could very well be a foreboding message leading up to our imminent end."

Becca chokes on her sip, coughing as she says, "Wow, dramatic much?" She raises her eyebrows. When she sees that I'm completely serious, she removes the smile from her face. "Molly, really, I don't think he's going to break up with you, *but*—and I mean 'but' in the very, *very* small chance that he will—I know you can turn him around. You would want to turn him around, right?"

"Yes."

"Then there you go. Problem solved. But to be honest, I didn't think you were that into him for a while. Glad to see you've changed your mind. He's a rare find in these parts—gotta keep those types close. Just like I gotta keep Rae," she adds with a wink.

Her last words make me falter, but I force myself to smile in return.

⋅⟶⟩ ⟨⟵⋅

I make my way toward Jared's apartment after getting off the phone with my mom, explaining that I'd be going away with him for a few days. She was all bubbly and excited for my make-believe time with Jared, asking more than once if I could bring him home soon. The idea depressed me given that I might be going to break up with him this very minute. Or, more accurately, getting dumped.

I couldn't have planned all this craziness to happen at a better time though, because my mom informed me that she and my dad are going to visit my grandfather for a few days. He's been having some freak-outs, and his live-in nurse has called more than once in concern, so they're going down to see him and figure out what exactly is going on. She also told me that he's been asking for me and I should really make a visit soon. All of this adds to the already-large mound of guilt I have accrued in my stomach.

With Becca and my parents taken care of, I just have one more thing on my list to figure out, and with each step I take, I want to run five miles in the opposite direction. Jared lives in Tribeca in one of those newer, fancier buildings with a doorman—living quarters that come with the same territory as his job. I've only been to his apartment a couple of times in the three months we've been together, but I'm always intimidated while I'm there. It makes the salary difference between us very apparent, and while he *is* older than me, I still feel a sense of imbalance between us. And I'm nothing if not a fan of equality in relationships, maybe even tilted a bit more in my direction. Like I said, equality.

After Will—the lovely doorman—announces my arrival to Jared, I walk toward the elevators, tucking my hair nervously behind my ear.

I check myself over in the reflection of the car as it makes its ascent. My yellow sundress––that I thought was cute this morning––seems to wash me out against my flushed, pale skin, and my eyes seem a little too big in my head. Great, I look absolutely terrified. I fix my hair again even though there's nothing to fix, and plead desperately for the butterflies to stop doing Taekwondo inside my stomach. I don't think I was this nervous on our first date.

Stepping out of the elevator, the long hallway seems to stretch endlessly to Jared's door that looms at the end. Something about this moment gives me a weird sense of déjà vu as I remember following Dev down to his apartment. The memory of the other world I'll be visiting for an extended period of time does nothing to calm my nerves. In fact, I'm practically shaking with anticipation for both events.

The sound of my sandals hitting the tiled floor reverberates around the empty hallway, making me cringe. The very presence of my shoes tainting the ground here feels like a faux pas. Did I mention how this place makes me uncomfortable?

Finally, after what feels like a lifetime, I reach Jared's apartment. Taking in a breath, I knock. There's the sound of footsteps making their way to the door, and in that instant I want nothing more than to disappear like the girl from *I Dream of Jeannie*. I blink my eyes just in case I've suddenly been gifted the power of poofing away. No go.

The door opens and I stop breathing.

Chapter 29

"Hey." Jared smiles.

"Hey," I say as my heart pounds erratically, taking in his appearance.

And God, what an appearance. His dirty-blond hair is immaculately disheveled, like he just woke up but had it styled. His jaw showcases stubble that's asking to be touched, and gazing into his hazel eyes makes me feel like I taste honey. He's wearing a light greenish-gray T-shirt that hides none of his perfect physique, along with the tailored dark jeans that he knows I'm a fan of. His feet are bare and for some reason, staring at them has me thinking of sex, but maybe I was already thinking of sex as soon as I saw him.

This is going to be more difficult than I thought. Whatever *this* is.

Jared gestures for me to come in, and my stomach turns into a pretzel shape, more than aware we didn't do our usual kiss-on-the-lips hello. I glance around his apartment, feeling the most out of place I've ever felt here. Everything is steel and tile and dark man colors. I've always wondered if they had a Man Apartment and a Woman Apartment they let people rent here, because I can't imagine any girls would want to live in a place like this. Have sex in, maybe, but not live.

Why do I keep thinking of sex?!

"Do you want anything to drink?" he asks like a good host. I follow him with my eyes as he strolls toward the kitchen area that is styled in an open floor plan.

"Sure, I'll have some water, please." It's like we hardly know each other. Each of us obviously has our walls up, which leads me to the conclusion that this is a breakup.

Oh God, I'm going to throw up.

I still haven't moved from where I'm standing when Jared returns with bottled water. I thank him, extremely interested in removing the cap and taking a sip, not wanting to look up into his face and see what I fear is a look of indifference. Even though I told Becca I'd try to change his mind if he wanted to end things, at this moment I would definitely just nod my head and run toward the door. When did I become such a wuss?

Finally growing a pair, I meet his gaze and am caught off guard to see him regarding me with a small smile.

"What?"

"You're nervous," he says without question.

"Yeah."

"I've never seen you nervous before." His smile grows.

"Well, I'm glad someone is enjoying it," I say dryly.

He nods. "I am."

I eye the door, wondering if I should just leave it at that and make a run for it. He follows my gaze and chuckles. I've missed that sound, and my heart sinks further.

"No, you're not going to escape that easily." He puts his hand behind my back and guides me to his living room. I feel like a thousand arrows just popped up and are pointing to the contact that's finally going on between us, and with every blink of their neon bulbs, they cheer.

Leading me to the couch, he sits on the ottoman directly in front of me, our knees a hair's width away from touching. I wonder if this proximity is his tactic for letting me down gently. I'd much rather him rip it off like a Band-Aid so I can get on with my mourning.

"How have you been?" he asks. I stop playing with the zipper on my purse and shoot him a glare.

"Are you serious?"

He looks confused.

I let out a sigh. "If you asked me over to break up with me, I'd rather skip the formalities of talking about the weather and just get to the point." I'm not sure why I'm so snippy, probably because I've never been very good at talking about feelings, more importantly my own.

His brows pinch together, and then he does something that surprises me—he laughs.

Uh...what?

"I've missed you, Mols." He leans forward, placing his hand on my knee.

"Come again?"

"I've missed you," he says more seriously, holding my gaze.

I glance from his hand on my knee back to his face, trying to understand what this means. "So...you didn't ask me here to break up with me?"

He shakes his head. "Why? Did you want me to?"

"No," I don't hesitate to respond.

"Good, because I have no intention of ever doing that." He puts his other hand on my other knee, securing my legs between his. The word *ever* plays in circles in my mind as the days of tension that I felt between us begin to crumble. Sparked by the contact of his hands, a fluttering feeling of hope gathers in my chest. "I asked you here because, yes, there are some things we need to discuss since we last saw each other, but mainly because I'm sick of this thing between us being so...untitled."

"Untitled?"

"Yes. I've done a lot of thinking these last couple of days, and I've come to the conclusion that I want to call you my girlfriend." He looks me square in the eye, and I forget to exhale. "When people ask me about you and when I introduce you, I want to say, 'This is my girlfriend.' And I'd like you to call me your boyfriend. I want to be able to do things for you that only a boyfriend can do, and take claim in things only a boyfriend can take claim in. Like taking care of you when you're sick," he says wryly. "I want us to be each other's."

Well, I obviously didn't see that coming.

"What do you think of that?" he asks, watching me patiently but with extreme confidence in his words.

What do I think of that? I think I want to cry—and that's just what I do. I cry.

Pathetic, right?

As I lay my head in my hands and let the unexpected tears pool out of my eyes, I know I must look insane. I must have looked insane the past three times we've hung out, but I can't help the enormous amount of relief I feel at this moment. These past weeks have felt like I've been twisted and twisted until finally, right now, I unwind.

The couch cushion dips with Jared's weight as he sits next to me, pulling me to his chest. Breathing in his familiar cologne makes me cry harder. I've missed him more than I realized. I've missed how his presence makes me feel so secure and calm, like I can do no wrong. And if I do, he likes me despite of it.

I need to get a grip.

"I didn't think that would make you sad," he says into my hair.

"No, no." I push up from him and wipe my pitiful tears from my cheek. "I'm not sad—I'm *happy*."

"Happy?" He laughs lightly. "Then why are you crying?"

"I'm just so relieved. I didn't want to lose you, and I know the way I've been acting lately has been…odd. I just didn't know what was going on with me. I've been dealing with a lot internally, and I'm just…I'm sorry." The words spill quickly out of my mouth.

"I know," he says soothingly, holding me tight. "I know."

Even though he doesn't *really* know, I have a feeling he knows enough about me to understand. To understand and accept whatever I'm dealing with and see me through it, for better or for worse. He's too perfect and I know I don't deserve him, but I hold on tight anyway. In this moment, the space I was making for him in my heart expands.

"It was so hard not talking to you these past few days," he whispers softly into my hair.

I lift my head from his shoulder and face him. It was so hard for me too, but I don't admit this; instead, I'm distracted by his gaze dropping to my lips. When he looks back up, his eyes are dark and filled with desire. I would never have thought I'd be in his arms again, friggin' crying, but in his arms nonetheless. I become very aware of their strength and the hardness of his chest against my side. Before I think any more about any of this, I bring his lips to mine and let go.

Starved—that's the only way I can describe how Jared is kissing me. Like he's starving and I'm his favorite meal. He stands with me still wrapped in his arms and walks to another room. Our lips only part when he gently lays me on his bed and rips off my jacket. I frantically tug off his shirt with the same sense of desperation. He's nothing but bare chest and jeans hovering above me before his lips slam back to mine, and I groan in pleasure.

With the scent of his skin mixing with his cologne, it takes all of my strength not to lick him. His hand moves up my thigh, hitching up my dress and cupping my bottom. I move my hips into him even more and gasp. *God, how I missed this man.* As our lips continue to move together, I feel his hands tugging my underwear down my legs, and I help by kicking them off. He stands, and I frown at the sudden void of his body.

He chuckles at my reaction and doesn't take his heated eyes from mine as he unzips his jeans, taking them off. My body practically croons with desire seeing him standing there, bare as the day he was born, the tan skin covering his defined chest calling out to be touched. He leans back over, rubbing his hand from my calf up to my thigh as he teasingly pulls at the bunched-up material of my dress. "I like this dress," he says darkly with a grin.

"Do you?" I respond with an air of innocence.

He nods slowly. "We're keeping this on."

"Whatever my *boyfriend* wants," I tease, and if the strength of words could be measured, mine would be astronomical given the reaction this elicits from Jared.

From that moment on, there's nothing but sounds and sensations and the euphoric pounding of each of our hearts.

⋯⊱═◉ ◉═⊰⋯

I watch the slow descent of light from Jared's floor-to-ceiling windows. My eyelids want to follow the movement of the dimming sky, but I know I can't let them—I still haven't talked to him about where I'll be going for the next two days. Remembering what I'll be doing brings back all the nervous tension that was removed by the distraction of the man lying next to me.

It's like I'm being pulled in two different directions. One part wants to stay right here in Jared's arms and refuse to accept what I know is inevitable, and the other part is swimming like a fish to a baited hook, straight toward this giant change that's about to take place in my life. And I'm welcoming it forward with excitement.

I take a deep breath, preparing myself to lie once again to someone I care about. Jared is soothingly playing with a strand of my hair and has his eyes closed. The corner of his mouth tips up, knowing I'm watching.

"Yes?"

"How did you know I wanted to say something?"

He doesn't open his eyes but keeps smiling. "Why else would you be creepily watching me?"

I lightly smack his chest. "I'm not creepily doing anything."

He peeks at me, taking in my wide-eyed, offended expression. "Yup, creepy." He closes his eyes again.

"You ass!" I shove him, and with a laugh he quickly flips me on my back, nuzzling his face into my neck. His scruff tickles my skin and I squirm, pleading for him to stop. Chuckling, he eases off me.

"Did I tell you that I've missed you?"

"I think you might have mentioned that."

"So what have you been doing these past couple of days?" He runs his fingers along my collarbone.

"Being pathetic."

He grins against my shoulder and moves his face above mine. "Me too," he says and kisses me.

My chest is heavy with how happy he can make me, and I resist the urge to frown as I think about how I'll have to leave soon. Wrapping my arms around his neck, I bring him in again for a more passionate kiss, one that he readily returns. After a little more delicious procrastinating, I lightly push my body away from his. He still hasn't removed that adorable grin from his face.

"I don't want you to be mad, but I made plans to go home tonight before I knew all this was going to happen between us."

There goes the smile. Jared's brows move together, and he props his head on his hand.

"Home? Why?"

I repeat what I said to Becca about some R & R with the 'rents and getting some proper rest since the accident. He seems to understand this logic but still doesn't look too thrilled.

"How long will you be gone?"

"I'll be back Tuesday morning."

"That long?" He pouts, wrapping his arm around my waist and pulling me closer. I laugh.

"Jared, it's only two days."

"One day would be too many days." He slides his hand up my stomach. "You just officially became my girlfriend. I wanted to start doing those things only a boyfriend can do," he whispers into my ear as he kisses the soft spot right underneath.

"And what would those things be?" I ask breathlessly.

He places his lips to mine and coaxes them open, massaging my tongue with his own. His hand that was gently grazing my skin starts to move south. I breathe heavier with anticipation.

"Let me give you a little preview," he murmurs as his fingers travel lower and lower. "So you'll want to come back for the main feature."

I gasp as he finds what he's looking for, and as he begins to expertly send my mind spinning, I know without a doubt I'll be back for the feature *and* all the sequels.

⋆⇒◉ ◉⇐⋆

Standing by Jared's front door, somewhat put back together, I brush my hands against his chest.

"I can't believe you managed to escape my bed."

"I can't miss my train." I lean up and give him a peck. I've started to convince myself that what I'm about to do is *technically* going out of town, so I'm not feeling as bad for lying. *As bad* are the key words.

"I think you can." He gives me a more thorough kiss good-bye, and I realize in this moment that this might be a much-bigger good-bye than I originally thought. Just like my good-bye to Becca.

This instantly throws me into a frenzy to get as much of Jared as possible, and I push into his body and fist my hands into his hair. He immediately responds by pinning me against his front door. Our lips move together, and I moan against his mouth as he moves one hand to grab my backside and squeeze. I'm so thankful that I spent most of the day talking and laughing with Jared—as well as not talking and definitely not laughing. This is exactly how I want to remember us together, exactly what I want to be excited to come home to, to hold on to. No matter what I experience in the coming days, I want to always be the same Molly that's in Jared's arms right now, happy and hopeful.

Jared is the first to detangle us from one another. He brushes my hair behind my ear, and his eyes twinkle with an emotion that I don't think I'm quite ready to admit to seeing.

"I'll see you soon?" he asks softly.

I nod. "I'll see you soon."

Chapter 30

THE ENTRANCE TO the Village Portal Bookstore is unlit, and the dream catchers hang with an eerie abandonment in the dark windows. I wonder if I'm supposed to knock. The whole place definitely appears closed. I know this is the right location, but the scrap of paper didn't say anything else about actually getting inside.

I glance up and down the street a little awkwardly, given that I'm practically in my pajamas on a Saturday night in the West Village. Even on this random back street, there are plenty of people dressed up for a night out, probably noticing me and deciding that I'm scoping out a stoop to sleep on. I didn't exactly know what to wear to this…thing, but the notion of sleeping for two days had me going in the direction of something comfortable.

"Hope I haven't kept you waiting," a deep, familiar voice says from behind me.

I turn to see Rae standing under a streetlamp. The light illuminates his long blond locks and casts a dramatic shadow over his dark features. He's wearing the same black shirt and jeans I saw him in the first night we met and again when we bumped into each other in the bookstore. I wonder if these are his version of traveling clothes.

"No, just long enough to get the judgmental eye from some girls who probably thought I was searching for one of my three cats."

Rae laughs deeply and moves his large frame from the spotlight. "Yeah, I can see why they might have come to that conclusion. What are you wearing?" He glances at my outfit.

"My pajamas," I say like he should already know this. I look down at my gray sweatpants and hoodie. Is it really *that* bad?

"But why?"

I furrow my brows. "Um, because…" I glance around to see if anyone else is nearby and lower my voice as I continue. "Because I'm about to go to *sleep* for two days. What was I suppose to wear, a dress to go clubbing?"

He laughs again, like that's the funniest thing he's ever heard. I can bet him a thousand bucks that it's not. He places an arm around my shoulder. "Come on—I've got stuff to show you."

He pulls keys from his pocket and lets himself in.

"So…do you know the owner or something?" I ask as I follow Rae through the empty store, which is looking even creepier with the lights turned off.

"Something like that."

I want to ask him what that means, but I bump into a low display table and curse as I grab the books that spilled over. "How can you see where you're going in here?" I ask in a whisper. Even though the shop's closed, and Rae's obviously allowed in here since he has keys, I still feel like we are breaking and entering.

"Oh, sorry." Rae gently grabs my arm. "I can see a little better in the dark than you can." He walks us toward the back of the store.

"What do you mean? Like you have night vision?" I have to remember that these people are not normal...well...people.

"Not so much night vision as advanced eyesight in the dark." I fail to see the difference. "Remember what Elena said about how the Navitas gives us certain qualities that humans don't have?"

"Yeah."

"Well, I guess that's one of them. We can't see if there's absolutely no light source—then we're just as blind as you—but as long as there's some light that can be used, we can see pretty well at night."

Interesting. It makes sense for the Nocturna to have this power, since they are always in the dark, but it seems like an added bonus for the Vigil, who can travel in the daylight.

Rae stops in front of a doorway that is blocked by a gaudy purple velvet curtain. Parting one side, he gestures for me to walk through. The space beyond is a typical store backroom. There's a ratty couch in the corner and used coffee mugs littering a stain-covered table. There are hooks for coats, and used books stacked everywhere on the floor and against walls. There are two more doors in the room, and if I had to guess, they would be for a bathroom and a closet.

Rae walks to the door on the far right, and I follow, my nerves resurfacing. Turning the knob and flipping a switch, he illuminates the interior. I peer in and am disappointed to find a regular closet—a dirty one at that. Rae watches my reaction with a hidden smile. He walks forward and steps over boxes, beckoning me to follow. I step into the closet that turns out to be decently sized, but because Rae is practically a giant, it feels smaller than a doghouse.

Moving to a circuit breaker, he pops its cover open. "You didn't think I'd just open that door and we'd be where we needed to be, did you?" he asks as he runs his hands down the switches until he pauses over one in the corner.

"Yeah, I guess I kind of did."

He chuckles. Instead of flicking the switch, he pulls it back from the panel to reveal a button. I feel like I'm in a James Bond film. He pushes the button, and I step back as a huff of air escapes from the top of the wall and the whole partition starts to descend into the floor.

Okay, maybe I *am* in a James Bond film.

I squint at the sudden stream of bright light that's released as the wall comes down. When my eyes finally adjust, my jaw drops. I'm now standing in front of a giant white room, very similar to the white rooms I found myself in at City Hall. The reason it looks so big is because there's hardly anything inside. In the far left corner is a circular blue-and-white pod that I've seen people walk in and out of in Terra—I guess it's some sort of teleportation device. Against the left wall is a white padded rectangle that looks creepily like a futuristic coffin. And that's it. Just those two things.

Rae steps inside and heads to the white coffin, which is what I'll now be calling it no matter what he says it is. Touching a panel on the wall, a keyboard lights up and he types in some numbers. Other panels around the room begin to illuminate in that strange bluish glow. The glow that I now understand to be synonymous with the power Terra harness from the Dreamers.

I quickly find out why there's nothing else in here: the rest of the equipment sits in the walls and floor. Rae walks back and forth, touching different images on multiple panels, causing the white coffin to move to the center of the space. Strange apparatuses ascend from the ground and surround it. All of this is so alien, and I start to shake from the adrenaline that's coursing through my body.

I don't think I can do this. Actually, I know I can't do this. My heart wants to jump out of my chest, it's beating so hard. I can't get in that coffin. Is that even what it's there for—for me to lie in? How am I supposed to fall asleep in this creepy room? And what are those strange white posts that came up from the ground? When my foot bumps into a box, I realize I've been backing up.

"Molly," Rae calls to me. "What's wrong?" He's stopped typing at a keypad that's next to the coffin and walks toward me.

"I don't know if I can do this," I whisper.

Rae's brows come together and he glances around the room. An understanding passes over his features. Letting out a sigh, he reaches for me, and I subconsciously take a step back, almost falling over the box behind me. Rae catches my arm.

"Whoa there," he says, steadying me and reassuringly places a large hand on my back. "Sorry, Molly. I kind of jumped the gun there and forgot to explain all of this to you." He nods to our surroundings. "I didn't realize how crazy this might look. It's my first time acclimating a Dreamer." His expression is sincere in his remorse. "It's really all harmless. Can I show you?" He manages to coax me forward with a small smile. "Can I take your bag for you?" he asks as he points to my death grip around the strap. I'm not even sure why I brought it—it's not like I'll be able to get at any of the contents while I'm in Terra. It just felt weird to leave my apartment without it. A girl needs her purse.

I nod and hand it over. He places it in a drawer that pops out of the wall. "I'm going to store it in here, okay?" he says like he's talking to a child, which I kind of understand because I certainly feel vulnerable and small at the moment.

"Sure."

"Oh, by the way, I heard from Becca that you'll be going away for a couple of days to stay with your parents down in Pennsylvania."

"Yeah, I took care of my alibi," I say as I poke the fluffy material that surrounds the interior of the white coffin. It molds to my finger like a Tempur-Pedic mattress.

"I still don't know what to do about the 'no texting' though. That might be an issue."

"No worries," Rae says unconcerned. "We'll figure something out. I'm sure Elena has a fix."

"Who exactly *is* Elena?" I ask, slowly walking around the room, inspecting more of the strange panels that display symbols and numbers that hold no meaning for me. The longer I'm in here, the more I begin to relax. Most of this stuff merely seems like computer equipment. No dissecting knives and scary needles—at least, not yet.

Rae watches as I do my inspection, seemingly pleased that I'm not backing out of the room again. "Elena is very important to both the Vigil and Nocturna. Really to all of Terra. Think of her as the queen bee to the honey hive." He walks to the closet door, which is still open. "I don't want you to freak out, but I'm going to close this now. We need it shut since we won't be coming back for a couple of days, and it would be weird for anyone to open that door and see all this back here."

"Okay," I respond, still thinking about his comment regarding Elena being the queen bee. I always thought she had a monarchical disposition.

"So what? Does she produce all the offspring or something?" I ask sarcastically and am rewarded once again with Rae's deep infectious laugh. I know for a fact I'm not that funny.

"Not quite like that," he says while he presses another invisible button, and we both watch the wall rise from the ground. Not until the opening disappears and we are now in a four-sided doorless, windowless room do I feel the onset of another panic attack.

"Molly. Molly, look at me," I hear Rae say, and I strain to focus on him. I can't breathe…I just can't breathe. There must be no air in here. When the door closed it took all the air with it.

Something cool fills my hand, and I glance down at a glass of water. How did he get that in here? Rae opens my other hand and drops a very small white pill in it. "Here, take this. It will calm you down."

Without question I drop the pill in my mouth and swallow, chugging all the water with it. After a moment, my heart rate slows and my mind regains composure. "Feel better?" Rae asks. I nod. "Man, I'm really sucking at this on-boarding, huh?"

I don't respond, because I suddenly feel drained and need to sit down.

"Molly," he says again, and he's so close that I feel like I'm going to fall backward from craning my neck to look him in the eyes. "I just want to say that I think you're really brave for doing this."

I manage a small smile. Am I brave? From the multiple panic attacks I've just had, I would have to say no, but then I did fare rather well after the Metus run-ins. Still, I find myself saying, "I don't know if you should call me brave just yet," while glancing at the white coffin.

He wraps an arm around my shoulder. "No, you're brave. If you weren't, then you wouldn't have been chosen for this."

I shudder slightly at his ominous words. "You think?"

He gives me a squeeze. "I know."

Rae walks around the room and explains how many of these white panels are exactly what I thought they were—a form of computer screen. What he's been typing in are coordinates to his dimension and setting up my sleeping pod, a.k.a. white coffin, to hold me in my dream state for the next few days.

He also explains how the weird poles that originally freaked me out next to the coffin are sensors that will monitor my body as well as allow me to nourish and relieve myself while I'm sleeping. He actually had to explain this a couple of times, because the very idea that eating and going to the bathroom in another dimension will affect my sleeping body here is insane. I'm extremely thankful that I don't need a catheter or anything uncomfortable like that. It's going to take me a bit to wrap my head around how this other dimensional stuff works, at least in the rules of Terra.

After I ask why I can't just walk into the portal that Rae himself uses to go between worlds, his face grows serious and he gives me the short answer: It's too dangerous for my molecular makeup. Once through, I most likely wouldn't be able to come back—if I made it there in one piece to begin with. I'll be sure to ignore that side of the room.

"Are you ready?" Rae asks after he's done setting everything up.

Oh God. Am I ready? No, I don't think I will ever be *ready*. "Yeah, I'm ready."

"Good." He smiles. "Do you have a T-shirt under that hoodie?" I'm confused by his question but nod.

"Perfect. You'll only need to be in your T-shirt and pants. You'll see why it wouldn't have mattered if you *were* in your clubbing clothes once you're in the sleeping pod."

After taking off what needs to be taken off—careful of my nervous sweaty pits—Rae assists me into the pod. As soon as I lie down, I let out a sigh.

Holy baby angel wings, this is comfortable! "Wow."

"Right?" Rae says.

"It's almost like I'm floating in water. And it's so warm! But like...perfectly warm."

Rae nods, and I want to laugh because I feel so silly lying here and looking at him hovering above. "Yeah, this is a new material you guys will be seeing out on the market in a few years. It feeds back your body temperature, but at five degrees higher, so it's like being wrapped in a blanket. It also molds to your body, similar to a Tempur-Pedic mattress but with ten times the receptor structure."

"Sure, whatever you say," I agree distractedly, nestling my head into the material. "All I know is, this feels awesome."

He bends closer. "This was made from a dream, you know."

"You guys made this come true?" I ask in awe.

"No, *you guys* made this come true—we just gave a little push."

"Always so humble." I feel like I'm a little girl who's about to be tucked into bed.

"Okay, let's get this show on the road." He stands and disappears from my view. I realize now how difficult it is for me to sit up in this thing, even if I want to. It feels almost like it's pulling me down.

"Molly," calls Rae from somewhere out of view, "I can see your heart rate accelerating. Try concentrating on your breathing to slow it down. And remember, there's nothing to be worried about." His voice gets louder, and he pops his head over me. "You'll be back in Terra soon, and I'll be right there with you. So will Dev," he says with a grin before he disappears again.

Dev. I hadn't thought about Dev really at all today, and now suddenly lying here knowing he's waiting for me on the other side has me in a weird panic. Not because I don't want to see him, but because there's a large part of me that is excited to, and that somehow feels wrong. How will it be between us, now that Jared and I are most definitely exclusive? Those stolen kisses can't happen again. My body grows deceptively warm thinking about the last time that happened and the fact that I won't be able to wake up to get a reprieve if it gets to be too much. What if it's *all* too much? What if I never find the strength or the power to fight the Metus like everyone expects me to? Both times I've fought them and survived have seemed like flukes. What if I really get hurt? Will I wake up then, unharmed in my own world? Why didn't I ask any of these questions before?!

My breathing grows erratic despite my better efforts to control it. Fear for my health flashes through my mind as there's a prick in my arm. I blink up to see Rae removing a syringe from one of my veins. My heart rate spikes.

"What the hell was that?" I glance at him, wide eyed.

"Don't worry—it's safe," Rae assures. "You're going to start to feel tired now. What I gave you is a sort of anesthetic."

"Well, next time friggin' warn a girl before you stick her with a needle. That's not really acceptable behavior around here," I scold shakily. My reprimand seems pathetic given that I'm yelling from inside a marshmallow bed.

"Sorry." Rae cringes. "I'll definitely warn you next time. But don't worry—this really is all safe, part of the protocol."

I nod, my anger slowly slipping away into sleepiness. With great effort I have another quick rush of uncertainty, really hoping this is the right thing to do. But I trust that Rae is telling me the truth, that this is safe, that I'll be fine. And surprisingly, I find strength when I think of Dev. As much as we fight and he annoys me to no end, I know deep down he would do anything to protect me.

"If you want, count down from ten. It will help you relax," Rae instructs.

Ten. I count in my head. *Nine...*

Soon what Rae says takes place, and I start to relax.

Eight... My eyes begin to droop and my limbs grow heavy.

Seven... I feel the sensation of being wrapped in warmth, and I'm slightly aware of the dimming lights of the room.

Six... My breathing slows, and any fear I felt seconds ago lifts away like a fog.

Five... "I'll see you soon," says a male voice, but I can't place where it came from.

Four... My life leading up to this moment feels very far away and hazy, like a distant memory.

Three... I don't know what my new life will be like, what tomorrow will bring, but for the first time, that hole that's always been inside my chest fills up. It sits full and warm and ready.

Two... I blink slowly to darkness, then Rae smiling reassuringly, then darkness. I lift my eyelids fleetingly one last time, trying to hold on to this place that has always been my reality.

One... My eyes close.

For an unknown amount of time, all I feel and taste and see is black.
And then...
My eyes open.

And all I see is blue.

THE END

(For now)

Acknowledgments

Well, here we are. The sort of end, but actually very beginning, of something I've been working on for many, many, *many* moons. Five hundred warehouses full of moons. Okay, maybe more like three hundred, but you get the point. I couldn't have arrived here without an armful of some pretty amazing people.

Right out of the gate I have to thank my family, to whom part of this book is dedicated. Ma and Pa, you always nudged us to color outside the lines of life, and I am forever grateful. Please always stay your crazy, wacky, artistic selves. Alex, Phoenix, and Kelsey, what can I say? You are my sisters beyond sisters. You were the first eyes and ears to this crazy adventure I've been determined to go down, and I thank you in the squishiest of hugs for reading the first draft of this book and all the other short stories and beginner manuscripts that came before. I shudder at the writing you've had to endure along the way. Thank you for being kind!

To Dan, my midnight peanut butter and cereal companion. Thank you for sticking with me through my morning, midmorning, afternoon, midafternoon, and nighttime freak-outs that have come with writing this series. You are always the light I see at the end of my neurotic-filled tunnel. I could not have come so far without you. I love you.

To Corinna Barsan, I am forever humbled that you took the time to read and give notes on the first draft. Your mentoring and insight with everything in life and literature means the world to me. I owe you a lifetime supply of morning coffees.

Julia McCarthy, my editor extraordinaire who made this book pretty, thank you for all your amazing suggestions and notes and for being my biggest fan. You are one of the smartest and most loveably talented people I know.

To Dori Harrell from Breakout Editing, your proofreading is what made this book so shiny and clean. I smile in anticipation every time my inbox dings with your name. I am forever grateful for finding you!

To Mercy Lomelin, your typography skills took my cover from humdrum to hell, yeah! Thank you for being my companion in all things nerdy—I don't feel as lonely wearing my cape when you sit beside me in yours.

To my book club ladies, Jessica, Lauren, Alicia, Erin, Nicky, Meg, and Eman, your support is what keeps me breathing every day. I love you all tremendously.

To my beta readers, specifically Brittany and Brianna, thank you for being my sounding board.

To the self-publishing community, the RWA, and all the writers who've been there to powwow and commiserate with on the long process of writing, specifically Todd Dillard and Shannon Wixom. Thank you for calming my fears, cheerleading my ideas, and sharing your talents. Pen pals for life!

To Emma Raveling, your genius, kindness, and general all-around badassery (yes, that's a word), inspire me daily in my own work. I'm so grateful for the day I found you and your incredible books.

To my high school English teachers, Micheline McManus and Katy Kenney. Your passion for the written word saturated my every pore, and I am forever honored to have been one of your students. Everyone go hug a teacher! They are the foundation of everything that's possible in our world.

To all the other friends and family that I am unable to list individually here (only because it would be another novel in length), your words of encouragement make doing this a lot less scary. I am bowing in gratitude for being around so many wonderful people.

And lastly, but without a doubt most importantly, I want to thank you, the reader. Thank you for taking a chance on an indie author (and for making it to the end of this). Your support is what gets me up in the morning. I hope you like it, because there's more to come!

About the Author

E.J.Mellow is a fantasy writer who resides in Brooklyn, NY. When she's not busy moonlighting in the realm of make-believe, she can be found doodling, buried in a book (usually this one), or playing video games.

The Dreamer is the first book in her NA contemporary fantasy trilogy, *The Dreamland Series.*

Made in the USA
Middletown, DE
25 March 2016